A VAMPIRE ROMANCE

BLOOD RED KISS

USA TODAY BESTSELLING AUTHOR
JADE WEST

Blood Red Kiss copyright © 2022 Jade West

The moral rights of the author have been asserted.

All rights reserved. No part of this publication may be reproduced, distributed, or transmitted in any form or by any means, including photocopying, recording, or other electronic or mechanical methods, without the prior written permission of the publisher, except in the case of brief quotations embodied in critical reviews and certain other non-commercial uses permitted by copyright law. For permission requests, write to the publisher, addressed "Attention: Permissions Coordinator," at the email address below.

Cover design by Letitia Hasser of RBA Designs http://designs.romanticbookaffairs.com/
Edited by John Hudspith http://www.johnhudspith.co.uk
Paperback formatting by Sammi Bee Designs
All enquiries to jadewestauthor@gmail.com

First published 2022

*To all vampire lovers out there.
I hope you enjoy the Blood Red Kisses.*

1

I'd always loved Halloween. There was something about the scary costumes, the eerie thrill in the air, and the nights drawing in through the autumn that drove me wild. I loved cauldrons and broomsticks and ghost stories, but more than that – more than *anything* else – I loved vampires.

Yes. I, Katherine Jane Blakely, at eighteen years old, was still absolutely *crazy* about vampires. Just as I had been from a little girl.

I was pouring a wine for Frederick Brust when a group of the younger members came in through the main entrance. They were out on a guys' social after a polo game earlier, and usually I'd have given them little more than a polite *hello* as they got seated and ready to order some drinks, but tonight was different. They were dressed up in Halloween costumes, even though there was still a whole week to go, and Max Eggerton, the very hottest young guy of the bunch, was dressed up as Dracula.

Max's fangs were shitty white plastic, and the fake blood dripping down his chin was almost as cringeworthy as the flimsy red satin cape around his shoulders, but that didn't matter. The very sight of fangs gave me tingles right the way up my arms. He looked twenty times better to me as an immortal vampire than he did as the young, hot kid on the block. Even in a cruddy costume.

He stepped up to the bar along with Stephan as soon as I'd handed the merlot to Frederick.

"What can I get you?" I asked them.

Stephan leant forward, checking out the selection of spirits despite the fact he already knew them by heart. The people here at Regency Gentlemen's Club were the same crew of posh guys every single weekend. I almost laughed out loud at Stephan when I got to check out his costume in greater detail. He was clearly supposed to be a mummified corpse, but in reality he was swirled up in shabby toilet roll.

I was dressed in white myself, but my outfit was the total opposite of shabby. I was in a barmaid's uniform of the highest calibre, fitting me nice and neatly. My hair was up in a tight, dark bun to make the most of the neatness. Understated, but nicely natural.

I always needed to look prim and perfectly proper in this role. A little mascara would do ok, but that was about all. Even my lipstick was nothing more than a natural sheen.

"I'll go with a gin and Coke, please, Katherine," Stephan told me.

I got another tingle as I looked at Max standing beside him. His teeth appeared even worse up close, but that made no difference. Plastic fangs still made my heart race.

My eyes were on Max's mouth as Stephan ordered drinks for the rest of their group, on autopilot as I presented the bottles and glasses on the counter. My fingers were jittery on the bar tab screen as I tapped in their totals, still eyeing up the crappy red cloak around Max's shoulders as he disappeared with their tray of drinks.

I was so caught up in the approaching Halloween air that I hadn't noticed Hans appear at the bar. He was a pale, tall figure with the most glorious dark hair I'd ever seen. Way, way more worthy of my attention than Max Eggerton ever could be, fake fangs or not.

Hans Jacob Weyer was his full name.

When I noticed him there I knew I'd fucked up – ignoring a club member who was waiting to order drinks. Inadvertently or not, it made no odds. It was incompetent. If my manager Eliza caught me, I'd be getting a stern telling off when the night was through.

"Sorry, sir," I said, but Hans shook his head with a smile.

"It's understandable to be distracted by vampires. I'll forgive you this once, Katherine."

I felt even more of an idiot for my distraction when I saw the pure perfection of Hans' teeth rather than fake plastic ones. His beauty didn't just lie with his teeth, either. His brows were sculpted dark, and his cheeks were angular in the most stunning of ways, and his lips were nicely filled out. Not only that, but he had the lightest green eyes in creation, and it only added to his presence. Striking – that's one word you could use to describe him. Stunningly striking. Not least because of the gorgeous suit he was wearing. Black tie, white shirt, black tailored jacket. He could have been on his way to a funeral, but it looked great on him.

I was staring mutely at Hans when Frederick arrived back at the bar holding his glass of blood-red wine, and slapped his friend on the back in a friendly greeting. They shook hands and I noticed how lean Hans' fingers were. His hands were as gorgeous as his face. Strong, yet delicate somehow.

I realised I was staring at fingers not faces when their *hellos* turned to distant silence, and there I was, being a crappy barmaid all over again.

Both men looked across as I stumbled back to my senses. I met Hans' eyes, finally giving him the professional barmaid attention he deserved.

"Sorry again, Mr Weyer," I said. "What would you like to drink?"

"The same for me, please," he told me, gesturing to Frederick's glass. "A large merlot."

"Of course."

I got straight to it, feeling his stare burning my back as I turned and uncorked a fresh bottle. Maybe it was the approach of Halloween, or Max's plastic teeth, I didn't know, but I felt prickles in weird places as I poured the wine.

Frederick was chatting about something with Hans, but his words sounded blurry behind me. All I could feel was the heat of Hans' green eyes on my back. Turning to face him with his drink in my hand only confirmed he was watching me. I realised I was blushing, and I blushed even more as I handed him his drink.

"Katherine, thank you," he said with a slight nod of his head.

I wondered again where his accent was from, just as I had done every night that I'd seen him. His voice was fitting of this posh London community, but not quite as British as the other aristocratic bloodlines that usually frequented this bar. His speech was impeccable, his tone low and confident, but different to the others. Hard to place.

It was Frederick doing most of the talking, not Hans, which wasn't unusual. I busied myself slicing some lemons, trying not to focus on either of them as I pretended I was comfortable in my role, even though I was still trying to find my feet in this new city life I was living. It was hard. Some days harder than others. Some nights harder than ever.

This night felt like one of them.

Frederick was only chatting with Hans for a few short minutes before Benjamin Hastings made his appearance in the doorway.

"*Ahh! Ben!*" Frederick exclaimed, then went on over to give a *good evening* as Benjamin hung up his coat. I was left with his strange, beautiful friend at the bar.

"You like vampires, then?" Hans asked me out of the blue, and I gave him a stupid smile.

"Yes, you could say that. I've loved vampires since forever."

I wasn't lying. I'd been besotted with them for all time. Cartoon vampires as a toddler turned into gothic horror movies as a teenager. I'd even loved a cartoon duck called *Count Duckula* when I was growing up.

Hans smirked at me. "Which is your favourite?"

"My favourite vampire?" I laughed. "That's not an entirely fair question. Picking a favourite sure is hard…"

"Go on, at least give it a try," he pushed. "If you had to pick one single vampire to drink the life out of you, which one would it be?"

I swear my heart skipped a beat, and I burnt up. Hot and bothered.

Hans tipped his head, seeming to notice.

"It is warm in here tonight, isn't it, Katherine?"

I blinked, wiped my brow, cringed. Shouldn't have done that. "Warm. Yes."

"So, your favourite vampire?" he resumed.

"Dracula, of course."

He laughed a low laugh.

"Which version of him? There must be at least two hundred versions or more. Novels, movies, TV. You must have your favourite."

"Ok, yes. I have my favourite." I paused. "Gary Oldman. Bram Stoker's Dracula. The movie."

Hans gave a nod of his head as he sipped his wine.

"Good choice. He plays Dracula so very well."

"Yes, he really does," I agreed. "Don't get me wrong, I love Keanu, but seriously. It would be Gary for me, most definitely."

"I am guessing you wouldn't be slaying him at the end of the movie, then?"

I shook my head, grinning. "No. Definitely not."

I thought Hans would be done with the vampire small talk at that point, but he shot a glance over to find Frederick still chattering with Benjamin. He leant his elbows on the bar, leaning in closer.

"How about the 90s Interview with the Vampire movie? Did you like that one?"

"Yes," I said, then pre-empted his next question. "Armand for me. Number one choice."

"Very nice. Louis or Lestat in second place?"

"Lestat."

Hans' smile was as beautifully dry as the red wine he was drinking. "You'd still enjoy Louis, though?"

I nodded. "I'd adore Louis. I'd adore all of them. Even the evil smug guy who kills Claudia."

"Ouch," Hans said. "That's quite a statement."

Hmm, he had a point. I pictured Claudia scorching to death under the sunlight and changed my mind.

"Actually, no. He pushed it too far. I take that back…"

Hans took another sip of wine before he quizzed me some more.

"How far does your love of vampires go? How about Buffy the Vampire Slayer?"

I rolled my eyes with a smile as my polite barmaid mask began to slip down.

"Is that even a query? Doesn't everyone love Angel? And don't get me started on Spike."

"I'm not interested in everyone," Hans said. "I'm interested in *you*."

The whole room felt like it disappeared in that instant. Hans' green eyes were fixed on mine, and his lips were perfect as he raised his glass to them, and I couldn't breathe, couldn't think, couldn't break myself from the spell in his words.

I'm interested in you.

Did he mean more by that? Was there something pointed in his tone?

The flush blooming on my chest told me the answer.

I didn't have time to think about it. The noise of the bar returned at full volume along with Frederick and Benjamin and put an end to our little exchange as they took their seats beside him. I got Ben a double whisky, and then I faded into the background, getting a fresh round of ice for the tray once Eliza joined me back from the lounge.

The guys talked, and we served drinks, and I did my best to be a good barmaid, but still, all through my shift I couldn't stop thinking about Hans. My eyes shot him a glance every time he was in sight, even though I kept my attention on service as best I could. His words were an unending swirl in my head.

I'm interested in you.

It made my skin prickle.

Later into the evening the regulars began to disperse. Max and Stephan's gang were off back to Finley's, and Kristoff Kelly was hitting the casino with Leroy Marsden and his crowd.

It was Frederick and Benjamin who rose from the bar together, and I expected Hans to be up and out of there with them, but he waved his goodbyes and remained in his seat, just the other side of the bar.

"See you soon, gentlemen," he said.

"See you soon, gentlemen, thank you," I offered as well, but my voice sounded timid somehow.

I looked around for Eliza, but she was out of sight. It was just me and the gorgeous man and his beautiful green eyes.

He finished up his glass of merlot and stared right at me.

"One final question for you on the vampire front, Katherine," he said. "Would you really, truly want to get bitten by a vampire, if given the chance?"

I smiled. "One that looked like Dracula, or Louis, or Lestat, or just anyone?"

He didn't laugh.

"An attractive one, but one in real life. Someone who would be genuinely desperate to sink his fangs into you and take your blood."

The words came out before I'd had time to think.

"Yes, I would."

"Really?" he asked. "You are sure about that?"

"Yes," I said again. "I'm very, very sure about that."

Once again, Hans didn't smile, just nodded. He got to his feet once Eliza appeared at the other end of the bar.

"I hope that one day, you get to live your fantasy," he told me, this time with a smirk. "Goodnight, Katherine."

There was a glimpse of something in his eyes. A sense of knowing. A sense of power. Something that would have sounded nothing but crazy to myself if my heart hadn't thumped so hard and fast. It just didn't make any sense. The prickles on my chest ran riot as I watched Hans Jacob Weyer walk away.

On reflection, I should have known something was coming.

2

The feelings from the bar wouldn't leave me alone that night. I got home to my tiny bedroom in the house I was sharing with other tenants, but there were no distracting conversations to be had there. I was living with people I barely knew, even after three months. Our hours were different. They were early starters. The four of us were like passing ships in the night.

I could have really done with a friend to chat with. Such a shame I didn't have any yet in London, and as for family. Well, I'd have been better off grabbing a stranger from the street to talk with than calling my mum up in Orcop. Grandma would be hissing in the background behind her, calling me a *stupid girl* yet again for moving away from home.

London is crawling with sinners, Katherine!

The other tenants were already locked away in their bedrooms, no doubt fast asleep as I made jam on toast. I took it to bed and munched while I watched mindless videos on my phone. Snippets of The Vampire Diaries came up amongst random funny cat videos, which wasn't all that helpful in shifting the prickles. Usually mindless scrolling was enough that I'd sink away into dreamland, but the edginess, and the heat, and the flushes wouldn't ease off.

I'd picture Hans' face and I'd get crazy flutters, heart pounding as I remembered his words.

I'm interested in you.

His smile. His perfect teeth. His laugh. I could see him speaking those words with crystal clarity.

No.

I was going insane.

Scrolling through videos stood no chance whatsoever of distracting me, so I ran a bath, praying that the steam from the water would relax my mind, but still nothing. The prickles kept on coming.

I was so hot that I put on a satin slip of a nightdress for bed instead of cosy PJs. A white flimsy thing I hadn't worn since the height of summer.

It didn't help. I tossed and turned, covers on and off, cursing my brain for churning.

I'm interested in you.

There was only one thing for it – to embrace the vampire fantasies and let them work their magic. Hans was the obvious choice, but imagining him biting my neck was just too much. It sent shivers through my whole body, so intensely that slipping my fingers down between my legs felt like vicious electric, so strong that I couldn't bear it. It was so bizarre that I kept on trying, only to reinforce the truth.

I couldn't touch myself thinking about him.

It didn't make any sense. It felt like my body was punishing me for daring to think about it. As though some weird force was forbidding me to touch myself and think of his voice.

Insane. Just... no. No.

I gave myself a shake, determined to put Hans out of my mind.

I reverted to my usual fantasy fuel and put on the beginning of Interview with the Vampire, watching as Lestat dripped vampire blood into Louis' desperate mouth, which would invariably work like romantic filth for me. It was a whole fresh round of shock when it didn't work. Not even Lestat and Louis could take my mind away from Hans Weyer.

I couldn't handle the disappointment of Gary Oldman failing to distract me, so I abandoned my phone and kept on tossing and turning, cursing sleep for giving me the middle finger.

I have no idea when sleep did finally hold out a hand and grace me, but the transition into dreamland was sharp. I was tumbling deep and fast when I felt cold cobblestones under my feet. Yes. I recognised them. *Hyde Street*, on the way home from Regency. I'd walked along that street plenty of times on my way home from work, but never barefoot. It was cold and mossy, and the place looked different, despite the buildings being similar. It was hard to make out for certain in the dark, but it felt older, as though I'd stepped back in time.

I turned around on the spot to check things out, goosebumps up my arms and freezing cold, since I was still in a satin slip that barely grazed my thighs. It felt so real that I looked down to find my nipples were hard in the chill, and true to life – just like in bed – I wasn't wearing any panties. Even in dreamland it freaked me out – feeling so exposed.

I glanced around, checking the road. Thank God, there was nobody there to see me.

Nobody there in view didn't mean there was nobody there in the flesh, though…

I felt the gaze of someone. *Something.* And in one cold, hard flash I was slammed with memories I'd been trying to forget for years. So many shivers up my back that I'd had at random points through my life, always getting the feeling of being watched by someone. *Something.*

Mum would tell me I should stop making up stories, with Grandma cursing behind her and saying I was a *silly little girl* who should be *told off* more, and so I'd stopped voicing them. Stopped daring to speak them out loud.

Tonight, that feeling was stronger than I'd ever known, and my heart took on a life of its own, ready for fight or flight.

When I heard footsteps on the cobblestones my senses made the decision for me. Flight. Most definitely, definitely FLIGHT.

I bolted as quickly as I could, hair loose and tumbling as the soles of my feet took the force of the ground. Wet moss, and cold stone, and the sound of my breaths running as wild as I was.

I was being chased.

The footsteps behind me were heavier than mine, and much, much faster.

Shit. Shit. SHIT.

I ran harder, trying to scream, but it didn't work. My screams were silent, even though I could feel the force of them slamming right through my throat.

That sealed my fate, and I knew it. Nobody was going to save me – nothing except my own determination.

Panic and terror were enough to give me an insane energy rush. I sprinted with everything I had, but the turning onto Keel Avenue didn't come. The street kept looming ahead, but no matter how hard I tried, and no matter how fast I ran, I just couldn't reach it. There were only cobblestones and desperation, with an increased sense of knowing.

I knew I was going to get caught.

I knew my running was futile.

Still, my spirit fought on.

It felt almost as though the heavy footsteps behind were playing with me, holding back just enough to enjoy my efforts. Still, I tried to scream. Still, there was only silence.

The cobblestones kept on coming, the buildings reappearing on loop. I kept giving everything, gaining nothing, and slowly, slowly, slowly, I could feel my spirit weakening.

No. NO.

I fought it some more.

My silent screams were louder but useless. My feet were hurting, but kept on running, running, running until I couldn't take it anymore.

Finally, I buckled and stopped.

I pressed myself against a timber framed building, my back against a thick wooden door. My hair felt tangled and my nipples were like bullets, still freezing cold despite the fact that I was sweating and panting for breath, clouds of steam around me like fog in the air.

I looked up and down the street, preparing myself for my attacker, but the footsteps had stopped. A fresh prickle ran up my spine.

I was being watched. They were still there. Waiting in the shadows.

Panting, heart pounding, I glanced around, waiting for the inevitable...

Who the hell was watching me?

Who the hell had been watching me like this my whole life?

My instincts knew the answer before I did. I recognised his voice before he stepped into view.

"Have you finished fleeing yet, Katherine?"

I folded my arms over my breasts. His smirk was enough to make me shudder.

He looked even more striking under the moonlight. His smile was brighter, his eyes piercing green. His suit immaculate. His dark hair sheening. But he looked different in these surroundings, as if we'd been transported back a hundred years.

"It's you," I managed, pointing out the obvious.

"Yes," he said, and stepped up closer. "It's always been me."

Of course. The sensations came tumbling. The instinctive recognition when I'd first seen him step up to the bar in Regency. The pounding of my heart as though I knew him, even though I'd never seen him before in my life. I'd blocked it out as nothing, and it had worked. I'd busied myself in my working life, just like I should have.

I kept looking up and down the street, contemplating whether my feet would be willing to carry me.

Hans tutted as he read my mind.

"You really want to run, do you?"

I nodded in a flash, adrenaline buzzing.

He tutted again, placed a hand to his heart.

"Really, Katherine. I held you true to your word."

Oh no.

NO.

Any instinctive recognition I'd had before faded to nothing in comparison to how I felt as he stepped closer and smiled. I saw... fangs. And they weren't shitty plastic.

My voice was barely more than a whisper when it came out of me.

"You're a vampire."

"Bravo," he said and applauded with slow claps, but there was no malice in it. "So, now you have to ask yourself, which came first? Me, or your vampire crushes? The chicken or the egg?"

My thoughts swirled, trying to make sense of it. I tried to put it into words, but I sounded like a fool.

"You mean you're the reason I'm obsessed with vampires? But how? I've been obsessed with vampires since I was a kid watching cartoons on TV."

I could feel the heat from him as he stepped up in front of me, held my arms tighter to my chest, one hand to my throat.

"Trust me, fate and bloodlines are a lot deeper running than you could imagine. Your obsession with vampires isn't something that you randomly fell into. It was in your veins from the very moment you were born."

My questions were scary, even to speak them.

"And how about you? Were you watching me from the very moment I was born?"

"I've been watching you a lot longer than that, little girl. I've been watching you since you were nothing more than a tiny spark of life in a family chain."

I couldn't fathom it, so I didn't even try.

This is a dream, I told myself. *Wake up, Katherine. This is a dream!*

Hans read my mind again.

"At least you're using the word *dream* and not *nightmare*."

"Stop it!" I said. "I can't think straight."

"Don't be so hard on yourself. I don't think many people would be thinking straight in your position."

Shit. I was so confused. My blood was throbbing so fiercely that I could feel my pulse in my neck, but of course I would. I was standing in front of a freaking vampire.

Hans' voice was much lower this time.

"The question is, little one, did you really mean it? Would you truly like to be bitten by a vampire?"

I shook my head, but the pull was magnetic. I let out a whimper that sounded nothing like fear.

Hans ran his hand down my shoulder, and I shot a glance at his beautiful fingers at the same time as my arms dropped to my sides of their own accord.

"I don't just bite," he said, his eyes moving to my nipples, poking through the fabric of my slip. "I have many more needs than blood."

"Like what?" I whispered back, my breasts tingling like crazy.

"How about you let me kiss you and find out?"

He tipped my chin up, his face so close I could feel his breath on my lips.

"Let me kiss you, Katherine."

I was frantic with terror under the bliss of tingles, but the pull was too strong to deny. His mouth moved closer, and mine opened just a little, and his lips brushed hot but gently against mine.

And then he kissed me.

Hans Jacob Weyer, the vampire, kissed me.

His body pinned mine, and his mouth claimed me, his tongue dancing in brutal rhythm. I responded like the girl who'd been dreaming of vampires since I was young, desperate for more.

I moaned as I tasted him. Moaned as his fingers stroked over my nipples. Parted my legs as his fingers trailed their way down my slip, crying out against his mouth as he found the right spot.

He was even better with my clit than I was.

"So, did you mean it?" he whispered between kisses. "Do you really want to be bitten by a vampire?"

Desperation knew no bounds. I was squirming against him, panting with need. My clit was alive, and my skin was thrumming all over, and my head wanted to nod with a life of its own.

But that's what it was in me. *Life.*

I was *alive*. And I definitely didn't want to let that go.

My spirit fought back like a burst of flames.

"NO!" I screamed, and shoved him away from me. "NO! I don't want to be bitten by a vampire!"

I expected Hans to pull me back to him, or run after me, but he didn't. I charged away up the cobblestones with painful feet, and this time around Keel Avenue came into view, just like normal. The street was lit up with the regular street lights, and my shared house was exactly where it should be at the end of the road.

The front door was wide open. I didn't need keys.

My steps were thumping on the stairs and my breaths were loud on my way up, but nobody stepped out of their bedrooms.

I threw myself in bed and pulled the covers up high, repeating my thoughts like a mantra.

This is a dream. This is a dream. This is a STUPID FUCKING DREAM.

And then I woke up.

I sat bolt upright in bed, knowing that the illusion was over. I was back in my body, for real.

It was a dream. A stupid fucking dream.

Fuck, it took some time for me to calm down. I flicked on my bedside lamp and cursed the night terrors. I called up the time on my phone to find it was 4 a.m. and London traffic was rumbling a little outside, just like usual.

What a fucking dream that was.

I wondered if I'd had some kind of reaction to jam on toast, like processed strawberries had even the slightest chance of being a hallucinogen. That at least made me giggle a little out loud.

Eventually, it was time for sleep round two, so I opted for a trip to the bathroom first, to save the urge to pee before breakfast.

I didn't need to see my feet as I dropped them down onto the carpet. The sensation told me all I needed to know.

I held my breath and closed my eyes, bracing myself to take it, and then I faced it.

I opened my eyes and looked down, and yes. I was right.

There was dirt all over the carpet, and moss still trapped between my toes.

3

*I*t's hard to convince yourself *it was only a dream* when you're washing fresh dirt off your feet in the shower.

Was it sleepwalking? Sleep-running? Was it really a strawberry fuelled hallucination that sent me out into the street in nothing but a flimsy satin slip?

Who knows, but I slept with the light on for the rest of the night, tossing and turning even worse than before.

Sleep eventually found me again, and this time Hans did not. I woke up to the sound of a car horn tooting on the street. With a groggy head, I pinched myself hard, half-expecting Hans Weyer to step out from my wardrobe. But no.

Just a dream.

My housemates were at work when I pulled myself out from under the covers at just gone midday. The house was empty, and I was like a ghost as I mulled around, getting myself a breakfast-lunch. I most definitely avoided jam. Strawberries could leave me alone for the foreseeable. Possibly for ever.

My toes were still sore from the pounding on cobbles, and I felt like I really had run a marathon. All of my muscles were aching. It was crazy, what I'd done, running around the streets in nothing but a satin slip. I wondered if I'd been seen, flashing myself as I ran. I could have been arrested – or worse.

I was shaking when I got dressed for work, trying to talk rational sense into my stupid imagination.

The dream wasn't real. Hans Weyer wasn't chasing me. Hans Weyer didn't hit the spot. Hans Weyer most definitely isn't a vampire. Vampires don't even exist.

I buttoned up my freshly washed and ironed crip white blouse. I made sure my bun was tight and neat, and made sure my foundation was solid enough to keep my skin glowing, as though I hadn't just spent a night on the run.

I wished it was summer as I set off on my way to Regency. The nights were already drawing in, and the air was chilling more every day. It was especially eerie when I reached the cobbled street, and I made a dash for it on instinct, despite getting strange looks from passers-by.

I figured I'd calm down when I reached the other side without anyone chasing me, but I jumped a mile when a bus pulled up and a group of girls climbed off, cackling and dressed up as witches.

I needed to get a hold of myself before I got to the bar. I'd be the worst barmaid in creation if I was wide-eyed in panic, too shaky to so much as hand over a beer. Eliza would probably fire me on the spot if I spilt red wine over someone's tailored suit across the bar.

Red wine.

Blood-red wine.

Hans Weyer drinking blood-red wine.

I could have screamed at myself. On some level I even wished my grandma was standing there next to me, pulling her usual nasty face about how stupid my fairytale reality was.

I did my best to imitate her.

Katherine, grow up. You're being a fool over a ridiculous night terror.

You probably embarrassed yourself in front of half of Hyde Street. They were likely peeping through their curtains at you. Stupid girl.

I gathered myself at the staff door of Regency, my last chance at coming back to my senses. I took a breath and braced myself, pasting on the closest attempt at a natural smile I could manage.

I stepped into the hall, closed the door heavily and hurried to the staffroom. I hung up my coat on the hanger, hung up my bag alongside it, and then I made my entrance into the bar, praying to hell I didn't look as scatter-brained as I felt.

Here goes…

I was ready to face it…

Face *him*…

But no. There was nothing to face.

The anti-climax was powerful. Hans was nowhere to be seen. Neither were Frederick, or Benjamin, or Stephan or Max or the gang. The place was virtually empty, with Eliza serving a solitary George Miller his regular whisky.

"Where is everyone?" I asked her when she was done.

She shrugged. "You tell me. Something must be happening somewhere else in the city. The place has been dead since I opened the door."

I wanted to feel relief, but I didn't. I got the most bizarre sense of disappointment as I scouted the empty seats, a distant part of me aching to see my dream stalker.

Stupid girl.

I shrugged it off along with Eliza.

"Maybe there was a polo game over in Cirencester?"

She shook her head. "Nope. I checked the calendar."

"Is it someone's birthday? One of the Barons?"

"Not that I know of. We'd normally get to know in advance."

"Strange," I said.

"Very," she agreed.

George Miller was known as an eccentric, but I'd never heard him laugh as he laughed across the bar at us. His grin was almost feral as his hand clutched his whisky.

"They've been barred," he cackled. "All of them, forbidden."

Eliza pulled a face at him.

"Forbidden from here? Who?"

"Everyone." He kept on laughing. "But I like breaking the rules."

She walked on up to him, with genuine concern on her face.

"Are you feeling ok, George? Do you want a mineral water instead of your whisky?"

"Nah," he said. "I'm not drunk, just wise. Or maybe stupid. One or the other."

It was me who took hold of the conversation, the prickles coming back to me as I met his gaze.

"Who barred everyone, George?"

He looked right back at me, then rolled his eyes.

"You know who. Don't pretend you don't."

Eliza shot daggers at me.

"Did you know anything about this, Katherine?"

"No!" I said. "I don't know what George is talking about."

George cackled some more. A guy in his 80s, laughing so hard he was leaning on the bar to stay upright.

"Honestly!" I insisted to Eliza. "I know nothing more than you do."

"Hmm," she said, obviously suspicious. "I'll head on out the back and make a call to the management myself to be sure."

I almost asked her to stay, the prickles were so bad, but she probably wouldn't have heeded my request if I had. She paced away with her arms swinging, and I stayed mute, still reeling from the situation as much as she was.

George was staring at me. He stopped laughing as soon as she was out of view, and beckoned me over. I did as I was told and stepped up close.

His eyes were beady and dark. Not the guy I'd come to know at all. He seemed older than his 80s, skin drawn and pale, like he was made-up for Halloween and not for the Regency club, without the costume. His words were a whisper.

"Do you want to see him?" he asked me.

"Who?" I replied, and he laughed again, just a little.

"You know who. Stop playing dumb."

I felt static in the air, senses tingling. I knew exactly who he meant, even though it felt like I was in a world gone crazy. I wanted to pinch myself to make sure this wasn't another dream gone wild.

"Answer me," he said. "The clock is ticking. Tick tock."

I should have said no. I could hear both my mum and grandma in my head, demanding I stop being a *stupid girl* and get some *common sense* into me, but I was on autopilot, unable to deny the truth.

"Yes," I told George. "I want to see him."

"Excellent," he said.

He clicked his fingers, and all at once the front door opened and a big crowd of members came bustling inside.

Max and Stephan and the gang stepped in first, in suits this time, not costumes. Richard Scott, and Baron Taylor, and the Westminster trio close behind them. Mr Kelly, and Edward Warren, and Killian, and Cedric Quentin, too. And then finally, bringing up the rear, were Benjamin and Frederick.

…And Hans Jacob Weyer to follow.

My heart leapt and it was like a switch had been flicked, the bar back to life just the same as it would usually be. People took their regular seats and spoke in their regular voices, and George looked like George again, sipping on his whisky.

Eliza came dashing back in at the sound of clients, looking at surprised as I was, but she hid it better. She put on her smile and got to service, supplying people with beverages as quickly as she could.

I felt like an idiot struggling alongside her. My hands were jittery, making me a clumsy clutz as I tried to pass myself off as normal.

I served the Westminster trio first, and then Edward, Killian and Cedric, but I was burning up like a beacon as Hans took a seat at the bar alongside Frederick, just a few seats down from George.

I couldn't look at him.

I couldn't dare face him.

I kept on serving and smiling, with a rush of crazy, silent gratitude as Eliza handled their orders instead of me.

The rush at the bar died down after a few long minutes, but still I kept my distance from the men at the end, glad when Eliza beckoned me over with a grin on her face.

"You were right, there was a polo match. The coach just got back in from Cirencester. It was quite a day of it."

"Who told you that?" I asked her.

"Baron Taylor," she replied. "He was telling me what a good match it was. The Wesleydales won."

I knew little about polo games, apart from the fact that the players rode on horses, but I smiled like I was pleased at the news.

"Excellent. That explains it, then."

"Yes," she said. "Thank God for that. I thought we were facing some kind of management crisis, or some Halloween terror had cursed our club!"

I laughed too loudly, but she didn't seem to notice it was fake.

"I'll handle the lounge," she told me. "Stay here and take care of the bar."

I did as I was told. I cut up lemon after lemon and stocked the ice trays back to full. I cleaned down the sides, and cut up yet more lemons, and the whole time I was as flushed and tingly as I could be.

I tried to summon Mum and Grandma's voices some more, telling myself I was being a ridiculous girl with a fantasy brain, and it may just have been beginning to work for me – until Frederick got up to make his way to the bathroom and Hans summoned me over.

"A merlot for me, please," he said.

Blood-red...

"No problem, coming right up," I replied, but he called me back with a *wait a moment, Katherine.*

The only other person in earshot was George.

"You seem a little uneasy tonight," Hans said. "Are you feeling unwell?"

I shrugged it off, screaming inside that I was nothing but crazy, and that Hans Weyer was just Hans Weyer, a normal human. The newest member of our club and nothing more.

"No," I assured him. "I'm fine, thank you."

I thought that would appease him, but it didn't. He kept his bright green eyes fixed right on mine.

"Are you sure about that? You look as if you've seen a ghost. As if you're living in some horrible night terror."

I thought I'd known prickles before, but they were nothing like these fresh ones. The room started spinning, and the only thing that was steady was Hans' beautiful white smile.

"Did you have a nightmare?" he asked me. "Honestly, Katherine, if you aren't feeling well, you should go home."

I swallowed and braced myself on the bar.

The prickles were hot and fierce. The memories of racing across the cobblestones came back with a vengeance, but Hans' words still transfixed me, surpassing it all.

I'm interested in YOU.

His vampire fangs, his perfect touch, the way he kissed me so fiercely.

His hand...

Stop!

My voice found itself, and the world stopped spinning. My spirit held firm in my body.

"I'm fine, thank you," I told him. "I didn't have a nightmare."

"No?" he asked. "Are you sure about that? They call night terrors *terrors* for a reason."

I held his stare, even though it was eating me up.

"It wasn't a nightmare," I said, and my words sounded more assured than I thought they would. "I had a dream last night, and nothing more."

I poured his merlot, confident, even though my fingers were shaking. I handed it over with a smile.

"Thank you," Hans raised his glass to me. "Here's to more sweet dreams, Katherine. We all have plenty of them. A whole world of dreams out there worth living for."

And dying for.
That's the voice that came into my mind.
His voice.
Some dreams are worth dying *for.*
The question was…
Were mine?

4

It turned out to be a busy night at Regency, considering it started as a dead zone. The regulars were drinking hard, chatting into the early hours, and even Eliza was sneaking glances at her watch, clearly wishing everyone would fuck off so we could close up the bar.

Hans had already left with Frederick several hours before Max and the crew waved their goodbyes and stumbled out with boyish cheers.

"Thank God for that," Eliza said once she'd locked the door behind them. "I thought we were going to be here until breakfast."

We cleared up the empty glasses together, loaded up the washer and got to wiping the bar clean. She was on the opposite side to me, working hard when I cleared my throat and chanced a conversation. She knew the member accounts a lot better than I did.

"Hans seems an interesting guy. What does he do for a living?"

She shrugged. "I don't know."

"You don't know?"

"No," she said. "His membership application had nothing on it beside the essentials."

I stopped wiping the bar.

"Really? How did he get approved, then?"

The application process was normally rigorous, I knew that much. The criteria for acceptance here was high.

"He's an associate of Frederick's. Frederick went to management and they accepted Hans without question."

"I guess maybe Hans is a client of Frederick's?"

"Well done, Sherlock," she laughed. One of the few times I'd seen humour from her.

Frederick was one of the top accountants in the country. He worked for the elite at levels that barely anyone knew about. Eliza had told me that right from my first shift. He was one of the most prestigious members, from a very prestigious group, and was to be treated with utmost respect and consideration.

The bar was archaic and all of the members were wealthy, but Frederick was a prize amongst the rich of the country, no doubt integral to them maintaining their already huge financial estates.

Eliza seemed to take pity on my curiosity as I carried on working.

"Hans moved back to London recently, I believe, from the countryside over by Wales. Quite a rural gentleman."

"Really? Where from?"

"Herefordshire, actually. Like you. Who knows, maybe you ran into him in the corner shop, and didn't notice him." She huffed out a laugh. "Scrap that, you'd have definitely noticed him."

I stopped moving, staring at her with the bar cloth in my hand.

"Herefordshire? Really?"

"Yes."

"Do you know where from exactly?"

My legs were trembling at the thought, because it seemed so weird. Hans from Herefordshire? Surely not.

She paused, with a hand on her hip.

"Let me think. Somewhere with weird churches."

My turn to scoff. "That could be anywhere in Herefordshire."

"No, there was one of them he was talking about with George… One with some weird things on it. Carvings of a serpent, and a green man, and an upside down hand."

I stopped in my tracks. "Are you sure?"

She looked at me. "Um, yes. I'd say that's pretty memorable."

"Garway," I said. "That's the church at Garway."

"Possibly. I don't remember the name."

"It is," I told her. "That's the Garway Templar Church."

"I guess so, then," she replied, unaware of the coincidence.

Or synchronicity.

"It's only a few miles away from Orcop," I went on. "Where I grew up."

She laughed. "Maybe you did run into him at the local shop at some time. I don't imagine they have all that many around there."

She didn't even say *wow, that's strange, don't you think?* Nothing. She got straight back to work, passing it off as nothing but two people living in the same county, but she didn't know Herefordshire. The village communities were so small and interconnected that it was insane to think a man like Hans could have lived in Garway without me never so much as hearing about him. It gave me shivers.

If I'd have had anything like a decent relationship with Mum I'd have called her on the spot and asked if she knew him.

"When did Hans join the Regency?" I asked.

Eliza shot me a piercing stare this time.

"What's the interest in Hans all of a sudden?"

"Nothing," I said. "It's just a bit close to home. Literally."

"Not all that long," she said. "Just a few weeks before you started. Like I said, I don't know all that much about him yet. None of us do really, bar Frederick."

Those eyes. His smile as he reached for me...

I got a wave of something so deep in my stomach I thought I was going to be sick on the spot. I put my hand on my belly and held back a retch, but Eliza saw me.

"Are you alright? You look like you're going to throw up."

I nodded, but I was lying. I wasn't alright at all.

She moved a little closer, but I held out a hand shaking my head.

"I'll be fine, don't worry."

"Hardly. You're as white as a ghost."

I'm sure I was. A ghost from the past.

The room started spinning, so I closed my eyes. I heard a ringing in my ears as pictures of Garway church flashed through my mind one after the other. The carvings. The altar. The way I'd been lighting candles there on visits since I was a little girl. My mother and grandmother were religious women. Garway was the church they would pray in, every Sunday for years. I used to play around the gravestones, making up stories.

Had Hans been there?

Of course he had. The memories were flashbacks, streams of the forgotten like lightning bolts right through my head.

The evening choir singing around Christmastime. The man under the yew tree, watching as I left the service early, bored of Mum and Grandma chatting bullshit with the locals.

The man looking up at the Hand of God carving on the outside of the chapel, standing in the darkness and looking over at me with a smile.

It was him.

I couldn't remember his face, only his presence, but it was him. I knew it for certain.

My God. Hans had been there. In Garway. All those years ago.

"You need to go home, Katherine," Eliza said, breaking through my thoughts. "I'll finish the bar. Go call yourself a taxi and get to bed."

I nodded with a *thank you* and stumbled out to grab my phone from my bag, my fingers shaking so badly I could barely use the screen.

I dialled the taxi firm I normally used, but its lines were all busy. I tried the reserve taxi cab firm, but the operator told me they had no cabs available for at least the next hour. I called up some more from the listings. Three, four, five, all ringing out to nothing.

Fuck.

I tried the original one again, but the lines were still busy, over and over again.

The waves were still rushing through me, the spirals of memories still coming. Me in the darkness at Garway church as a little girl, the man on the sidelines always standing there.

No. It couldn't be. This was fantasy.

Stupid girl, Katherine.

I gave up on cabs. I had to leave. Now.

I grabbed my coat and put it on, took my keys from my bag and set off on shaky legs. My phone was still in my hand, I kept dialling the cab number as I walked down the street, becoming oblivious to the *line busy* tone that was beeping in my ear.

It was gone 3.a.m. as I walked up the street, that much I knew. Far too late for every taxi cab in London to be busy. That was reinforced by the fact that there wasn't anyone in sight as I made my way home.

Home.

It wasn't home though, was it? I was living in a room in a house I hardly knew, with people I'd barely spoken to. My home was in Orcop. My family had been living there for generations. I'd traced my family tree back as far as it would go, hoping for signs of more relatives to ease the constant burden of just me, my mother and grandmother, wanting my life to be more than just the three of us, when both of them clearly dismissed me as nothing.

My search had shown up generations, all tied back to that one part of the country. *Georgina, wife of Thomas, agricultural worker, Orcop. Josephine, wife of Phillip, agricultural worker, Orcop. Elaine, wife of David, agricultural worker, Orcop. Lillian, wife of Matthew, agricultural worker, Orcop. Ruby, Georgina, Margaret. Jane, Deborah, Kerry-May, Mary... so many women in the chain, all of them from Orcop.*

So many women in my family line I'd thought of, and wondered who they resembled most. Were they more like my mother and grandmother or more like me? I'd been needing something, *anything*, to believe I wasn't the black, lonely sheep in a very scathing family.

I kept on walking, so caught up in the memories and my pounding heart and the constant taxi firm unavailable tone in my ear, that I was at the cobbled lane of Hyde Street before I realised it. I stopped in my tracks the moment I felt the first bump of stone under my feet, staring at the dull street lights lying ahead of me. Barely more than an orange glow.

There was not a soul to be seen. Just like in my dream.

The air was misty, and my breaths were raspy, and I could have taken the longer route around Brooke Avenue, but it would have added at least ten minutes to my journey. I didn't think my shaky legs could handle it.

The final scrap of *stop being ridiculous, Katherine* rose up and took hold of me, and I stepped forward onto the cobbles. As soon as I'd done so, I felt another lurch deep in the pit of me, knowing that the *stop being ridiculous, Katherine, stupid girl* rantings had always been nothing more than a lie. Mum and Grandma had known I wasn't a stupid, ridiculous girl living in a fantasy world. I should never have believed them in the first place. I felt it right down in my soul.

There was more to this. So much more.

My thoughts were interrupted by a jolt.

"Lovely to see you, Katherine."

Hans' voice came out of nowhere, his footsteps appearing behind me. I spun to face him, dropping my keys and phone without a thought, and he kept on pacing towards me, even though I had both hands held up in panic.

"Stop it, Hans! Leave me alone!"

"Oh, please." He laughed. "I've been leaving you alone for eighteen long years. It's high time we became properly acquainted."

"It was you, wasn't it?" I squeaked at him. "You were the one at Garway!"

He had his hands clasped behind his back so naturally, circling me with footsteps, his bright green eyes fixed on mine as I turned around to keep him in view.

His voice was so low and powerful.

"Strange, don't you think? How you didn't remember those encounters at Garway until a short while ago. Recollections can come back in a flash. Just like that!" He clicked his fingers.

I was playing around the gravestones, ran straight into a man's legs, fell back with a yelp. His smile. His slender fingers reaching to help me up.

Be more careful amongst the dead, Katherine. Those were his words. Then he'd vanished.

I'd forgotten all about…

"What the hell is going on?" I asked him. "Really, Hans. What's going on?!"

I was terrified, and my heart was thumping so hard I could feel it in my ribs, my legs shaking harder than ever, but underneath all of that there was something different. A recognition, as though I'd known this man my whole life.

"You know what's going on," Hans said. "Trust your instincts and not your brain, like you should have done since the day you were born."

Rational Katherine was losing all hold of me, but I still felt like a fantasist fool when I spoke the words out loud.

"You really are a vampire, aren't you?"

He smiled his perfect smile.

"Indeed, I am."

"And last night… that wasn't just a nightmare, was it? That was real?"

"Ouch. I see you're using the term *nightmare* now. It was a *dream* earlier, if I recall?"

"A dream, then. It wasn't a dream at all, was it? It was real."

He tipped his head, as though he was curious, still circling me. "Call it a trial run."

I backed up against a door, ignoring my discarded phone and keys. I wasn't surprised to find it was the same large wooden door I'd backed into in my dream.

"A trial run for what?"

His hand between my legs.

He moved a step closer, his eyes so fierce yet so beautiful.

"You have a choice to make, Katherine."

"What kind of choice?"

Fingers sliding over my nipple.

"A simple one, really. Tell me you want me to leave you alone and I'll walk away. You'll have no memory of this, just as you've had no memory of our encounters before. All of it will be forgotten, and you'll be free to continue your new life in the city, trying to run away from the shadows of the past."

"And if I don't?"

"You're asking me questions you already know the answers to, you just don't have enough faith in yourself to accept them." He paused. "I blame your mother and grandmother for that. They've been feeding your self-doubt since you were old enough to start believing in fairytales."

"You know my mum and grandma?"

"Well enough to stay on the sidelines of their sad little world. I'm glad you opted to up and leave before they could crush your spirit even further."

My thoughts were spinning so fast my mind couldn't keep up. I closed my eyes and tried to focus, begging my head to take control.

"Stop fighting it," Hans said. "Instincts over brain, remember?"

"I don't… I don't know what to say…"

My voice sounded like a whisper, my whole world spinning and crashing in tidal waves, until there was silence.

Just like that, there was silence.

There was only me and Hans, the beautiful man standing in front of me, all London noise faded and gone.

"Tell me to leave you alone, Katherine," Hans whispered. "Or tell me you want me to stay. Your choice, but make it now."

My voice sounded more assured this time, without the chaos of thoughts there to lead me astray.

"And if I tell you to stay? What happens next? You suck the life out of me here on the cobblestones and I get the grand exit of my dreams?"

The thought seemed surprisingly enticing.

He smiled his stunning white smile, long pointed canines shining bright.

"I think you might be quite surprised by the outcome, Miss Blakely. Why don't you make your choice and find out?"

5

*T*wo choices. Two very different outcomes.

"Come on, Katherine," Hans said. "You must know what the legend says. For a vampire to enter your home, they must be invited."

"Yes, I do. And once a vampire has been invited in, there's no way you can get them to leave."

"Absolutely."

"This isn't my home you're talking about though, is it? This is my life."

His stare was so steady. "Your life *is* your home, and your body is your temple."

My breath caught at his words.

My body is my temple.

He smirked at me, clearly reading my thoughts.

"Yes, little one, I have every intention of entering the temple as well as the home. I showed you that last night." He paused, his eyes bright in the darkness. "You enjoyed it though, didn't you?"

I felt so inexperienced there before him. If the streetlights had been brighter, it would have been obvious I was blushing like crazy.

"You were very good at it," I said.

He laughed. "You'd certainly hope so. If you weren't a master after seven hundred years of practice, you'd be quite ashamed of yourself, I think."

"Is that how old you are?" I asked him. "Seven hundred years?"

"Stop avoiding the question."

My whole body was tingling when he took another step forward. He was so close, I could feel his breaths, and I was hot. So hot I wanted to tear my clothes off.

"Yes, or no?" he asked. "Go? Or stay?"

My body already knew the answer. Every part of me was aching for him. In that moment it didn't matter what the outcome would be. He could have sucked me dry and left me for dead on the cobblestones, and I'd still have made the same decision. I couldn't fight the battle anymore.

"Stay," I whispered.

"Good choice," he said, and tipped my face up to his.

I could hardly breathe as he dropped his mouth to my throat. I whimpered as his teeth grazed my skin, craving it, even though I was truly petrified.

I wondered whether the sensation would live up to my fantasies. I'd spent so many nights playing with myself, imagining blood-red kisses and the pleasure of pain.

"Do it," I whispered. "Bite me."

I felt the smile of his lips against my neck, the heat of his breath.

"Oh, Katherine. Do you really think I'm going to sink my teeth into your throat and take your blood, just like that? This is only the beginning. I've been dreaming of this moment for centuries."

He kissed the most sensitive part of my neck, just a touch below my ear. A kiss that sent a flush of sparks through me, right down to my clit. His thigh pushed between mine, and I cried out, desperate.

"That's it," he whispered as I began to move against him. "Trust your body."

My skirt hitched up so easily, leaving just a sheer pair of tights between Hans' thigh and my panties. I wished I could tug them aside myself, to give my myself the full sensation.

"Don't worry," Hans said. "I'll do that for you."

I yelped when he tore my tights free so easily and hooked his fingers in the lace of my panties.

"So beautiful and wet," he whispered as I worked against him like the needy little girl who'd been playing over vampire stories for years.

"Follow your instincts," he told me.

My instincts were already running wild. I was a fumbling mess as I tried to get out of my clothes, burning up, despite the chill of the night. I shrugged off my coat, and unbuttoned my blouse with clumsy fingers while Hans was teasing me so gently with his. I leant back as far as I could, and offered him my breasts in my white lace bra.

"Is that where you want to feel my teeth?" Hans asked.

I nodded, breathless. "Yes. Please."

"You're going to be such a dirty little girl. I knew it."

My depths were coming to light. I'd been fantasising for so long, and over time those fantasies had got dirtier, and dirtier... and filthier, and filthier.

Hans smiled as he looked at my offered flesh.

"So tempting, but I have a blood-red kiss to take of my own first. Your pretty tits can wait their turn."

My nipples tightened at his words. "Ok," was all I could say.

Even in my terror there was a strange sense of peace, and I thought back to so many vampire novels and scenes that had shown the submission of victims to me. The moment they accepted their fate and embraced it. Wanted it. *Needed* it.

Hans brushed his lips against mine, and I was ready. I cried out as he nipped my bottom lip, just a little. A sharp pain that felt nice. I tasted my own blood, and he let out a moan that set my heart alight.

"Delicious," he said, and his mouth met mine.

His kiss was so deep and fierce it ate me up. His tongue felt amazingly sensual, and I was kissing him like I had done in my dreams, wrapping my arms around his neck and asking for more without words.

I felt another sharp pain as he bit again, but I was too caught up to notice where the blood was coming from. Lips or tongue, or a mixture of both, I didn't know and couldn't care. The kiss was rich with a metallic taste and he was moaning, sucking. Drinking. He was drinking blood from my mouth.

I felt a little dripping down my chin and he licked it up in one swoop of his tongue. Then he pulled away far enough that I could see his mouth in the orange glow of the streetlights. *Blood.* My blood.

My first ever blood-red kiss.

I licked my bloody lips and opened my mouth for more.

He gave me more.

Bite me, I screamed silently, and he whispered in response.

"Patience, little one. You don't want to have glaring bite marks on your face in the morning. People will definitely notice."

So, he wasn't planning on killing me tonight.

He smirked at my thought.

"I'm not going to kill you. We're going to have a lot more fun than that. I can drink from strangers in a heartbeat, and leave them to their fate. Some want it, some don't. I don't care. I'm long past the days of regret and pity. I am who I am, and I need what I need. Human lives come and go, but mine does not."

I smiled with relief.

"Time to give you your wish," he said. "Give me your pretty tits. Offer them like a sweet little girl."

He sounded much dirtier than I'd expected him to.

"Trust me. I'm a different creature than you might think. I've lived a long time, I've experienced a lot of things and played a lot of games. There is very little I haven't done, and nothing I can't show you."

"Bite me then, please," I whispered, my mouth still tasting of blood. "Show me."

"Ask me to bite your tits, say it."

I'd never been in this position before. Not without my hand between my legs. It felt difficult, like I was on display, and about to be the *bad girl* my mum had called me when she'd seen the dirty vampire stories on my bookshelf.

"Let me make it easier," he said, and I was getting used to it. Him reading my mind.

His thumb brushed against my clit, and the feeling was so strong I panted.

"Say it," he told me.

"Bite my tits, please." My voice sounded so weak.

"Give it more. Trust yourself."

I swallowed my fear, took a breath. "Please bite my tits and make me bleed. Make it hurt."

"That's much better. No one has ever played with your tits before, have they?"

I looked him right in the eyes, still panting.

"You already know the answer to that, don't you?"

"You're a fast learner." He smirked.

I thought of the times I'd been courting guys back in Orcop, and how every one of them had backed away. I'd been such a loner that I'd given up. Nobody had wanted me. But it was a lie, wasn't it?

"Yes," he told me, speaking straight to my thoughts. "It was a lie. Plenty of people wanted you, but I wouldn't let them have you. I was saving you all for me."

He took his hand from between my legs and used his thigh instead. His fingers came up and he brushed my nipples through my bra. I arched my back further, pushed my chest out.

More. Give me more.

He didn't tug my bra down at first, just teased me through the lace as his thigh ground against me, and I was lost to him. I moaned as he got rougher, squeezing.

Bite me!

He lowered his head to my chest and I braced myself. But he didn't bite me, just lapped at my nipples through the lace and had me panting for more.

Please.

He tugged at the lace, freeing one breast. My nipple exposed to the cold air and his hot gaze made it tighten even more.

"Beautiful," he said then yanked the other the cup away, exposing the rest of me.

The hunger in his eyes had my heart racing, back arching as he lowered his mouth.

His tongue was so good, swirling until he began to suck. I couldn't stop moving against his thigh. He caught a nipple between his teeth and tugged. I gasped when he let go. Gasped and rubbed harder against his thigh.

"Ask me to make you bleed," he told me.

"Please, bite my tits, Hans. Make me bleed."

"Your voice is so wonderful when you speak like that."

His praise felt divine.

"Thank you."

I felt the points of his teeth, so sharp as he lapped at my tits, switching from one to the other. He teased me as his thigh worked, until I was a mess on the edge of coming.

And then he gave it to me, sank his teeth right into my flesh, and it hurt. Oh God, it hurt, but I didn't cry out, just held in my pain and took it, still bucking against his leg in solid rhythm.

He sucked and I felt my blood flow into his mouth. He drank from my breast and it felt so good I held him to me.

More, please. More.

He bit me again, and this time I was prepared for the sensation. It hurt, but I moaned.

Yes, yes... please.

My other breast was crying out for him. His thumb was brushing my nipple, getting it ready.

I was moaning as he moved his mouth. I smiled as he sank his teeth into fresh skin, both tits bleeding free, him sucking at me like he was as desperate as I was.

That's when he shifted the angle of his thigh, just a touch, changed the rhythm ever so slightly and it drove me absolutely crazy.

I came for him on the street, with my back against a thick wooden door and his thigh between my legs. I came with a vampire sucking at my breast, feeding him with blood. My mouth was still bleeding, and I loved it. I was grinning as I bucked against his thigh.

His teeth remained in my flesh until I'd stopped bucking. He pulled away with a smack of his lips as soon as I was done.

"Delicious," he said again. "As I hoped, your blood is perfection."

He kissed me with another blood-red kiss, and mine was full of gratitude.

Thank you, I said in my head when he was done.

"You're welcome. Now it's time for you to go home and sleep. I've taken quite a lot of blood from you for your very first time."

I nodded, felt weak on shaky legs, but I didn't care. I'd have done it all again in a flash, whatever the consequences.

Hans picked up my keys and phone and handed them to me.

"Go now," he said. "Don't tempt me."

I took my clothes from the floor and held my blouse to my chest, no longer caring if anyone saw me. I walked away from him in a daze, but he called after me. I shot him a glance over my shoulder.

"Remember your invitation, Katherine. You're mine now to take as I please. That invitation cannot be withdrawn."

"Yes," I replied. "I understand."

I was glowing all the way home until I flicked the light on in my bedroom. I flinched when I saw the blood smeared all over my bra, but I relaxed into it, stepping closer to the mirror to check out the bite marks. They were deep.

I got into bed and the inevitable happened. I slipped my hand down between my legs for another play, but no. His voice sounded loud in my head, and my fingers were held in a vice, even though I couldn't see him.

You can no longer pleasure yourself. Your body belongs to me.

I nodded in the darkness, accepting my fate. And somehow, I knew my soul belonged to him too.

6

My bottom lip was sore and a little bit swollen when I woke up, but it was nothing too obvious. Hans was right. Nobody would notice the blood-red kiss he'd blessed my mouth with.

The red raw teeth marks on my tits were a different story, though. My flesh was wounded deep and bruised, but it didn't freak me out as I stared at the aftermath in the mirror. I ran my fingers over the marks and felt a strange rush of pride for taking the pain. So many fantasies over so many nights, come to life. I could only imagine the beauty of every other fantasy Hans had the power to make come true.

I put on my dressing gown and wrapped it up tight, making sure my tits were well hidden before I went downstairs. I needn't have worried of course, since as per usual the other housemates were all out. Not a soul in sight.

Once again, I wished I had someone to share my stories with. A friend. A family member. Someone close that my mother and grandmother had always failed to be. I didn't have any extended family. I'd never known my father, and my poor grandfather had died when I was just a baby in arms, and there were no aunties, uncles or cousins to share my life with.

Maybe Hans could be everything, all in one? It was a stupidly optimistic thought that should've seemed crazy but didn't. How could anything about my fantasies possibly feel crazy anymore? I just needed... someone.

Him.

I made myself breakfast. Porridge with plenty of sugar, followed by toast. I tried to relax and let my strength come back to me, lying in bed through the afternoon, watching Buffy reruns on my laptop with a whole new perspective. It was when Spike slammed Buffy against the wall and she wrapped her legs around him that my hand dared snake into my dressing gown. It had been a shocker at the time. Spike was actually fucking her. And damn those kisses were hot. Blood-red kisses. My hand froze just an inch from my pussy, once again gripped like a vice.

Damnit.

I now knew what it felt like to be the victim of a blood-red kiss. I knew what it felt like to have a vampire's fangs sinking into my skin. I knew how it felt, being a vessel of flesh they were taking their life from.

I knew how it felt to be... *owned.*

Knew how it felt when your heart ached for someone. I simply couldn't wait to see him again. To kiss him again. To give myself to him.

If only I could play with myself thinking about it. But no. Definitely not. My hand wouldn't budge.

I was feeling a little more steady by the time I showered and got ready for work. My bra was sore over my bite wounds, and my blouse felt starchy as it rubbed my skin, but I liked it. The pain was a constant reminder of what Hans had taken from me.

I wasn't afraid of the cobblestones when I walked through Hyde Street that evening. I was grinning all the way.

My smile was still bright on my face when I stepped into the staffroom and hung up my coat on the rack. I felt surprisingly confident when I pushed my way through the door into the bar to find Eliza there, busy at work. Confidence wasn't something I was usually blessed with.

She turned to me when she was done serving Richard Scott, and her eyebrows raised up high.

"I expected you to be calling in sick today." She looked me up and down, still in disbelief. "You look well recovered, though."

I nodded. "I feel much better today, thanks."

She was still staring at me.

"Actually, you look absolutely bloody amazing," she said out of the blue.

Her compliment gave me a flush. Her expression was so genuine but so confused, as though she was staring at an entirely different person than the one she'd come to know.

I was the same girl with the same dark hair wrapped up tight in the same neat bun, wearing the same neutral gloss lipstick, in the same crisp white uniform, but I didn't feel like it. Not one bit.

"Thanks," I said, burning up so bad that I was grateful for the distraction as clients came up for drinks.

I served Kristoff and Edward with a happy smile, and then I walked over to George, who was sitting at the side of the bar. It was great to see him there.

"Thank you, George," I whispered. "For last night. I really appreciate it."

"Appreciate what, exactly?" he asked.

I gave him a grin. "You know. For fixing things."

He pulled a face, confused.

"Fixing what, Katherine? I have no idea what you're talking about."

My surprise must have shown, because he looked at me piercingly.

"Katherine, what are you talking about? Tell me now, please."

I didn't know what to say as he glanced around the bar.

"Nothing much," I lied. "Eliza and I were talking about how the place was quiet, and you told me people would be in soon."

His eyes came right back to mine.

"Oh, I did, did I? And tell me, who showed up afterwards?"

I shrugged. "Everyone."

"Everyone?"

"Yes. Everyone."

"Including Frederick and Hans, I imagine, yes?"

I felt cold, as though I'd blurted out a secret.

"There was a polo game," I said on instinct. "In Cirencester. Everyone came in afterwards."

"And Frederick and Hans were amongst them?"

"Yes."

"I see."

He drank down his whisky and shoved his empty glass at me for another. I felt like a naughty kid who'd done something I shouldn't, especially when I handed his fresh whisky over and he shot me a glare. He took his phone from his pocket and headed off to the bathroom without another word. I got a shiver as the door closed behind him.

What had I done?

I didn't know.

I didn't have much time to dwell on it before the entrance door swung wide and Frederick appeared. I held my breath with a silent *please,* and my skin caught alight when Hans walked in after him, dressed immaculately in another black suit with black silk tie. He looked even more stunning than ever. Oh how my heart raced.

"A merlot for me, please," Frederick said when he arrived at the bar.

"The same for me, please, Katherine," Hans added, and his smile was so perfectly white that my legs almost buckled underneath me.

I felt like a child giving a performance on stage when I uncorked the wine and poured out two glasses. I handed them over with trembling hands.

"Thank you, gentlemen."

The sensations were overwhelming as they zipped through my body. I didn't know what to do or say, or where to look. I was almost relieved when Baron Taylor stepped up and ordered a merlot for himself. I got to work with a *coming right up, thank you,* but then something niggled me from nowhere. A tickle down deep that drew my attention to the closed bathroom door. George was still in there, his whisky still sitting on the bar counter.

I got the weirdest pull to say something to Hans, but I didn't know where to start other than to close the distance between us. Every step felt heavy, the butterflies in my stomach going insane.

His eyes were so green, and I should have known it. I didn't need to say a thing.

"Where is George?" he asked me, with a piercing gaze.

I gestured behind him. "In the bathroom."

"And how long has he been gone?"

"A few minutes."

Hans didn't look at me this time, he looked at Frederick sitting right beside him, and Frederick gave him the slightest nod before he got to his feet.

Frederick smiled at me. "I'll say hello to George when I'm in there. I need the bathroom myself."

I didn't get the chance to ask Hans anything once Frederick was out of his seat. He took the action for me, fixing me in another perfect stare before I could speak.

"Don't trouble yourself with this. Please stay out of it. And stay away from George."

"But George…" I blustered. "What about serving him?"

"You won't need to serve him," Hans told me, and I got an ominous shudder up my spine.

"Is George going to be ok?"

Hans looked genuinely curious. "Would it bother you if he wasn't?"

My words were a stutter. "Well, I… I like George… George is—"

"Old," Hans said. "George is a very old man."

"But—" I began.

"But what?" Hans asked, and he was so cold, so detached.

I looked at the bathroom door and back again.

"Is Frederick going to, um…"

"Kill George?" Hans laughed a little. "No."

"I don't understand what's going on here."

"You don't need to understand," Hans said. "Trust me, and stay out of things you don't need to be involved with."

I got a flood of relief when George stepped back out of the bathroom. I was straight over to him when he took his seat.

"Are you alright, Mr Miller?" I asked, but he held his hand up.

"That'll be all. Greatest thanks." He drank down his whisky in one and got up to leave. "I'll be seeing you."

But he was lying. I knew in my heart I wouldn't be seeing George Miller again, and I felt bizarrely upset about it. I marched over to Hans when the door closed behind the old gentleman, and to Frederick beside him, who was taking his seat, back from the bathroom.

"What's going on?" I asked them, and Frederick looked surprised at my question.

He held back, and it was Hans who answered me.

"Katherine. Leave us, please."

But no. I didn't want to. I didn't speak it aloud before Hans repeated himself, with a lower tone this time.

"Katherine. Leave us. Now, please. This doesn't concern you."

I knew from his eyes that there was no room for negotiation, so I backed away, feeling trapped in a corner. I had the urge to say something to Eliza, or to chase George down the street to make sure he was safe, but I got another shudder, and a sense of something deeper.

No.

I shouldn't do that.

I stopped in my tracks on my way over to Eliza.

No.

I spun back and caught my breath to find Hans staring at me.

No.

I nodded silently, then turned my attention to an approaching Max and Stephan instead.

"What can I get you, gentlemen?"

The rest of the night was busy and bustling, and Hans was continually caught up in conversation with Frederick and Benjamin, who joined them shortly after. Every time I looked Hans' way he would flash me a glance in return, with a smile always waiting to greet me, but there were no more words between us. Eliza was the one to serve them every time they had a request.

The hours passed, and my skin grew hotter. The minutes ticked by and the wounds under my blouse began to glow, sore, and with every second came an increasing feeling of desperation, until I was as needy as I'd been in the alleyway.

It felt like I was craving something. That's the only way to describe it. As though I was an addict craving some kind of fix, and that fix was Hans and his teeth. I needed his teeth in my flesh.

If only I could tell him so, but I didn't get the chance.

Hans, Frederick and Benjamin left the bar together at just gone midnight with nothing more than a *thanks* and *goodnight*.

Jeez, I needed the other clients to fuck off and leave me alone. Two more hours until closing felt like a lifetime. I was on a frantic mission as Eliza and I cleared the bar together, trying to get out of there as quickly as I could.

"Steady on," she said when she saw me scrubbing like crazy. "You'll take the veneer off at that rate."

I tried to slow down, but it was hard. So, so hard. I had so many cravings, and questions, and needs. All of them piling up inside me like a squirming mess of sensations.

Hans.

I needed Hans.

Finally, after what felt like a lifetime, the bar was cleared and washed up and it was time to go. I got my coat on as quickly as possible, waving goodbye to Eliza before she'd even reached the coat rack, and then I was on my way, practically running down to Hyde Street and the cobblestones where I prayed to God Hans would be waiting for me.

As it turned out, I didn't need to get that far. Hans was waiting on the corner before the cobblestones began, propped against one of the marble pillars by the banking chambers.

"You have questions," he said.

"Yes," I panted. "I have questions, and I can't walk away from them, Hans! I can't play ignorant. I just can't!"

"I know that, little one. You are so beautiful in your curiosity. It's one of the things I love about you."

I love about you.

His words hit me like a lightning bolt, but it didn't make any difference in that moment. I was shaking like an addict. His smile was so affectionate it gave me flutters, but I didn't want his affection right then.

"I need you to bite me," I said. "Please, Hans, I need you to bite me. I can't take it anymore."

He was up against me in a heartbeat, backing me against the stonework of the building before I could take a breath.

"Oh, don't you worry. I know."

7

"Just a little appetiser for now," he whispered. "To take the edge off the craving."

I didn't care where he bit me. It didn't matter. I was so desperate it was driving me insane. *Teeth.* That's all I could think about. *I need his teeth.*

"Shh, little one," he said, even though I wasn't speaking a word.

He slipped my coat from my shoulders and unbuttoned my blouse so slowly, my chest was prickling and my nipples tightening. He opened my blouse and checked out my bite marks and bruises with a smile.

"They suit you so perfectly."

"Please…" I whispered. "I need you to bite me."

His warm fingers slid into the cups of my bra and tugged them down, freeing my tits. The cold of the air gave me goosebumps.

"Wonderful," he said, admiring the wounds and bruising around my nipples. Just his stare had my pussy tingling.

Please bite me…

"Soon," he said with a fanged smile. "Is it hurting yet?" he added. "The need? The craving?"

I shook my head with a rush of fear.

"Is that what happens? Am I an addict now? Addicted to bites?"

"No." His voice was a breath. "You're addicted to *me*."

Somehow that thought was even more scary, but even more beautiful.

"Brace yourself," he told me, but I was ready for whatever was coming.

I held on to his shoulders as he leaned in, moaned when he licked around a nipple and ran his hot tongue all the way up to my shoulder.

I shuddered, and braced myself as his teeth grazed my collarbone, gripped his shoulders hard as he sank his fangs straight into tender flesh, just around the bone. It was purposefully painful, and I knew it. He was testing me. Pushing me. Seeking out just how much I wanted him.

I cried out loudly, but it didn't matter, not to him and not to me, either. He had me pinned and kept on sucking, so I closed my eyes and took it, grateful when the emptiness of craving began to subside. Then came the relief. The relief and the pleasure. Such gorgeous pleasure it rippled through me and ate me alive.

It was me who shifted myself so his thigh was between my legs. Me who started to grind against him like a dirty little whore.

He hitched my leg up higher and tore my new pair of tights apart at the crotch, and then his thumb brushed me. Oh God, his thumb brushed and played me so well I could hardly breathe, and still he kept on sucking.

Bliss and pain. Grinding and sucking, and I was moaning. Whimpering. Lost.

My mouth was hungry for his when he pulled his teeth out of me. I tasted my blood on his lips and then he gave me his tongue, so wet with my blood it made me shiver. Blood-red kisses, hot and deep.

He lifted me up so my feet were off the floor and I wrapped my legs around his waist. He positioned himself so he could rub his cock against my pussy, and I felt him, hard through his trousers. Fuck. He was so big. Way bigger than I'd expected a cock to be, not that I'd ever seen one in the flesh.

He smiled against my mouth.

"The more I drink, the bigger I get, but don't worry. You'll be able to take it. I'll make sure you're begging wet before I claim you for the first time."

The first time...

My tummy fluttered and my pussy clenched at the thought of his huge cock inside me.

"When will that be?" I asked him, and he kept on smiling, kept on grinding.

"Patience, little one. It'll be time when it's time."

I was a slut as I rubbed myself against him as best I could. I knew my clit was swollen and I'd be dripping in my panties, and I wished, *prayed*, he'd fuck me right there on the spot.

Please. PLEASE. I need it.

"Patience," he repeated.

"But I can't… I can't wait."

"You don't have a choice."

I got the impression that would be true about a lot of things from here on in. A lot of choices would belong to him now – but I'd given him that invitation.

It didn't feel all that bad.

He dropped me to the floor as I contemplated my new reality. He pulled my bra back into place and buttoned up my blouse for me, then picked up my coat from the floor and held it for me to put my arms in the sleeves – as though I was a little girl.

A little girl who'd never got the same care from her own father, since he'd disappeared before she was even old enough to know his name.

He took hold of my hand. His fingers were so long, they felt so comforting in mine.

"Are we going to my place?" I asked him.

You could fuck me there.

"No. We're going to mine."

That gave me tingles.

"Where is it?"

"Holland Road. A little way from here. The air will do you some good."

I felt better now he'd bitten me, still riding the waves of sated bliss. I soaked in the cool breeze as we walked.

"Are you going to tell me about George?" I asked.

"No. Not yet."

"Is he going to die?"

"All mortals die, Katherine."

I stared up at him. "You know what I'm talking about, Hans. Don't pretend you don't."

"Yes, I do. So maybe you should start asking proper questions."

I was nervous as I voiced the unspoken.

"Is George going to die tonight because of what happened in the bar? What did he do wrong?"

"George is indeed going to die tonight, yes. But it's his time to go. We're saving him pain in the long run, despite the fact he may not realise it."

I had so many questions spinning through my brain.

Dying? Pain? Him not realising? Who the hell are 'we'? And why?! So many whys.

"Calm down," Hans said. "You'll get the answers to your questions. Slowly, one step at a time."

I tried to calm myself down, but my mind was still whirring. Hans' pace was slow and steady, in a lovely rhythm under the streetlights, and he was unfazed, in such contrast to me.

"Breathe along with your footsteps," he told me. "Feel the energy and trust it."

I didn't know what he was talking about, but turned my senses to how we were walking. My breaths went in and out to the pace.

"Do you feel that?" he asked. "The night?"

I felt the cool of the air.

"No," he said. "Deeper than that. Close your eyes and trust me to guide you."

It felt weird closing my eyes and walking, with no idea of what was in front of me, but the feeling was exhilarating. Alive.

I began to feel the power of his pace, his presence beside me and the strong grip of his hand in mine. I felt the flow of energy between us, merging as one. I felt my pulse beating, already craving his teeth again.

And then the rest of the world came into play.

I felt the glow of the streetlights, even though my eyes were closed. I heard the silence in the night, underneath the hum of London city. I felt the silver of the moon, even though it was hidden behind the clouds.

The questions stopped fizzing, and my mind stopped whirring and there was only footsteps, heightened senses and the rhythm of life.

It was a hymn I'd loved as a girl in the school choir.

The rhythm of life.

"I told you, didn't I?" Hans said. "You can open your eyes now."

I did what I was told, and my vision only added to the cold, beautiful intensity. I found I was smiling, like a child exploring the world through fresh eyes.

"Gorgeous," Hans said, looking down at me, smiling too.

We were stopping at a tall, grand townhouse before I knew it. The place had iron railings outside, and steep stone steps climbing up to the heavy black wooden door. The door knocker was solid brass.

"This is yours?" I asked him.

"Yes. It's one of my houses."

"Do you have many?" I asked as he took his key from his inside pocket and opened the door.

"Yes," he said. "I do."

It was time for me to cross his threshold, and I felt like I was about to step into a curiosity shop, filled with treasures. I wasn't going to be disappointed. That much was clear as soon as I walked into the hallway.

Beautiful ebonised antique furniture. Paintings of gold on the walls, abstract and stunning. A black and white Victorian style tiled floor, in perfect checks.

A home that would live up to the most dramatic gothic vampire novel I'd ever read.

"I'm glad you like it," he told me. "I hope you'll be spending a lot of time here."

I gave him my coat when he held out his hand for it. Proud at the way my nipples poked through my blouse. Proud that I was starting to understand his world – my new world. Proud that he'd chosen me. He was going to take me with his huge cock, make me beg, make me so wet…

"Earth to Katherine! Be still those filthy thoughts and listen to me, please. It's important."

"What? Sorry. What did you say?"

"I said, your days at Regency are over from now on," he told me. "And so are your days in the soulless room you've been trying to call home."

I struggled to digest it, all thoughts of rampant sex gone.

"Really? What? Just like that?"

"Yes," he answered simply.

"But what about–"

He smirked. "What about what?"

"What about my notice period?"

"You don't need to work your notice period. There are other staff waiting in the wings, don't worry."

"Ok, so what about the tenancy agreement on my rented room?"

"You don't need to worry about that, either. It'll be paid until the end of the agreement."

"By you?"

He took off his jacket and hung it on the ornate coat rack.

"Yes."

Another simple answer.

I was stunned.

"Is that not what you want?" he asked me. "You invited me over your threshold, remember?"

"Yes, but I… I didn't expect this."

"I'll repeat my question." He smiled a beautiful smile. "Is this not what you want?"

I listened to my heart, dancing under my surprise. I was soaring high.

"Yes, it's what I want," I said. "I'm just… shocked."

He laughed. "There are plenty of things that will shock you. This is only the beginning. Call it a nice surprise."

He led me through to the drawing room, off to the right from the hall. It was definitely a nice surprise. The ceiling was beautifully high, and the fireplace was grand in deep, dark marble.

"It's a little cold in here, isn't it?" he said and I jumped when the fire suddenly lit up in huge flames.

"What other things can you do?" I asked him. "You start up fires, and read my mind. What else can you add to the collection?"

"Not as many as one of the mages can," he replied. "They are another league altogether."

"Mages? What? Like wizards?!"

"Yes, and a lot of witches."

I was taken aback at the craziness, even though I was standing in front of a vampire.

"There are witches and wizards, too? Are you being serious?"

He laughed a rich laugh, and his green eyes were so full of affection.

Love.

"Oh, little one. You truly have no idea, do you? Your mother and grandmother have crippled you even more than I gave them credit for."

He gestured to one of the sofas, in deep blush burgundy brocade. I took a seat awkwardly as he paced back and forth in front of the fire. I felt so out of my depth in this space.

"Have you ever heard the tale of the nine witches between Garway and Orcop?" Hans asked me.

I remembered something vaguely from my memory.

"Kind of."

"Kind of?"

"Yes. I heard there are a group of them or something. It's a myth, right?"

"It's more than a myth. Your family line is inherent in it. Unfortunately, your mother and grandmother turned their back on their own heritage, and took yours from you, too."

"Stop," I said, trying to catch up with him. "I just… I can't."

My thoughts felt uneasy, like something was buried deep. Something I didn't want to surface yet, like a dark trapdoor deep down below.

He read me. Of course he did.

"We'll save this for another day," he told me, and I didn't argue.

I had other questions to ask him. Ones that didn't give me so many instant triggers.

"So, what about George? What's going to happen to him tonight?"

Hans took a seat beside me. His skin looked so stunning in the glow of the fire.

"Would you like the full truth?"

"Yes, please. Why wouldn't I?"

"A lot of people shy away from the truth on all levels. That's what culture has become now, a facade over the deeper meaning. Myths and legends have become little more than dusty fairytales. Everyone is now focused on the surface, racing around, looking for meaning where none can be found."

I looked over at the fire, taking in the height of the flames. Reaching, consuming. Part of my soul felt like that. Reaching, searching, wanting to consume and – to be consumed.

Just so long as that searching didn't include the trapdoor in my own subconscious.

"Shall I tell you what you want to know?" Hans asked me. "Call it another invitation on your part. You tell me you'd like answers, and I'll answer your questions. But once you start knowing those answers, you'll never be able return to ignorance again."

I weighed it up. It felt like I was on the edge of some kind of abyss, ready to jump and fall, or stay, forever wavering on the edge, wondering.

Considering I'd had a vampire suck my blood and was already an addict for more, it felt quite a strange thing to be wary of. I was already in way too deep to back out.

"Yes, I'd like answers," I told Hans, the creature who now owned my soul. "So, how about we start with George?"

8

I tried to get my thoughts in some kind of rational order.

"You said George is going to die tonight, didn't you?"

Hans' expression was so calm. Not a hint of trepidation in sight.

"Yes. I did."

"You said he was being spared pain. What did you mean?"

The vampire sitting beside me answered without a hint of concern.

"George is on the edge of death regardless. He's eighty-six and his health has been declining for years, but he doesn't want to get treatment for it. He wants to live an independent life, right up until the very end. Understandable."

"And the very end will be tonight?"

"Indeed, and it will save him suffering. George only has a few weeks until his heart gives up, but his heart will fight, because he's a fighter. That fight will put him in hospital, plugged into machines while doctors attempt to give him just a few more days of a miserable existence. He stopped enjoying his life a long time ago."

"How do you know that? About what lies ahead for him?"

"We have heightened senses. We read a lot of things about people, but we particularly read a lot about the flesh. It's our food source, after all."

"By *we*, you mean vampires? I guess there are a lot of you?"

He smiled. "That depends what you mean by a lot."

"Ok." I framed my question differently. "How many vampires are there in the world? Roughly?"

"There doesn't need to be a *roughly* about it. There are four hundred and ninety seven vampires in the world at present. We're quite a close knit community, spanning over thousands of years."

I tried to imagine four hundred and ninety seven vampires. It wasn't all that many. The population of Orcop was just over four hundred – a very small village.

My next question sprang up naturally.

"Is your friend Frederick a vampire?"

"No. He isn't. He's a mortal man associated with vampires."

"Associated how?"

"He's a financial asset manager. He ensures our estates pass down through generations when it comes to official paperwork. His family have been in the trade for a long, long time. His father was an excellent accountant before him."

"Is it Frederick who is going to kill George?"

"No. Frederick will just alert someone who will. George is likely already dead by now. I hope his passing was a peaceful one. God speed."

I got a pang of grief so hard it made me blanch. The very idea that George was dead already. It was just–

"Horrible, I know," Hans said. "I still remember how painful the ending of mortal life seemed to me in the early days, especially some. They can cripple your soul. But you adjust. Your perspectives change as your experiences change you."

I tried to get back on track.

"Why is George being killed? Is it because of what happened in the bar? Did I do something wrong?"

Hans reached out and squeezed my knee.

"You didn't do anything wrong as far as I'm concerned. I am in debt to you, actually. As are the rest of the vampire community. There are always hunters out to get us, and people who get scared and run to them. George was one of those people. He's been too familiar with

Frederick through Regency for quite some time. He's heard plenty of things he shouldn't have." He paused. "People are like an interconnected web and rumours whisper through silky threads. George tapped into two sides of a long waging war, and he picked his side. A lot of people choose the *righteous* hunters. That's understandable. There are always two sides to every story."

I had a horrible rush of terror at the mention of vampire hunters, the pang of grief for George buried under panic.

"You got to him in time, did you? The hunters won't be coming for you?!"

"It's good to see your priorities are where I'd hoped they'd be, little one." Hans squeezed my knee again. "No, I don't believe any hunter will be coming for me. I'm sure Frederick will have things under control by now. George was only on the outskirts of the hunter network. He was splashing in a shallow pond, thinking his depths were deeper. He had a long way to go into the ocean before he found the central ship he truly needed to find where hunters are concerned, but that's all over now. George is at rest. His splashing is over."

I took a breath of relief.

"Thank God for that."

Hans smiled. "Indeed."

There was something that glowed deep underneath the bright green of his eyes, and I couldn't place it. *Spirit? Soul? Belief?* I didn't know, but it gave me another fresh new sensation, striking a chord in my chest. My brain spun, trying to understand, but failing. I was growing weary of the confusion, and much more needy of the basics. I needed... time. I needed–

"We can pick up questioning tomorrow if you'd prefer," Hans said. "I'd strongly recommend you leave your mind to catch up and work things through. There has been a lot of revelation in a very short space of time."

I nodded. I'd trust Hans to guide me from here on in. I felt like a loved child at his side, which was a new one for me. A happy place to be.

"You need sustenance before I drink more blood from you," he said. "Let me get you some dinner. What do you like?"

I laughed, surprisingly light hearted. "You mean you don't already know? Jam on toast, please."

He laughed along with me. "Of course. I should have known that. I'm afraid I don't have any jam. I'll make sure to get some in for you."

He stood up from the sofa and held out a hand. He pulled me to my feet so easily.

"How about a nice, rare steak, Katherine? That's always good fuel to feed the fire."

I couldn't remember the last time I'd eaten steak, but the idea sounded a good one. My stomach rumbled at the mention.

"Wonderful," he said.

He guided me through to the kitchen, which was another impressive room with high ceilings. This one had rich terracotta floor tiles and black marble counters. Hans opened one of the thick oak cupboard doors and an inbuilt fridge appeared. Quite a contrast to the antique decor.

"Do you eat food? As in food, food?" I asked, and Hans shrugged.

"Very, very rarely, and usually only as a token display when in public. I don't enjoy it, and usually spit it out again as soon as I'm out of view. My appetite for blood soon wiped out my appetite for almost every other food in creation. Blood is my only necessity. It's like being an addicted wine connoisseur with a million different bottles of red to sample. Everything else pales into insignificance." He smiled. "And that's putting it mildly."

I took a seat at the kitchen island as Hans took a steak from the fridge. A huge piece that looked like rump.

"Did you get that in especially?" I asked. "Did you know I'd be coming?"

"Yes on both counts."

"Thank you."

He had heavy steel pans and lit one up and seasoned the steak like a master. Very confident and skilled for someone who rarely ate anything.

I grinned. "Were you a chef in a past life?"

He smirked back. "I enjoyed cooking food in a very distant part of this one. It's a hobby I've kept alive in the background. If not for myself, then for other people."

"Do you have many non-vampire friends to cook for?"

He shot me a glance full of humour.

"I thought we were done with questions for this evening, but since you asked. No, I do not. I have many non-vampire acquaintances, but not many I'd call friends. A life passes by in a finger click. Broken bonds can hurt for a lot longer."

I sighed at my own stupidity for asking, another round of *what, what, whats* running riot in my head.

"I really am going to stop asking questions now," I told him. "Every answer you give me leads to a thousand more questions."

"I'm sure that will be the case for a long time to come."

I got a fresh tingle. *A long time to come.*

"Yes," he said. "I'm hoping we will be acquainted for a long time to come. I wouldn't have introduced myself if I didn't."

I almost waded straight on in with another question. *Almost.* But I stopped myself. I needed to stop digging at the quicksand.

Hans started chopping up onions and I walked over to watch him. He had peas and broccoli, too. He took out some peppers and mushrooms to add to the collection.

"Is it really true what they say about garlic?" I asked him, and he rolled his beautiful eyes.

"Questions, Katherine."

I giggled. "That's hardly a serious question, Hans. Are you allergic to garlic, or not?"

"We don't appreciate garlic, no. It's an antibiotic. It doesn't do well for our blood, and it doesn't taste nice in other people's. You could see it as you see chocolate for dogs. They can eat a little, but it definitely won't agree with them. Too much of it will certainly put them in the veterinary clinic."

"What happens if you need a doctor? Do you have vampire clinics you can check into if you have a garlic OD?"

He grinned. "Not exactly, no. I'd have to retreat into darkness for a few days. Let the cold sweats take it out of me."

I became serious again, watching Hans' beautiful fingers chopping food.

"It's sunlight, isn't it? That's your biggest danger."

"Yes. It is. That's the killer. A very brutal way to pass, being burnt up into cinders."

I shuddered, hoping that never happened to him. The idea of having him gone from me was already unbearable.

He tossed the ingredients into a pan and added some spices, mixing them together like a pro. He really did know what he was doing with food.

"Plenty of health in this for you," he told me. "You'll need to keep your nutrient levels high."

He laid the thick, raw steak into the sizzling hot pan and within seconds it smelt absolutely delicious. I was definitely hungry for it.

"Take a seat and relax," Hans said, and I did what I was told, retreating to the island with my elbows back on the counter. Finally, I sat in silence, letting the questions slip away.

No more questions. Not tonight.

It was only a few minutes before Hans presented me with my dinner, arranged beautifully on a big porcelain plate, blood oozing from the steak. It made my mouth water. It had been a long time since I'd had such an extravagant meal. I'd been consuming jam on toast for weeks like a girl gone mad.

"Thank you so much."

"You're very welcome."

The first bite melted on my tongue. "This is truly delicious."

"Blood generally is, I find," my vampire chef said with another flash of humour. "But you could say I'm biased."

I felt my strength coming back with every mouthful of steak. Strangely vivid–

"Your body knows what it's lacking," Hans said. "You'll feel the digestion a lot more intensely than you would do without a vampire in the equation."

"That's good to know."

"Yes, it is. Since you're going to be needing that energy very, very shortly."

His smirk was divine. His eyes were like perfect green daggers. His tone was alight in a way that made every single part of me tingle.

I paused with my fork in the air. The rush of excitement was insane, even though I was still on the verge of exhaustion.

"Shortly as in tonight? More bites and more touching, and…"

My words dried up. I felt like the awkward virgin girl I really was.

"Sex, yes," Hans said easily. "Bites, and touching, and tasting, and sex. I'm going to fuck you, tonight."

The words sounded so filthy from such an eloquent mouth.

My fork was still in the air, hovering. My needs were still tingling, rising.

Hans grinned and gestured to my plate. "I'm going to take your innocence, hard and fierce, and I'm going to drink an awful lot of blood from your throat to go along with it. So, please. Finish up your steak and we can get started."

Wow. Holy fuck.

I've never gobbled up a meal so quickly in my life.

9

I'd had so many fantasies, but none of them had prepared me for the excited but abject terror I felt as I climbed the stairs up to Hans' bedroom. Every step made my heart pound faster. The reality dawning.

Hans was going to drink blood straight from my throat, and he was going to thrust his huge vampire cock inside me. That was the bottom line. Drink my blood and fuck me.

He was behind me with every step, close enough that I could feel the heat between us.

I was tempted to strike up an attempt at small talk to ease the tension, but I didn't. I made my way in silence with the vampire at my back, the tension still building with every pounding heartbeat.

"It's the door at the end of the landing," he told me.

I saw it, looming tall. A monster of jet-black oak. Yes. Black oak. Or so I thought until I turned the handle. I had to shove it hard to get it to move, shunting it wide with my shoulder.

It was obvious why when I stepped inside. There was thick steel attached to the wood. A huge solid panel on massive hinges.

"Yes, it's a heavy one," Hans said. "You'll get used to it in time."

I'm sure my mouth was open in awe when I saw the full extent of the bedroom before me. The bed was huge, made up in magnificent black damask bedding with satin cushions. The rug at the side was thick and plush, in glorious black and gold swirls, and the chandelier was wrought iron, hanging low. There was a dark wooden desk, and a beautiful gold banker's lamp, and antique bedside cabinets fit for a king.

"Wow," I said, because no true words could do it justice.

"I'm glad you like it," Hans said.

I jumped when he closed the door behind us. The thick steel bolts made tremendous clunks as he fastened them. There was no way we'd be getting out of here in a hurry.

And no way anyone would be getting in *here in a hurry.*

"That is true," Hans said. "We are very security conscious. Both of people as well as sunlight."

I looked around, trying to soak in every feature. There were old oil paintings – landscapes, and symbols I didn't understand. And a crucifix. There was a crucifix on the wall above the bed.

"But wha–" I began.

"Not all of the legends are true," he said. "That one is nothing but a fallacy."

I looked around some more, admiring a bookshelf filled from floor to ceiling with leather bound tomes. There was a beautiful velvet-covered armchair sitting beside them.

I walked up to the bed, still trying to comprehend the fact I'd be sharing it with the creature watching me. It felt like a very honourable place to lose my virginity. The header and footer were made up of yet more thick bars of iron. Beautifully regal. I touched the bedding, doing my best to believe this was really happening to me.

"Oh yes," Hans assured me. "It's really happening to you."

I gave him a meek little smile, then carried on past the bed to take a glimpse through a window at the street outside. The drapes around the glass were heavy black velvet to complement the bedding. It was when I stepped up closer to the sill that I realised just what was waiting behind them.

"As I said," Hans told me. "We are very security conscious."

The shutters behind the drapes were as heavy as the panel behind the door, with the same solid variety of bolts and latches.

"Let me get those," Hans said.

He closed the shutters with a tug, the metal thumping hard as the glow of the street outside disappeared. He worked the bolts and the locks in a flash, and it was clear we were sealed in so tight it was like a bedroom tomb.

After the dark metal shutters came a blackout blind that pulled down from above, and still came the thick damask curtains on top. He did the same with the other large window as I watched him, and if I was claustrophobic, I'd have been a wreck in this place, no matter the size of it.

"Just as well you're not." Hans smiled. "We're even more enclosed than you think we are right now, by the way." He tapped the oak floor with a heel. "Under here is solid steel, and there are matching layers in the walls to box us in."

"And in the ceiling?"

"Yes. In the ceiling, too."

"So, we're in a metal box?"

"Yes, effectively. No people, and no sunlight. They'd need an industrial team to get us out of this place."

I looked around through fresh eyes. Surprisingly, the place didn't feel all that eerie. I didn't feel uncomfortable at the thought of being locked in a London City tomb, bolted in tight by steel panels all around me.

"Let's get ready now, little one," Hans said, and I saw the hunger in his eyes. "It's time you learnt what it's like to truly be taken."

He gestured to the middle of the room, and I felt like I was walking onto a stage as I edged over with tiny steps. *One, two, three.*

But wait–

It was like something shifted in my subconsciousness on the journey.

Something primal. Wild. Crazy.

I mean, I wanted it. I wanted this...

But no.

NO.

My pulse was racing, and my legs were shaking, and the true force of what was about to happen seemed to hit me like an axe in the head.

"It's all right," Hans whispered. "Your body is scared. Let it be."

My body wasn't just scared, it was terrified. My eyes took on a life of their own as they zoomed around the place, realising in a new light that we really were sealed inside a bedroom tomb. *A vampire's tomb.* It was like being in the dream again with my feet wanting to sprint along cobbles, but here there was nowhere to run.

"This is natural, Katherine," Hans said. "Your body wants to flee because it fears what's coming."

"It's what I want, though," I said with a raspy breath. "I want you to bite me and take me."

He smiled with beautiful pointed teeth, but my legs were still braced for running.

"Your soul does, yes, but your body doesn't want to give in yet. Fight or flight needs to pass, so give it a moment. Take a breath and let it break its hold."

I took a breath, trying to calm myself.

"That's it," Hans whispered. "Your body must accept that it belongs to my will now. It must give up the fight."

My thighs tensed up, instinct still simmering.

"Give up the fight," he said. "Sink beneath your own survival instinct and tell yourself that your fate is mine to deliver."

"I… I'm not going to die though, am I?"

"No, but survival instincts don't work that way. Your body won't be believing you, especially when I sink my teeth into your throat."

It felt like a war was waging inside me.

"Breathe slowly," Hans told me. "Your body must accept it belongs to me now."

I breathed as slowly as I could, ears ringing. I zoned in on the pulse in my temples, and listened. Breathed and listened. *Slowly.*

My body belongs to Hans now.

Give up the fight.

"Good girl," Hans whispered. "No matter how much you think you want your life sucked from your slender throat and an undead creature's cock tearing your beautiful virginity away, it's going to be a very different experience when it comes to it. Tell yourself you want that experience. Make your body believe you."

His words sent fire searing through me. I felt his fangs stabbing my neck. His cock filling me up in one hard thrust.

Yes, I want it. I want that experience.

My body belongs to Hans now.

Give up the fight.

"That's it," Hans said. "So, bring your body into line. Give up the fight and strip naked for me."

My nipples tightened at his words but I wanted to whimper at the thought. I'd never stripped naked for anyone. My own mother hadn't seen me undressed since my breasts first started to develop. I was too uncomfortable to reveal myself, even to her.

Give up the fight. My body belongs to Hans now.

My fingers unbuttoned my blouse slowly. *He's already seen me like this. He's seen my tits offered up to him.*

"Yes, I have," Hans told me. "And they are absolutely beautiful. Just like the rest of you will be."

I used his words as extra confidence, still battling my body's urge to run. I unclipped my bra and let it fall to the floor with my blouse, then reached behind for the zip of my pencil skirt.

I felt so exposed. It felt like a whole audience of hidden eyes were watching me.

"You want me naked? Right here, in the middle of the room?" I was stalling and sounding pathetic.

Hans came to stand before me, eyes on my tits. The bruises looked worse now. I lifted my chest a little. He liked that. Smiled at me.

"Yes. I want you naked. Right now. This is part of accepting your fate. Losing your inhibitions to a higher force. Show me."

I felt the shift in me. The *want* in me.

His will. My will.

I unzipped my skirt and let it drop, standing bare apart from the tights he'd already torn at the crotch and the wet panties underneath them.

"Almost there," Hans said. "Go on, little one. Show me."

I closed my eyes as I took my tights off, and hooked my thumbs in the sides of my panties. It felt like there was something symbolic about it – presenting my virgin pussy to Hans.

"There *is* something symbolic about it," Hans told me. "Virginity is a sacred thing. A sacred gift of the body to be offered."

I opened my eyes to see his smile. The green of his hooded eyes was dirty but pure.

"Offer yourself to me," Hans said, and his voice was so self-assured. "Offer me your sacred little pussy like a good girl."

I no longer wanted to run. My panting had shifted from fear to want.

To need.

Oh God, I needed him.

"That's it," he whispered. "Acceptance of the body is so good for the soul. You want to offer me that sacred little pussy. I know you do."

"Yes," I said. "I do."

"So, do it. Be brave and show me."

With that, I took a breath and did what I was told. I pulled my tights and panties down and stepped out of the wet lace, and then I kicked the pile of clothes away, leaving just me, naked and vulnerable. His to consume and use however he chose.

The acceptance of my fate felt bizarrely liberating when the panic eased away. There was a level of peace under the terror that lit up my soul. Finally, it was coming. Truly. The time was coming.

"Spread your legs," Hans told me, and I did it.

I spread my legs and stood before him like a child standing before their teacher, desperate for instruction, and praise, and reward.

The look in the vampire's eyes gave me all the praise I could ever need.

"You're so slick and wet for me, it's beautiful," he said, and I smiled.

He gestured me to spin.

I turned for him like a naked ballerina, as dainty as I could be on nervous tiptoes.

"Perfect," he told me, and I believed him. For once in my life, I believed I was worth something.

The thought came hard and sharp.

I hadn't truly realised how little I thought of myself.

"Oh, sweetheart," Hans said, and pressed himself up behind me. "I can't wait to show you what it really feels like to be loved."

Loved.

"Yes," he told me. *"Loved.* I've loved you since before you were born. I'm going to show you that."

He's going to show me how well he can make me hurt, too.

"Indeed, I am."

His teeth grazed my shoulder from behind and I thought he might sink his teeth into my neck right there on the spot, but he didn't. He pulled my hair loose from its bun instead, so it tumbled free.

It made me feel even more naked and natural for him.

With that, he stepped away and gestured to the bed.

"I'm going to take it all from you now. Get yourself up there."

I was silent as I followed his command, at strange ease as I climbed up onto his mattress and laid down on my back for him, my arms above my head in perfect submission.

I didn't make a sound as he climbed up next to me and looked me straight in the eye.

"I'm going to take that sacred treasure from you now, little one. Open your legs nice and wide for me."

10

My skin burnt wherever his eyes roamed. The bite marks on my tits were still hurting, pulsing fresh as he looked at me.

And soon I was going to get more of them.

"Open your legs," Hans said again. "Show me your innocence."

I was nervous as I spread my thighs under the full glow of the chandelier overhead. I wished I was a girl who was better prepared. Who shaved or waxed, or–

"No," Hans whispered. "Your pussy is perfect as it is."

I spread my legs a bit wider, self-consciousness easing.

"Show me all of you," he said, and I did as I was told. I hitched my thighs as wide as they would go.

He smiled as he looked at the wisps of hair, and my glistening wetness, letting out a glorious moan. He wanted me so much it gave me flushes. They were gorgeous flushes to have.

Fuck.

It was going to happen.

Hans was going to fuck me.

My clit was tingling like crazy before he so much as laid a finger on me. I was lifting my hips from the bed as soon as he placed a hand on my thigh.

"See how fickle the body can be?" he laughed. "Wanting to run one minute, desperate for touch the next. We are more than our flesh, but our bodies truly are sacred temples, there to serve our souls."

His words hit me deep, but they were more of a rhythm of meaning rather than coherent thoughts. I was too caught up in the crazy moment.

I whimpered as he brushed the very tips of his fingers up the inside of my thigh.

Please…

"Wait," he said. "Patience."

He brushed my thigh again, getting closer. I squirmed, trying to get his fingers against my pussy, but he wouldn't give them to me.

"I said wait, Katherine," he told me, his voice lower this time. "Take what you're given."

I had to tip my head back and grit my teeth, hardly able to stand it. His fingers were almost touching me, so close I could feel the heat of him and my clit was throbbing so hard it was on fire.

"Time to see your secrets," Hans whispered and I gasped when his fingers spread my pussy lips, holding them wide.

"Beautiful," he said.

I knew what he must be seeing down there. I'd watched dirty movies, and I'd seen pussies spread open. I knew how exposed I must look.

I liked it.

I liked being spread and watched by a vampire.

Hans pressed fingers on either side of my clit.

"Feel this, here?"

I nodded.

"These are the points where my fangs will sink nice and deep. They'll make you bleed so beautifully, and the sucking will make your clit swell so much, you'll come with a just flick of the tongue."

I sighed, lost in the endorphins of his fingers on me.

Hans is going to bite my pussy.

"Say it out loud," he told me.

"You're going to bite my pussy…"

He pressed his thumb to my clit and I moaned.

"It's going to be so fucking delicious when I do. But it won't be tonight. It'll be a pleasure to savour another time."

I cried out in frustration as he pulled his hand away from me, but he gave me a *shh*. I looked up at him with a blaze of reverence as he tugged his tie loose and cast it aside. I was murmuring for more as he unbuttoned his shirt and stripped his chest bare. His flesh was so toned, muscles wired under pale skin, veins like pale-blue shimmers.

I could hardly bear it. He was too beautiful to soak in.

He shifted so he could undo his belt, and slipped off his trousers, and there it was. His huge cock was in his hand, his long fingers working his shaft as more blue snakes of veins appeared for me.

He'd never fit inside me. I'd never take him.

"You will," he said. "You'll take it all."

He was a lot bigger than the guys I'd seen in movies, but I'd known he would be. I'd felt his length through his trousers closely enough that I could tell.

I was transfixed. Staring. Desperate.

I reached out to touch his skin, and the muscles of his stomach tightened. He was the most incredible thing I'd ever seen.

He laid down beside me and his cock pressed against my thigh. His thumb returned to my clit and it made me heady, swimming in fantasies. *All of them coming to life.*

My vampire lover was in control. He lowered his mouth to my wounded tits and peppered them with kisses, his tongue digging into the bite marks.

More.

I want more.

"I want to bite your mouth first," he said. "Open those pretty lips for me."

My tongue was ready for his when his mouth met mine. His thumb kept pressing against my clit as he nipped and kissed, and there was the taste of blood again. My blood. I kept offering my tongue for more.

He must have trailed blood as he lowered his mouth away from mine, tracing kisses along my collarbone. He tongued the wounds there, and a part of me wanted to feel the pain again, in exactly the same place.

"No," he whispered. "So much fresh flesh to sample. Let me show you."

This time he sank his teeth into the side of my breast in a different spot, and it hurt so bad I wriggled underneath him, but still, I didn't want him to stop.

"More, please," I begged him. "More bites!"

He tugged his teeth from my skin. His smile was red.

"You're pain drunk." He looked into my eyes. "Oh, Katherine. I didn't imagine you'd be such a bite seeker. What a wonderful surprise."

I didn't know what pain drunk meant, but the sentiment rang true to me. I was already offering my tits for more.

"Please, Hans. Bite me!"

"I was going to take it steady," he told me. "But, if you insist."

He was rougher when he bit me this time, teeth plunging deep and hard. I cried out, panting and heady, loving the feeling of my blood flowing free into his mouth. His sucking was so fierce it would have scared me, if I wasn't so blindly needy for more.

Three hard bites, all around my tits, and I was grinning through the pain as he drank from me. His thumb was just a whisper against my clit as it circled, like a master playing a piano at the highest notes, so gently you could barely hear them. I bucked and squirmed, and reached down to brace myself, tangling my fingers in his hair. I loved the way he groaned as he sucked, as desperate for it as I was.

"Enough," he said once he'd pulled his teeth free from the last bite, but I'm sure he was saying it as much for himself as he was for me.

His breaths were heavy, and his lips were swollen, my blood dripping down his chin.

I coaxed him up to kiss me again, and this time there was no biting, just thick bloody mouths and tongue on tongue.

He positioned himself unspoken, and my body knew what was coming. My thighs strained to stay open, even though they were trembling, and I whimpered as he ran the huge head of his cock up and down my pussy.

It would never fit. It couldn't.

"Trust me," he whispered. "Trust me and give me your innocence. Keep your legs open wide."

I nodded. I'd try.

He soaked his fingers with some of the blood from my tits, and used it to lube up his cock. I stared down in fascination as he raised himself high enough that I could see it.

"Is this what you want?" he asked me. "Are you going to keep your legs open wide like a good girl? I want to claim you in one deep thrust. One solid ceremony of sacrifice."

"Yes," I told him. "I'll keep my legs open."

He rubbed his big, heavy dick up and down my pussy lips some more and I tried to prepare myself for what was coming.

Surely it couldn't hurt as much as being bitten deep? Surely it couldn't hurt as much as having blood sucked out from your tits?

"There are different types of pain," he answered. "You can't compare them, just accept them. So brace yourself. Now."

The thrust of his hips was so powerful I screamed. His cock was a vicious rod of iron flesh as he forced it inside me.

"Steady," he groaned. "Take it."

My eyes were watering, breaths hitching as the pain pulsed between my legs, but he stayed deep, his hold inside me firm.

"Good girl," he said. "Clench yourself around me."

"I can't…" I breathed. "I can't do it… it hurts…"

He smiled a blood-red smile.

"Yes, I'm sure it does. So, clench your beautiful pussy and embrace it."

I sucked in gulps of air, swallowed up by the raw burn inside me.

"Clench your pussy," he told me. "Accept the gift."

I groaned when I did it, and Hans groaned along with me.

"That's fucking divine," he said. "I'll move gently, but be a good girl and keep clenched, just like that. I want you to feel everything, as deeply and powerfully as it can possibly be."

He did move gently to start, but every inch he moved felt like miles of pain.

"Trust me," he insisted, and I nodded, keeping my muscles clenched as tight as I could.

It was craziness. I was soaked in blood, with a huge vampire cock deep in my pussy, almost delirious with both pleasure and pain. I looked into his eyes, and they were glowing. The smile on his face would be worth every scrap of hurt in the world.

His thrusts became long and slow, and he began to angle himself differently. It brought a pressure inside me that made me feel like I was about to wet the bed.

"It's all right," Hans said. "That pressure is a good thing. Let it keep coming."

I wrapped my arms around his neck and listened to him, not letting myself hold back.

"You're taking it so well now," he moaned at me. "How about we make my cock even bigger?"

I didn't say no, even though I was scared.

"There's one way we can do this," he whispered, his mouth still dripping with blood. "The final beautiful rite of initiation for a first time acceptance of fate."

"My neck?" I whispered back, and he nodded.

"Yes. It's time to bite your neck."

I tipped my head back on instinct, trusting him with everything I had.

"It'll flow a lot faster from your throat," he said. "Your body will want to fight at first, no matter how prepared you are, so I'm going to pin you down, you understand? You'll be pinned tight, with nowhere to go, and no way to pull your neck away."

His cock was still hurting me so fucking bad, and the pressure was still building, but it felt nice now. Really, really nice. Primal, right through to the core of me.

"Katherine," Hans said. "Are you listening to me?"

I nodded. "Yes. I understand. You'll be pinning me down."

"Hold your hands above your head. Wrists together."

I raised my arms and did as he wanted me to. Wrists tight together.

He gripped them in one of his big hands, and then he pinned me with his weight on mine, his hips still pumping. My heart was racing so fast I wasn't sure I could handle it, just whimpered like a scared little child, even though my soul was craving him.

His teeth were ghosts against my throat at first, his breaths heavy.

His dick kept thrusting, and my pussy kept taking him, my muscles still clenching tightly like he wanted them to be. I was managing to do what he asked of me.

I'd be able to manage this too.

"Ready?" he asked.

"I'm ready."

"Good girl," he said, and sank his teeth straight into my neck.

It was as though I was underwater when my body fought the fight, trying to thrash against him. I heard screams from my throat, but they sounded distant, as though I was deep in my psyche, clutched tight.

I heard my own heartbeat over all of it. A thump, thump, thump that sounded like wet boots stomping on dirt. Natural. Primitive. Real.

My blood was like a river flowing into his mouth. I could feel the waves as they pulsed, his sucking mouth nice and steady as he drank from me.

My body was prickling, lights exploding behind my eyes, and those wet boots kept on stomping in my mind. Thump. Thump. Thump.

Then my body gave up with the thrashing. The screams dried up from my throat.

I took a breath and I was back in myself, senses heightened beyond all reckoning. And I was smiling. Smiling as his cock swelled and stretched me.

Pain drunk.

I didn't care about how sore my pussy was or how much bigger he was growing inside me. I wrapped my legs up around his waist and ground my hips up for more.

Take me. Hard.

Harder.

Harder.

He moaned against my neck, and fucked me harder. He loosened his grip on my wrists and snaked his hand down between his body and mine, his fingers managing to play with my clit as he pounded.

And still he kept sucking.

Still I kept smiling.

It was like a house of cards tumbling all at once, so many sensations playing in harmony.

The thrust of his cock and the pressure inside me. The dance of his fingers sparking my clit. The way he was drinking the life from me.

Yes.

More.

Yes.

MORE.

I lost myself to everything, my soul exploding, and there was only him giving me life at the same time he was taking it. A paradox I'd never fully understand.

YES. MORE. PLEASE.

He thrust harder. Played faster. Swirled his tongue as he sucked at me.

MORE.

YES. YES. YES–

And then I came. A beautiful explosion of an orgasm so strong it blew my mind.

So did he. He came at the same time.

He groaned and snarled and slammed, and I could feel it. I could feel him coming inside me.

I came with Hans' fangs in my neck and his blood-red cock inside me. I came with his flesh against mine, no longer caring if I lived or died. I'd have given it all for one more moment.

But he wouldn't.

He pulled his teeth free and turned my face to his, eyes digging into mine.

"Katherine?"

His voice was beautiful, but so far away.

"Katherine, focus on me."

I was smiling, that much I knew.

"Come back here now," he told me. "Stop drifting. Focus your eyes on me."

But I couldn't…

Something else was calling.

Deep…

"Katherine, focus. Look at me."

I could see the trapdoor under the water in my subconscious, and it was tempting. It had a thick round handle, and I tried to open it, tugging it up just a little.

And then there came flashes.

Memories.

Hans standing by the tree in Garway church while I danced around the tombstones in the dark. Just a little girl.

His shins as I crashed into him by accident on the church pathway, when I was staring up at the moon and not where I was going.

Him watching me singing hymns from the back of the church.

Deeper.

A woman with dark hair I didn't recognise, but she looked like me, smiling at him.

A crowd of spinning girls on Orcop hill, chanting names I didn't understand.

The woman again, with eyes like mine. A smile like mine. Kissing Hans like I kissed him.

Then deeper.

The trapdoor began to open...

"KATHERINE! HERE! NOW! LISTEN TO ME!"

I snapped back to myself and the vampire holding me. A fear in his eyes I hadn't seen before.

"I'm ok," I told him. "I'm back now."

He tipped my face from side to side, checking out my vision.

"I'm ok," I insisted. "I just got pulled away. Somewhere weird."

His gaze was fierce.

"Pulled away to where? Tell me!"

I shrugged. "Nowhere that makes sense. Just some women spinning, and things from before... you in Garway church. You with a woman who looked like me. Just... *things.*"

I got a shudder as the trapdoor slammed shut in my subconscious. Its ripples made me cold.

"What happened there? What happened in my mind?" I asked Hans. "You know, don't you?"

For once, he didn't answer my question.

11

"Tell me, Hans," I pushed. "What's underneath that trapdoor in my head? Dark secrets, right? Something lurking?"

He stroked my cheek, his lips still bloody, dripping red.

"Let it go for the moment. Your body needs to recover, to give your mind the fuel it needs to process things. Especially levels like that one. They will take a lot of energy and faith to understand."

My pulse was still pumping, and everything was glowing, but I was growing tired. Really, really tired.

"It's normal to feel like this," he told me. "You need to sleep, but first let's get you replenished and cleaned up."

He opened one of the antique cabinets at the side of the bed to reveal a fridge.

"Water," he said and presented a glass. "Drink, little one."

I drank it down gratefully, watching as he loaded a plate with cold meat. More steak, oozing with blood. I didn't want to eat it, but I knew I had no choice.

"Replenishment," Hans said. "Your body needs to adjust. It'll join in rhythm with mine over time, spirit to spirit. Your flesh will learn to produce enough blood to keep on flowing, providing enough to play all the games we desire."

He held the plate closer. "Eat, please."

I reached for the meat, but my hand was shaky.

"Let me," Hans said, and picked it up for me, one cold piece of steak in his long, pretty fingers.

I felt like a little toddler as I took the food that was offered, but there was no shame in it, just trust.

Hans the vampire fed me, and I chewed and swallowed. He smiled at me and kept on giving, even though my senses were fading in and out. I guess it was a reversal of forces. Him feeding me after I'd been feeding him. A polarity of opposites, like yin and yang.

Or the opposite pillars of the temple. Black and white, with marble tulips on top.

I didn't know where that thought came from, but it gave me a weird sense of memory inside. And the figure of someone in the darkness, a silhouette, but this time it wasn't Hans...

"Keep chewing, that's it," Hans coaxed. "Nearly there."

Finally, the plate was empty. I saw it through blurry eyes. Hans gave me more water and I guzzled that too.

"Let's get cleaned up now," he said. "Don't move, just let me carry you."

I wouldn't have been able to move if I'd tried.

Again, I felt like a little girl as he lifted me into his arms, but I was comfortable. I felt so safe it was ridiculous, given that I was in the arms of a vampire who'd feasted like a beast on my blood.

He was still carrying me as he opened a doorway off to the side of the bedroom. There were no windows in here, just a glow overhead that lit up the bathroom. The bath was luxurious. A huge white tub in one corner. That's when I saw us in the big mirror over the sink. I half expected just to see myself, hanging mid-air, but no. It made my skin tingle afresh to see him holding me in his arms.

"Vampires do have reflections, then," I stated the obvious.

"How else would I manage to look this handsome," my grinning vampire laughed.

He sat me down on a stool beside the bath and set to, filling the bath with steaming water.

"Put your toes in," he said. "How does the temperature feel?"

I took his hand and eased myself over the side of the bath, loving how the heat soothed my skin. "Feels great," I replied, because it did. Lovely and warm. Perfect.

The cloth he used to wipe me down was soft and gentle. The water turned pink with blood as it loosened from my skin, but it didn't faze me. I could have stayed there for ever, even though I was tender and battered and bruised.

"That's better," Hans said. "Nice and clean. Now let me join you."

The bath was more than big enough for both of us. He scrubbed himself as I watched, and I was smiling in waves as I drifted, admiring the strength and the beauty of his body. He was glowing even brighter now he was full of blood. I felt so proud that I'd fed him.

"So you should be, sweetheart. You blessed me with your body." He smiled. "And blessed me with your innocence, too."

I clenched my pussy as he said it, still raw inside from where he'd taken me. Even now, in pain, I couldn't wait for him to do it again.

"I guess I'm still *pain drunk*," I said, and he smirked at my words.

"Yes, but as with all cravings, we need to know when to stop."

"When can we do it again?"

"When you're ready. I'm yet to discover how well your flesh copes with it. This is the first recovery period to witness."

I was so curious.

"How does it work with that kind of thing? With getting my blood levels back to provide for yours? Is it like when women are living together and their periods start to hit them at the same time? Natural?"

"Yes, kind of. Although this is soul and energy matching, not hormones and moonlight."

I loved the thought of that, even though it was weird.

"Anyway, you need to relax now," he said. "Time to sleep it off."

I didn't want to sleep, despite the fact I let out a natural yawn. I still had so many questions.

The trapdoor.

"No," Hans said. "Not now."

If I wasn't so exhausted, I'd have pushed him to talk about it, but I had no strength left to fight, and none to focus. I was drifting in and out of sleep as he took me from the bath and wiped me dry.

"Bedtime," he whispered.

He sat me in the gorgeous plush armchair, wrapped up tight in a towel as he changed the bedsheets to a fresh set of the same.

"Time to sleep now," he said, taking away my towel and lying me down in his bed. He wrapped me up under the covers, like I was a dainty little girl.

Because I was to him.

I didn't want him to leave me, so I reached for him as he moved away, but he was only circling the bed to reach the opposite side. He slid under the covers to join me and pulled me close, flesh against flesh, his arms snaking around to hold me tight. He was so strong.

Sleep consumed me so easily, and I felt secure to go along with it, safe in his arms.

"You've never been held like this, have you?" Hans asked me, breaking into my dream state with a whisper. "Not even by your mother."

I felt the emotional pain in my ribs, remembering the many times I'd cried in the dark with nightmares, screaming for Mum's arms, even when she'd cussed along with Grandma and said I was *silly*. She'd told me there were no such thing as monsters, and witches, and wizards. No demons, or ghosts, or vampires.

Just a silly little girl.

My dream voice spoke in a tiny echo, straight into Hans' mind.

She knew, didn't she?

He sighed before he answered me.

"Yes. She's known your whole life. So has your ghastly grandmother."

I caught a glimpse of the trapdoor again, under the water, and this time it was glowing red around the edges. Its heavy round handle was calling me. But no. Not tonight.

I spun in my tracks like an underwater ballerina and swam the other way.

"Good girl," Hans said, full of pride. "Keep on swimming until it's time."

Time.

It faded in and out in a cycle, the trapdoor, the lake, the trapdoor, the lake.

Still, I didn't approach that trapdoor, just kept looking at it from a distance whenever it appeared.

"Where is the lake I keep seeing?" I asked. "Is it in the subconscious, or does it really exist?"

"It's symbolic," he replied. "But it's based on memory, yes."

"Have I swam in it? For real?"

"No. But your family have."

"Mum and Grandma?"

"No, but your family line did before them, for a long, long time."

I wished I had the strength to ask more questions, but my body forbid me. Or maybe it was Hans that forbid me.

"Sleep now, little one, we need you to recover."

I sank into his hold, drifting on a cloud of happiness. That's how it felt. Aware that time was ticking. Aware of my blood pumping, rejuvenating. Aware that I was totally safe and secure.

I came to lazily, stretching, sighing at the beautiful long fingers stroking my tits. I had so many bite marks, each one of them looking deep and proud.

"There you are, back from dreamland," my vampire said. "How are you feeling?"

My grin must have spoken for me, but I told him anyway. "Like a new woman."

He smiled, his fangs gleaming.

"Perfect," he said.

"Did I sleep for long?" It didn't feel long at all.

"Twelve hours exactly," Hans said.

"Twelve hours?! Wow. I usually struggle with six."

"Yes, twelve hours of the deepest, purest sleep. Just what you needed," he said, trailing his fingers down my stomach.

My thighs opened for him.

I felt his hardness against my hip as he moved his fingers down between my legs, and I felt the heat in my pussy.

Then I felt embarrassed when his fingers opened up my pussy lips and he repositioned himself for a view, as though I was being examined.

"Healing nicely," he said, and then pressed his mouth to my clit.

I squirmed, expecting this to be the hot prelude to another round of slamming, and I wanted it, no matter how much it hurt. But no. He cut me off in a heartbeat.

"No cock for you today. You're still healing. Don't worry though, sweetheart. Let me pleasure you with my mouth instead."

He didn't waste a moment, working me like a master.

I sank into it, shudders running through me when the points of his fangs touched my tender flesh.

I shuddered afresh as his tongue lapped at my clit.

"*Thank you*," I whispered.

I wrapped my legs around his neck, rubbed my pussy in his beautiful face, moaned for him. Moaned and whimpered at the press of his tongue.

"Come for me, Katherine."

I came for him, wave upon wave of gentle orgasm washing all over his face. And *fuck, FUCK*. It was incredible.

I floated down from the high, panting like I'd run a mile, and smiled at the grinning vampire between my legs.

"That was... perfect," I said. "Just perfect."

"As are you," He pulled himself up to lie by my side. "Your recovery was swift, a I suspected it might be. Such strength of spirit."

Again I felt pride. I was glowing with it.

With him.

He stroked hair from my brow. "What would you like to do next?

So many wonders to explore. So many questions to ask, and things to see."

"You could do *that* again," I said, laughing, but I meant it.

Hans laughed back, got up from the bed and held out his hand.

He pulled me to my feet, wrapped his arms around me and kissed me.

"There will be plenty of time for that. How about a change of scene? Get out of this steel box for a while."

He opened up the drapes, and the blinds, and the huge metal latches to reveal the beauty of the moonlight outside.

"Ok," I said, slightly disappointed.

Hans dropped a kiss on my forehead. "Sweetheart, the night is young, and you'll feel like a new explorer amongst it after last night's adventures. Step out into the world with me and see it through fresh, pretty eyes."

I wasn't sure. My skin was already tingling for more of his.

"Come," he said, and took my hand. "I mean it when I say you can trust me. You most definitely won't be disappointed. I have plenty of surprises in store."

12

I was stark naked as I stared at my crumple of clothes on the floor. My blouse was creased, and my tights were ripped. The thought of walking next to a gorgeous vampire through the crowded London streets seemed fascinating. But what was I going to wear?

Hans was smirking when I looked over at him.

"Don't worry. Frederick collected your possessions and delivered them here this afternoon."

I had to do a double take.

"From my room?!"

"Yes."

It should have seemed weird, but it didn't. I was already becoming accustomed to surprises from Hans.

I could have asked him for a dressing gown to conceal myself on the way downstairs to check out my things, but being naked around him already felt surprisingly comfortable. He followed me, happily naked himself, and I had to remind myself to keep an eye on where I was going, and not on him. His body would distract me from anything, damnit. I was already craving more of his teeth and touch, and… yes. Everything.

The constant sizzle between us was thrilling, enough to keep my nipples hard and my pussy wanting.

My clothes were in the drawing room, hanging neatly on a rail with cases packed up to one side. It was obvious that Frederick had made a thorough job of it. Hans took a seat as I scouted through them.

"Where will we be going?" I asked. "We could always stay in and eat more steak, don't you think? It would save getting dressed."

Hans smiled at me.

"I've spent a long time living in tombs. Taking you out to dine in the city tonight will be an honour that I have waited a very long time for."

I put my hands on my hips, faced him with tits proud, confidence beginning to bloom.

"Sounds amazing, so long as we spend a long time in your bed after."

He gave me another of his glorious smirks.

"There's no doubt about that. We'll be spending a long time in *our* bed for a long, long time to come. At least, I hope so."

Our bed.

I could have grabbed hold of him right then and begged him to take me upstairs again, but the thought of dining out with a vampire while the world looked on oblivious was a major pull.

"Choose your outfit, little one," he said.

There was only one obvious contender, so I picked out my finest. A dress in a beautiful dark blue, high enough at the neckline to cover my bite marks, and fitted nice and tightly down to my knees. I'd fallen in love with it but never had the confidence, or the occasion, to wear it before.

I'd need a bolero to cover yet more bite marks, so I picked one of those from a hanger too. Thank God I had a choker in a lovely black lace, just thick enough to cover my neck wounds. I chose my highest heels. A pair of stilettos with lovely black straps to match my choker. I just hoped I wouldn't stumble over on the pavement.

"I wouldn't let you fall," Hans said. "We'll take it steady tonight, how about that? No cobblestone sprints."

Something about that disappointed me. I got a tingle of a shiver at the thought of being chased up Hyde Street again. *The cobblestones. The bites with my back to the wall. The panting. The fear. His hand between my legs...*

"I'll need to get ready myself," Hans told me, interrupting my thoughts. "You can come upstairs with me, or feel free to–"

I didn't need him to finish his sentence. I was already grabbing my makeup and toiletries and following him up the stairs.

I brushed my teeth and combed my hair in the ensuite while he disappeared into a dressing room, and then I opted to push my confidence some more. I went for smoky eyes and deep, dusky pink lips – much more dramatic than I was used to, but my outfit deserved it. I was still checking myself out in the bathroom mirror when I heard Hans' footsteps approaching.

I spun around in a daze, and there he was, in a perfectly tailored tuxedo with his hair slicked back. He could have stepped straight from a vintage movie. I was a hot mess as he joined me and ran his thumb across my cheek.

"You are absolutely beautiful," he told me, and I couldn't help but laugh.

"Yeah, well that makes two of us then, doesn't it?"

"Just as well we're a couple then, isn't it?"

His words slammed home. *A couple.*

"That's how I'd refer to us," Hans said. "Would you agree?"

This was insane, surely? So soon, but so real. Yet, I couldn't fight it, and couldn't deny it. I didn't want to...

Hans kept on talking.

"It's a great relief, since I've spent a very long time waiting for you to be at my side. I don't want to wait any longer."

Because I've been waiting your whole life – that was the sense of emotion I got from his words.

It came with another vision of the trapdoor in my subconscious. A thump of the mysteries underneath.

NO.

I didn't want to face them, so pulled away from it, back to the present and hottest man on the planet.

"Steakhouse then, is it?" I guessed.

"Good guess. Steak will most certainly be on the menu where I'm taking you."

I felt like a queen on the arm of a king when we descended the stairs together and reached the front door. My teeth marks were pulsing under my dress, and I was buzzing live with them, already feeling the desperation for more. *So many more.*

I needed his teeth in me. I needed his vampire fangs, and his touch, and the pain of taking his cock like I did last night.

"Steady," he whispered as we stepped out onto the street. "We need to get you dinner first. It's still only 8 p.m., we have plenty of time ahead."

He already had a cab waiting for us on the street outside.

The Waterstone Restaurant, Westminster, he told the driver, and we set off on our way.

Hans had his hand on my knee in the back seat, and my skin responded with prickles. Needy.

I didn't want dinner. I wanted him. Even though my stomach was rumbling.

"Relax," he whispered. "You'll get me just as soon as we're done. Believe me, I'm as hungry for it as you are, I've just got more experience at managing it."

Every mile felt like it took a year, but the destination was a shock of brilliance when we arrived in Westminster. The cab dropped us outside the grandeur of a stunning restaurant, lit up with striking white lights. I was staring up, awestruck when Hans opened the door for me and directed me inside.

"Reservation for two," he told the girl at the entrance. "In the name of Mr Weyer."

"Of course, sir," she replied and led us to our table.

It was on the edge of the room, near to an orchestral quartet playing, out of earshot of everyone around. I was certain it must have been on purpose.

"You are correct, it's the most private table in the restaurant," he said once we'd taken our seats. "We vampires usually adhere to a code of silence about our affairs in public, as we'd prefer not to be sectioned or arrested, but I'm sure you must have a thousand questions brewing. For you, I'll make an exception."

I laughed. "You could say that I have a thousand questions brewing, yes."

He tipped his head. "So, go ahead."

I didn't have a clue where to start, and my thoughts were rambling like crazy.

Who was Hans? Where had he come from? Who had made him a vampire and why? When? How? What did it feel like? Where had he been? What had he seen, and loved, and wanted?

And lost?

Surely a creature like Hans must have lost a lot, too.

But, as all the questions kept rolling through my mind, the sensations kept rolling through my body. My flesh was still craving teeth and tongue like an addict, so I was relieved when one of the waitresses came over and took our drinks order, just for the distraction.

I needed to get my body back in line, before I drove myself crazy. I needed blood-red kisses, so I was more than happy when Hans ordered a bottle of merlot.

My attention was on him when he picked up his menu, even though I knew I should be choosing my meal. The questions were still forming as I watched him.

How? Why? When? Where? How? Why? When? Where?

He grinned. "It's all right. You can ask and choose at the same time."

"I'm not much of a multitasker," I admitted. "Menu choices and questions, wow, quite a task."

And cravings. Cravings for his teeth and touch.

"So, how about you opt for a nice rare steak and get the questions rolling?" he suggested.

I laughed. "What is it with you and steak? Is that some kind of ritual?"

He didn't laugh back, just smiled.

"It's the recommended nutrition for new blood players, yes. It helps the system adjust."

Sorry, what?

"Is that what I am now?" I asked him. "A blood player? Is that like a vampire addict?"

His gorgeous green eyes had the intensity I was coming to know, but it still gave me shivers.

"Oh, Katherine. You can already feel it, can't you? The desperation for me to drink the blood from your veins? The desperation for a nice, hard fucking as I suck on your throat?"

My breath caught. My thighs clenched.

"Yes," he continued, with a knowing smirk. "Then you are most certainly a blood player."

I felt nervous because his words were so true. I really was a blood player, then. *But I was also his partner, right? A couple... Did that make me... different?*

"Yes, you are my partner," he said. "Which is just as well, seeing as there is no way I'd want you to end up seeking your thrills purely through a blood house. As upmarket as they are, they are not nearly enough for a girl like you."

My curiosity was piqued more than ever.

"Blood house? What's a blood house?"

"Blood houses are places blood players go to surrender their blood. They are frequented by a regular clientele of people desperate for fangs, and quite often anything else that goes along with them. We have a few of them based around the world."

Wow!

"Really?! There are people desperate for bites that go to blood houses to get them? Like whore houses, but with vampires instead?"

His eyebrows pitted. "No, no. I wouldn't say they are like whore houses. These people and situations are most certainly consensual, no matter how intense the exchanges may be. They may well seek out consensual non-consent, but these people get what they need from us, and we get what we need from them in return."

People.

"Yes, people," he continued. "Your imagination won't be far from the truth, I promise. Call it a selection of filthy vampire novels in the flesh. Men biting men, women biting women. Vampires sharing *victims* all at once."

I was truly fascinated.

"Do you ever go to these blood houses?"

He looked me in the eyes, and I'm sure he was digging into my thoughts, ready to read me. Only this time I felt myself put a wall up.

"Never be embarrassed by your thoughts or fantasies," he said.

"I'm not," I replied, but he kept on staring at me.

"You've been very sheltered, but that doesn't need to be the case anymore. The world is a big place, and there are fantasies galore to be enjoyed in it."

He paused as the waitress delivered our merlot and took our orders. Steak and steak.

"In answer to your question, yes," he said, once she'd gone. "I do visit blood houses. Or at least I did until you came along. Now, my cravings are all about you."

"That's quite a statement," I said, with another flash of pride.

"Yes, it is," he agreed. "Now, how about we get some of your real questions out of the way? Shall we start from the beginning? How did I become the creature I am today? That's one of your most pressing curiosities, yes?"

He was right on that. The *who, why, when* questions had one clear place to start. That became a lot more clear as I downed a few decent gulps of merlot.

"Yes, please, let's go from the beginning," I said. "How did you become a vampire, Hans? And why?"

13

"*I* was a knight," Hans told me, and my eyebrows shot up. "A knight? An actual knight? On horseback with a sword?!"

"Not exactly. I missed the Crusades luckily, otherwise I'd have likely been butchered in the Holy Land on a battlefield drenched in blood. I managed to miss that stage of it, but yes. I was a member of the Knights Templar. I really did have an impressive sword. I still have it actually."

I saw the humour on his face and it made me laugh.

"You're blessed with impressive swords then, Hans."

"Indeed."

I flicked my attention back to his story with absolute fascination, like a girl hearing a fairy tale.

"You were really a knight of the Knights Templar?"

"I was, yes. A servant of God helping pilgrims in their travels to worship. At least for a short while. We were considered *old* at a much younger age back then."

There was something in his words that was so serious underneath the smile. It gave me a flutter.

"You were a holy man before you became a vampire?"

"I still am. Still, after over seven hundred years, the pursuit of faith still captivates me, but the more I know, the more I realise I don't know a thing." He paused. "It's been hard to reconcile the lifestyle of a vampire with my previous incarnation, but I think I'm doing an ok job of it."

I knew a little about the Knights Templar through history lessons at school. I knew they were powerful, and robed with powerful red crosses on their chests.

I also knew they were persecuted by the royals across the empire and destroyed for their sins.

"*Fake* sins," Hans interjected. "There was very little truth in any of it, they just wanted us dead and buried."

He cleared his throat and continued. "I was thirty-two years old when I became a vampire. The experience most definitely wasn't one I'd been expecting."

"Don't worry, I'm sure I wouldn't have either." I laughed, and took a sip of wine. "I may have watched almost every vampire movie ever made, but I didn't believe they existed. Not for real."

My vampire lover looked at me with a glint in his eyes.

"Ah, yes, Katherine, but the world exists very differently now. It wasn't so much that I didn't believe in vampires, but that I didn't believe a vampire would come for me. We were a lot more alive with myths and legends. We had no internet to distract us, it was all about tales around a campfire, whispered through the generations."

"So, what happened?" I asked him. "Who made you a vampire?"

"A friend. Someone I knew closely and had done for years, or so I thought. I had no idea that he was a vampire, even after all that time. He kept it very well hidden." He laughed. "We've become an awful lot closer since."

My mind whirred, remembering the *people* comment about the blood houses. Was the *he* a friend, or a *friend*? The idea was a surprisingly hot one.

Hans smiled. "He was purely a friend at that point. I had no experience of being bisexual at that time. Lord Neville was just a gentleman I knew through the Church, and talked through the gospels with. I'd spent many evenings at his manor, enjoying his company. *Evenings*, of course. It never occurred to me that I'd never once seen him in the day."

Purely a friend at that point. I wondered if that was still the case now.

"I've had sex with Edwin, yes," Hans answered. "We've shared some blood games, and had some fun times biting and chasing. Quite a different friendship than the one we started with, but nothing less genuine or valid."

My mind was spinning at the thought of seven hundred years of religion and philosophy, and Hans being turned into a vampire by a Lord named Edwin. The sensation gave me a sense of doom, somehow. It reminded me of my mum and grandma preaching to me about being a *good girl* at the cost of everything else. Praying to God every single weekend without fail, but judging and scorning everyone around them.

Hans swirled the wine in his wine glass.

"Don't judge anything by them. They aren't an accurate representation."

I didn't want to delve into Mum and Grandma, so took a sip of wine and turned the topic back to him.

"What happened to you?"

"A lot of the Knights Templar were tortured, little one. Me included. The royals and their minions tried to force a confession of fake sins from me, but even until the very end, I wouldn't give in."

His words gave me a vile shudder. He nodded his head at my thoughts.

"Yes. I was beaten, and whipped, and stretched on a rack. Starved and lashed and burnt."

I despised the idea of people hurting him.

"And your friend saved you?" I whispered. "Thank God for that."

"Yes," Hans said. "Quite literally. I was crucified in the church grounds and left for dead. Edwin appeared at midnight and cut me free."

I let out a breath, not knowing quite what to say. Hans kept on talking.

"He bit my neck and drank from me, and then he slashed his wrist and offered it to me. Drink his blood and live, or refuse and die. My choice, he said. So, I drank from him. I wasn't ready to leave this world behind."

It was like a thousand scratches on my skin when he said that. My whole body was alive with the sensation.

"Did it hurt?"

"Yes, but not as much as being tortured, I can assure you of that." He was grinning, even though the memory still clearly hurt. "My body died, and that was a horrific experience, being fully conscious all the way through as your flesh gives up, but bizarrely it was quite liberating. A once in an immortal lifetime's experience."

Hans smiled, as though the story was done. Just like that.

"So, yes," he said. "In answer to your earlier question, I was tortured as a religious knight, crucified in the church grounds for being a sinner, and Lord Edwin Neville, the vampire, came along and saved me."

I tried to digest it. "When did this happen?"

"1309."

"Wow, ok. And where?"

There was a quizzical look on his face, as though I was asking the obvious.

"Garway church," he said, and my stomach dropped to the pit of me.

"Garway? Honestly?"

"Yes, but you already know the exact spot, don't you? You've spent a great many times sitting in that place, listening to the hymns from the chapel with your mother and grandmother inside."

At the top of the graveyard, looking down at the northern windows.

I could see it vividly.

"That's right," Hans told me. "Give your instincts more credit, little one."

"But I don't get it," I said. "How could I know what happened there in 1309? I don't understand."

Hans took my hand across the table. His fingers looked as gorgeous as ever in mine.

"One of the most important things you'll ever learn, is that it's more often the soul that has the answers. Listen with your soul and not your ears."

He took his hand away and I took another swig of wine, trying to focus on the orchestral quartet just a few feet away from us. The room was... heavy. The energy in the pit of me was... scared. It felt so horrible – the thought of Hans there, hanging on a crucifix, tortured, with blood pouring down his legs.

He switched the tone. "You can ask Edwin what happened yourself when you meet him. He'll be able to recount the tale better than me, I'm sure."

My eyes widened. "He's still alive?"

"Oh, yes. And he's still as funny as ever. His sense of humour has never changed. You'll like him. I'm sure you'll get on well."

I jumped in my seat as the waitress appeared with our steaks.

"Anything else I can get you?" she asked, but we both shook our heads. "Enjoy your meals," she said with a smile, totally oblivious, and walked away.

I looked at the meat on my plate, feeling a bit sick at the sight of it. Blood and flesh.

"Come on, eat up," Hans said. "You'll enjoy it when you get started. Don't let my tales put you off."

How could they not? The thought of chewing on steak made my stomach churn.

"Believe me," he said. "You'll be seeing a lot worse than blood oozing from a steak as time goes on."

We'd barely even scratched at the surface of the vampire's long journey, but the initial instalment had me reeling. I tried to compose myself, my fingers jittery as I picked up my knife and fork. I tried to eat, and my body managed it, even though my mind was still twisted in stories.

"Anyway, that's enough of me for now," Hans said, switching the focus again. "Let's talk about you."

I pulled a face in confusion, still chewing until I swallowed.

"I'm hardly a vampire with seven hundred years of stories," I replied. "There's nothing much to say on my side. I grew up in Orcop. Went to school. Lived with Mum and Grandma in the village. You know all this anyway though, don't you? You said it yourself. You've been watching me my whole life."

He smiled. "Yes."

"So, why ask me?"

He laughed at that. "Because you're squirming in your seat, so freaked out that you're paler than I am."

I laughed back. "Is it that obvious?"

"It is, yes. So let's change the topic. Onto you and your past, or onto some aspects of our... present."

He had the power to flick the moods between us like light switches. He was a master of energies and tones.

"It's all right," he said. "The past is the past, and time moves in cycles. Turn your attention to the now."

His eyes were lustful and deep with desire, and there was no point denying it. The magnetism between us was still burning strong, even under the nausea. If anything, his history made me more attracted to him, like something profound was going on under the surface. Some kind of knowing. *Wanting. Craving.*

"Tell me what turns you on, little one. Truly, deeply, from the depths of your fantasies."

I felt shy in my seat all of a sudden.

"I... I don't really know yet."

He laughed again. "I don't believe you."

I shrugged, striving for honesty. "Ok, so what do you want me to say? The thought of a blood house and some filthy hot people getting bitten for fun? Running across cobblestones while you chase me, so out of breath and desperate I can't get away? You fucking my pussy so hard I can barely stand it while you suck my blood like a monster?"

"Yes. If that's the truth of it."

"You know that's the truth of it. You've seen how excited I get."

He flashed me a gorgeous white smile.

"Yes. I just wanted to hear you say it out loud. I love it when you speak like that."

It was just like being in my dreams again, but my fantasies had more of an eerie quality to them when they were out in the open, even with the thrum of the restaurant trying to mute out my words.

I looked at my steak, trying to focus again on what I should be eating, but it was pointless. My body was already buzzing with need. My excitement was already making me wet, my thighs clammy.

"Keep on eating that steak," Hans said. "You'll need your strength for later."

I grabbed hold of his statement with both hands.

"Why? What are you going to do to me?"

"I'm still deciding. I'll let your body guide me on that, but I do have a penchant for the chase. There is a great thrill to blood being taken that way, in chase and submission, even if it's only playacting. As I said earlier, a lot of blood players like consensual non-consent. It's quite a staple fantasy. I know you have it too, Katherine, as do I." He smiled. "It's you I want to play the games with now though, little one. You and only you. You drive me so wild I can barely stand it. I could get up and pin you on this table right now or chase you right out of this restaurant. Luckily, I have slightly more restraint than that. I don't want to end up in a jail cell tonight."

I nearly dropped my cutlery at the heat in his eyes. My heart was thumping even louder than the quartet. It was the stare he gave me, like the creature in the dark and not the gentleman opposite me. My thighs clenched. My bites throbbed sore. He was speaking to a part of me below the surface.

The part with my feet pounding the cobblestones.

It was the way he was so confident with it, too. The power in his smirk of *I know what you need.*

"Go with it," he told me. "Feed your fantasies."

I was there again... with my back against the door... caught in the stare of a vampire. And wanting him. Needing him. Begging him for his teeth in my throat.

"Don't worry," Hans said, just loud enough to be heard over violin and cello. "There is no sin in the pleasure of the chase. There is such a mortal pleasure in the freedom of running free for a lot of people, even if you know it will end in capture. So many years of your life you've been constricted, forced to behave and think what you're *supposed* to think. But that's all done now. You can run free."

"And you'll chase me…"

"Always." His tone was so primal. "You liked that, didn't you? You ran with such spirit. It was beautiful."

I remembered the panting. My heaving chest. His hand between my legs.

And that's what I wanted now. I wanted to run, away from here, and the images of the past, and the tight reins of my mind. I wanted the fear of the vampire opposite me in the most beautiful of ways, and the certainty of knowing that no matter how fast I ran, he would catch me.

I was his now.

Under the spell of a vampire named Hans.

The strangest urge possessed me. A flash of rebellion so strong it was straight from the core of my soul, fighting against the *do as you're told* orders of my past, hissed by my mother and grandmother like I was just a stupid little girl.

Hans tipped his head, reading my thoughts.

"Run now, if you want to."

But did I want to? Did I want to leave this plush restaurant and dash away into the London streets on a mission to outrun him? My body answered for me – my spirit ready to flee.

Yes, I did.

I shot him a smile before I stood up from my chair and walked away. I flashed him a backwards glance over my shoulder once I reached the doorway, and then I rushed away.

My stilettos were awkward and clacky on the pavement but that just served to make it more dramatic. My heart was already pounding before I'd even crossed the street.

I heard a thought in my mind as I reached the corner, giving one final look to the restaurant behind.

Run, little one. I'll give you a reasonable head start.

My chest flushed hot and my skin prickled with tingles so beautifully it made me grin.

Grin like a fool in the night. This was crazy. CRAZY, but I did it.

Run, little one, his thoughts came again.

And, oh, how I ran!

14

I had no idea where I was heading, but that only made the rush more exciting. My instincts were running free as I threw myself down the nearest steps to the London underground, two at a time, fearing for my life – or broken legs – as I somehow managed to stay on my heels.

There was no way I'd last more than two minutes in a cat and mouse game with Hans if I was reliant on my feet alone. I needed transport.

I took a one-stop journey, switching lines from District to Northern at the Embankment. I was hanging on to one of the carriage poles, my veins pulsing and my feet aching as the train pulled away from the station. I was still so new to London that I didn't have a clue where I was going.

I hoped my confusion would only spell the same for Hans.

If I didn't know where I was going, then how could he?

The Northern line took me to Tottenham Court Road, and I bailed from the carriage at the last possible moment, dashing up the escalator as quickly as I could. I glanced up and down the street at all the people around me, minding their own business like it was another easy night in the city.

For them, I guess it was.

So, where from here?

I saw signs for Covent Garden and made my choice, trotting on my heels like a girl gone mad, but barely anyone shot me a glance. I was spinning when I hit the park grass, checking for signs of an impending vampire attack, but none came.

Should I hide? Find another tube? Keep on running on foot as fast as I could?

I could see paths and benches, and people still walking on by... so which way? Which direction?

I guess I pondered my options too long, because when I looked back, I saw him there. Hans. Walking slowly towards me, like he had all the time in the world.

It took everything I had not to scream, but I kept walking, trying to blend in amongst some other people, even though I knew full well that Hans was watching me.

He didn't try to catch up, and in some ways that made my heart pound even harder.

He was playing a game he had no fear of losing, but still, I wasn't going to be an easy catch for him. Not this time.

I spotted an exit from the park and ran with everything I could, trusting instincts that were still fresh to me. My legs were already tiring, so it was a great relief when I saw signs for another tube station.

Leicester Square.

From that point, my race from the vampire was a blur of underground stations. I took random stops and switched lines, over and over. Sometimes I doubled back, and sometimes I ran across platforms, and I was panting, desperate, my heart crying out every second I had to wait for an overdue train.

I don't know quite when I ended up in Camden Town, but it was a fitting location for a vampire given its almost otherworldly nature, lined with goth shops on both sides of the road. Hans would blend in like a mega posh goth guy pretty well here, but me? I'd be visible in a mile radius, so fuck it, I kept on running.

Of course, when I turned around at the end of the street, there was

Hans, behind me, walking towards me with the same beautiful smirk on his face.

Fuck.

Running through Camden was even harder than running on the cobblestones. The people around me were unwelcome obstacles to avoid, made worse by my stupid heels. Fuck only knows how I ended up in Kentish Town, and fuck knows on top of that how I ended up back on the tube – destination Hackney – I was just grateful that Hans wasn't on the same carriage as me.

Hackney felt different from the other parts of London. It had a different vibe somehow, with less people milling around. I felt out of my depth as I chose the next street to take, because some of them looked darker, quieter... more deserted.

But now was the time. I had to choose and run for it.

I picked the nearest street, and the nearest one again after that. The underground option seemed distant now, as though I was a million miles away from another station, so I slowed myself down and tried to use my brain.

Think Katherine. Think.

Hiding. That seemed the best option.

I dashed into a yard behind a closed restaurant and repeated a mantra in my mind. Maybe that would confuse him...

Kensington. Kensington. I'm going back to Kensington.

Maybe I was clutching at straws, but I had to try.

Kensington. KENSINGTON.

Ah, but fuck it. I failed.

I heard the footsteps and gave myself up with a grin as I panted, grateful for the shiver of excitement at what was coming. I was too exhausted to run any more.

My thighs were already parting, and my veins felt ready to be taken, and I couldn't hold in just how much I wanted this. I only wished my hands could touch myself to get ready. My clit was aching for touch, screaming out to be played with.

I opted for as much confidence as I could, whispering out my invitation.

"Bite me, please," I whispered. "And make it hurt..."

"Shut the hell up and give me your fucking purse," a voice sounded out, and the tone of it gave me the horrors.

It gave me absolute, petrifying horrors, because Fuck, FUCK, the guy approaching me in the yard wasn't Hans. Hans wasn't the only one I'd been running from.

"I... I don't have any money," I managed to stutter. "Really, I don't. Even my bank cards are maxed out. There's no point in taking them."

I didn't know what I was doing, reasoning with a guy who was trying to steal from me, but I felt I had to try before I screamed.

"Please," I said. "I don't have anything."

"Give me your fucking purse," he snarled, and he was big as he stepped up, shrouded in a black hoodie so dark that I couldn't see him. He was drunk. His words were slurry.

"Give me your fucking purse! Now!"

"Honestly," I said, taking a step back, "I don't have any money."

The man stepped closer until I was backed against a wall. His breath smelt of whisky.

"Then I'll just take something else," he said and reached for my tits.

I put my arms up to protect myself, and caught a glimpse of the wild eyes under that hoodie. Fuck. I was terrified. I told myself to fight, to lash out. To give it everything I had to get him off me, but I didn't need to...

That hood of his was yanked back and the man went sprawling to the floor, Hans towering over him.

The brute of a thief leapt to his feet and tried to wrestle him, but it didn't matter. There was no way he'd ever have won.

I'd felt Hans' strength before, but I'd never seen the extent of it. I'd felt the power of his teeth, but I'd never seen them biting someone else...

Hans slammed the guy into the wall beside me, crushing the guy's heaving chest against the bricks with his face turned in my direction, right next to me. And then he tore the hoodie down far enough to free the thief's neck. The guy's flesh was pale and orange under the pathetic excuse for a yard light, but it was bright enough for me to witness the attack.

Hans' eyes were on me as he sank his teeth right the way into the thief's neck next to me. The guy tried to cry out, but Hans slapped a hand over his mouth.

Gloved.

Hans had gloves on.

The guy was muffled and flailing, trying to shove Hans away, but it was pointless. It wasn't just Hans' eyes on mine as the scene reached its peak. I stood mute as I stared into the thief's gaze, watching the submission of his soul as he lost the fight.

The thief gave up in front of me, his eyes draining of life along with his throat. His hands dropped at his sides, limp, and he tried to whimper but had no sound to give.

Neither did I.

I was fixated in a mash of horror and fascination, mute and useless. I didn't even try to help the man survive, but maybe I would have if Hans' eyes hadn't drawn my attention back to his with their glistening green. The glow of his stare was enough to drive me insane, but it wasn't in a bad way. Not like it should have been.

The vampire was a monster. He was killing someone right in front of me.

I should have been running again as fast as my legs could carry me, since he was cold, and ruthless, not giving a fuck about the life he was taking, but I couldn't.

He was too beautiful. A beautiful creature in the most beautiful form I'd ever seen him.

He gasped when he finally pulled his teeth free and let the thief's limp body drop to the floor. I could still hear the victim's ragged breaths, but they were so slow now that they were nothing but tiny little whistles.

"Time for you to see another vampire ritual," Hans told me, his mouth dark with blood.

With that he took a knife from the inside of his jacket. Long and thin and brutal.

I flinched, finding my voice.

"Hans? What the hell?!"

He dropped to his knees and tugged the dying guy's head back, staring up at me with blood still trailing down his chin.

"Do you think we can drain people to the point of death and leave our teeth marks standing proud when we walk away? Our reality wouldn't just be a whisper of folklore then, little one."

Hans slit the guy's throat open with enough force that it slashed through the bitemarks, and tore the evidence away. I had to cover my mouth with my hands.

Watching someone being butchered was a world away from seeing their blood being sucked by a vampire – bizarre, but true. I retched as I watched Hans wipe the knife clean with a handkerchief, then slip it right back inside his jacket.

"It's all right, Katherine. I know this is difficult."

I was shaking my head, trying to believe it.

He got to his feet and put his hands on my shoulders, still gloved and no doubt still wet with blood.

"Katherine, listen to me. The guy was nothing but a vile, corrupt excuse for a man. He was going to beat you, do you know that? After he'd raped you, of course. And plenty of innocent people after you. I've just saved plenty of people from a nasty fate."

I was still shaking my head, with my ears ringing. *I couldn't. I just couldn't handle it.*

"You *can*," Hans said. "Do you really want the truth of it? Do you want to feel the mentality of the vile excuse for a man lying on the floor there? Trust me, it'll do you some good."

I squeaked as the killer of a vampire took my head in his hands and placed his thumbs against my temples. His eyes stared into mine.

"Let me show you."

The thoughts came pounding into me one after the other – visions of robberies, and fights, and rapes, all from the dead man's point of view. It wasn't just visions that came to me, either. I felt the malice in the guy's memories as he committed his crimes...

And then came more.

Hans.

I felt the vampire's thoughts as he bit the evil man's neck and took his life from him. I felt Hans' pain for the people the guy had hurt. Hans' belief in righteousness and saving the guy's future victims from suffering.

It felt good. At odds with the man he'd just destroyed.

I tried to gain hold of myself when Hans pulled away, but I was trembling in shock.

"See?" Hans said. "He wasn't ever going to change his ways. I just did the world a favour."

I nodded. "I saw."

"Good."

We stared at each other. His mouth was still wet and bloody as the body of the man lay next to us, but that didn't matter. The charge of the magnetism came back between us. The fizz of need, and my pride at the creature in front of me.

I could see him in his cross fronted robe, protecting the pilgrims as they travelled. A knight. A warrior. A protector.

Hans wasn't evil. Just brutal.

My soul cried out for his, because it was obvious to me then that he still had one.

The beautiful, vampiric Hans Jacob Weyer had a soul.

A beautiful soul.

My words were a whisper, my body trusting itself.

"Kiss me, please..."

Hans kissed me with passion, and depth, and hunger, and I kissed him right back with the same. I tasted someone else's blood, but I didn't care. It felt erotic in the most insane of ways. Maybe because that was so much a part of Hans and his life. I was sharing the taste of his ways.

He hitched me up and I ground against him as he kissed me, back in the memories of the alleyway when he'd first shown his true colours.

"We have to stop," he hissed between kisses. "We have to get away from the body."

We were still kissing as we stumbled back towards the street.

"Wait," he said, before we risked the clear sight of people.

He licked the remaining blood from my lips, then wiped his own with a fresh handkerchief.

"Let's get around the corner and I'll hail us a cab," he said, and I followed meekly as he guided us away.

15

We sat in silence in the cab, with Hans' dark gloved hand on my thigh. The driver had the radio on, blaring out politics news, but still, we didn't risk a conversation between us. I wouldn't have known what to say if we'd tried.

The quiet between us only added to the tension. Whispers of thoughts, and images and feelings.

"Here, thank you," Hans said to the driver when we were a few streets down from his house.

He paid in cash, then led me in the opposite direction.

"I guess you're used to acting like a criminal," I said, realising how shaky my voice sounded.

He held my hand tightly. "Yes. Things have become slightly more skilled on the technical side of detective work in recent times, but we're still hardly dealing with Sherlock Holmes on our case, luckily."

He put us on the true route to his house once the cab was out of sight

Here goes.

I was tingling all over when his street came into view, the taste of the thief's blood still thick in my mouth. If I hadn't been so possessed by my need for Hans, then I would have been exhausted beyond all recognition, but I couldn't be. I was far, far too hungry for Hans' teeth and his kisses, not to mention his cock.

The perverse nobility in him was so attractive it drove me insane.

"I know what you need, don't worry," he whispered as we walked. "Just wait until we get inside."

My stomach did a fresh lurch as he turned his front door key with his gloved hand, and he wasn't lying in his promise. I was slammed up against the hallway wall the very second the door closed behind us, and his breaths were hot on my neck, teeth teasing.

It was torment.

"Please," I whispered. "Please, Hans, bite me now! Do it!"

"Patience," he said, and the authority in his tone was power. Absolute, total power.

He tugged my dress down with enough strength that it tore, but I didn't give a fuck at the sound of lovely blue satin ripping. I shrugged my bolero off and stripped the ridiculous choker from my neck, offering my wounds and secretly hoping, *praying*, he'd hurt me just like he had before – his teeth in the same clotted bite marks. His mouth fresh with another man's blood.

Fuck, I was feeling so... dirty.

"Don't chastise yourself," he said as he took his gloves off. "This is the natural reaction to lust mixed with shock. It's relief."

He ran his tongue over the very wounds I was thinking about.

"Blood play drives a lot of beautiful filth, Katherine. Needs and desperation certainly fuel the imagination. Yours is only just beginning to start roaming free."

"Imagine where the fuck it's going to lead me, then," I whispered.

"Don't worry, I imagine it plenty. I've been imagining it for years."

I couldn't take it anymore. I pulled my panties off and kicked them away from me with my torn excuse of an evening dress, aching to have my flesh next to him. I moaned as he shrugged his jacket off and let it fall. There was a solid clunk of the knife as it hit the floor tiles, and BOOM, the memory came back to me in vivid colour. A soulful beast like Hans slitting the throat of the soulless beast in the restaurant yard.

He helped me as I tore off his shirt and tie in a frenzy until his chest was naked and pressed up against mine. He pinned my wrists above my head, gripped tight with one of his long, sculpted hands.

"BITE ME!" I cried out like an addict.

"*Patience*," he said again, but I squirmed, every one of my healing bite marks screaming, screaming, screaming.

"Please, Hans, BITE ME!"

He tutted at me.

"I'm nicely full of a sweet, bloody drink already. It will be so beautiful to watch you begging to be my next."

"I'll do it now, if you want me to," I whimpered. "I'll do whatever you want, just please, Hans. Please bite me."

He let me wriggle and squirm against him, watching me with dark eyes. Finally, he gave me the chance.

"Get down on the floor," he said. "Prayers are said from the kneeling position. Only it isn't the hand of God who'll be blessing you tonight. It won't be the Lord Saviour you're praying to. It'll be me."

His words were so fucking horny they drove me insane. I fell to my knees as soon as he let my wrists free, staring up to him like he was my saviour.

I guess he was.

Hot tingles flushed through me when he freed his huge cock, but I felt intimidated as he worked it in his hand.

It won't fit in my mouth.

"It will," he told me. "But you'll need to open nice and wide for me."

He tipped my chin up.

"Show me how wide you can open your pretty mouth, Katherine."

I did it, feeling like a dirty whore on my knees as I stared up at him, but he didn't look at me like I was one. He smiled with pride.

"That's a good girl," he said, and eased the head of his cock between my lips. "Taste it."

I ran my tongue over him, lapping at the salty taste.

"That's nice," he said and eased through my open lips.

The girth of him filled my mouth right up, but he was barely inside.

"You'll have to give me your throat," he told me, and I murmured my agreement as best as I could.

I let him angle me, and he worked his hips nice and slowly, pushing deeper. My mouth was still bloody, and his cock was hard as steel, and I could feel the outline of his veins against my tongue.

"Do you like taking cock in your mouth?" he asked and I gave a slight nod.

"Show me, then."

My eyes were watering as he picked up pace, my throat beginning to retch in protest, but he didn't stop. I sucked as best I could, and used my tongue with every thrust, dedicated to being everything he dreamt I'd be.

"You are everything I imagined, don't worry," he said. "You're the horny little one I waited for."

It spurred me on. I licked and sucked through the retches, forcing my throat to take him. He took my hair in his hands to help me, and it was another form of submission. Another sense of giving up my everything. It felt liberating.

I gave him my throat at any cost, and he used me how he wanted to. Every grunt of his felt like a victory. Every thrust felt like I was giving him my all.

"I could come in your beautiful mouth," he told me, and I whimpered because I wanted it so much.

I wanted to taste a vampire's cum.

"Not yet." He smiled. "I've got other plans for you first. Your sweet little pussy needs to learn to take me, time after time."

I was still sore, but my clit was tingling like crazy.

I wish I could play with myself as he fucks my mouth.

"No," he said. "Your pleasure is in my hands from now on, not yours."

With that he pulled out, leaving a huge string of spit between my lips and his cock while I gagged again, catching my breath.

He didn't give me time to compose myself before he pulled me to my feet and scooped me into his arms, carrying me up the stairs like a dirty little trophy.

His bed was waiting.

He threw me onto it like a little ragdoll, but again there was no cheapness to it. He was looking at me like I was the prettiest girl in the world. It made me glow so much.

He stalked me up the bed, towering over me on rigid arms. My legs spread wide and I moved on instinct, my pussy calling for his cock, even though I knew it would hurt like hell.

As would all of it.

"Where would you like to be bitten first, little one?"

I smiled. "Anywhere."

His stare roved down from my neck to my tits, but he seemed to ponder before he gave me a smile back.

"Let me surprise you. I think your clit has earned its reward."

Was he going to bite my pussy? Really? Was he going to sink his teeth into the spots he told me about, right on either side of my clit?

"Patience," he said again. "Learn that sex works best when you use feeling before thinking."

Feeling before thinking, I nodded, gripping the sheets as he kissed his way down my stomach and yes, I was feeling it deep inside. I wanted him so much it hurt.

I sighed when his hot mouth reached my pussy.

He didn't bite, though. He lapped, right the way up my wet pussy lips.

Oh God, I'm feeling it. Feeling you, Hans and it feels so good.

I looked down to see him open his mouth ready to bite me. His fangs were so long and white they gave me chills, but they were good chills. Excited chills.

It wasn't my pussy he sank his teeth into, though. It was a spot right on the inside of my thigh, untouched and so tender that it sent shocks of pain right the way up through my ribs.

I cried out, but his tongue was swirling as he sucked, and I sank into it, *feeling not thinking.*

My legs were trembling, but my breaths slowed down, and I let go of the sheets, stretching my arms above my head.

I could take it. And I would. Anywhere he wanted.

"Yes," he growled through his bite. "You will."

He let go of my thigh and moved his bloody mouth back to my pussy, and this time he spread my pussy lips and swept his tongue across my tender clit, over and over. I gasped and I moaned and it felt like heaven.

"I'll get you nice and ready this time," he told me, and sucked my clit into his hot mouth.

I raised my hips from the bed, crying out for more, and he used my position to sink his fingers all the way inside me. I don't know how many he was using, but it hurt, stretching me.

He twisted his fingers and sucked at my clit, but every time I began to pant and peak, he'd ease off enough to keep me hanging – drifting on the edge of an orgasm in a timeless haze. My thigh was still pulsing and bleeding, and he used my blood as lube, stretching me more and more with his fingers.

I took it, like I was told.

He sank his teeth into my other thigh and I cried out again, but it wasn't as loud this time, the pain more bearable. I twisted into his bite as his fingers worked inside me, with a big heady grin on my face. *Feeling it... feeling it...*

"You're almost ready," he told me, and climbed back up until we were face to face, his huge dick thumping against my pussy. "Show me your throat now."

I tipped my head back and offered him my neck, my arms still stretched above me.

He kissed the spot first – brand new flesh – then speared me with his massive dick in one solid thrust.

He'd said I was prepared, but I wasn't expecting the force of the pounding his hips gave me. It felt like I was being torn apart from the inside out, so deep with raw pain and lust that I'd forgotten my offered throat.

He sank his teeth into me with such force that I screamed, but I was grinning, panting, needing.

Blood play.

I could only begin to imagine the crazy addiction players had in the blood houses. It must be frantic, desperate, frenzied.

Hans fucked me as he took my blood, fulfilling his needs as my body cried out for more. He became as frantic as I was, hips slamming as mine bucked, faster and faster. He ground in just the right spot, my clit so tender that it had me gasping.

Finally, gratefully, I was going to come, and suddenly, fuck, fuck, fuck. I was in the middle of the best fucking orgasm I'd ever known, and it was long as his cock pounded me. So fucking long I was groaning like a slut, and it was magic.

With his cock buried deep, he took his teeth from my throat, dripping my own blood over me as I smiled up at him.

"Like I said, little one. It's all about patience. The longer you wait, the better it feels."

I clenched around his rock-hard cock, still cresting on the waves. I arched my back, silently offering him my tits, and he gave me a fresh bite, right around my nipple. Perfect. It was fucking perfect as he sucked my bleeding nipple into his mouth. Just perfect as his thrusting cock set me on fire.

His fierce green eyes were boring into mine as he hissed and grunted and slammed into me as he came. I felt like a queen as he crested for himself with as much passion as I was. And then he slowed, dropped a kiss onto my lips with his dick still inside me. I could feel how ridiculously slick my pussy was when he pulled out. I must have soaked the bed.

"Open your mouth again," he told me and slipped his fingers back inside my throbbing pussy.

His fingers were glistening with both blood and cum when he held them in front of my face.

"Suck," he whispered, and offered them to me.

There was no hesitation. Just pride as I sucked and lapped them clean like a girl being given a reward, and he laughed with a gorgeous warm tone.

"Hungry girl," he said.

I nodded with a giggle, and he laughed again when he pulled his clean fingers free.

"We'd better get the hungry girl a steak," he told me. "Considering you barely touched the one at the restaurant."

He kissed me on my blood-red lips before he pulled me up and off the bed with him, holding me tight on my shaky legs.

I certainly didn't protest. My stomach was rumbling enough to eat a whole damn cow.

16

I couldn't stop staring at Hans as he prepared my steak. The sizzle of it in the pan had my stomach rumbling. I was ravenous.

He was dressed in a burgundy dressing gown that suited the gothic decor, and I was a stark contrast, in one of my oversized sweaters from the rail in the drawing room. Smears of blood were already showing through the fabric. It would make a fitting Halloween outfit.

"And you would make a fitting Halloween creature of the night," Hans said, giving me a smile over his shoulder. "It's only a few days away. How do you usually celebrate?"

I felt almost embarrassed to admit my lack of a social circle in Orcop.

I shrugged. "Watching movies and eating bat-shaped candy."

He laughed. "How about this year? How do you think we'll be spending it?"

"Maybe getting bitten and having another round of crazy sex in your boudoir."

"That's a staple from now on, Katherine." He presented my steak, oozing with blood. "Bon appetite."

I was straight on it, moaning as the bloody meat melted in my mouth. Even though the steak was a huge one I was done in a few minutes, tops.

"Excellent work," he said. "Shame I don't have any bat-shaped candy to follow, or strawberry jam for that matter, but we'll get the cupboards stocked up for you."

Who'd have ever thought I'd be in a vampire's house talking about the domesticity of cupboards stocked with strawberry jam? I almost laughed out loud, it was so surreal.

One thing that was already becoming less surreal was my easiness around Hans. Despite the crazy fact he'd sucked blood from me and taken my virginity with his huge vampire cock, plus actually killed a criminal before my eyes, it was already so natural to watch him across the breakfast bar. Me watching him as he watched me.

Maybe it was his smile, or his care, or the way he was so at ease with himself. Maybe it was because I was already a tiny bit familiar with him from Regency in my brief stint working there. Or maybe it was–

"Feeling not thinking, remember?" he said with a smirk. "Believe me, you can drive yourself insane with a mind running riot."

"I've got plenty to be thinking about, don't you think?"

"True."

I leant back on my stool, wincing a little at the pain. I was still staring at him.

"You must have been thinking so much that you were driving yourself crazy at some point?" I asked him. "Your mind must have been in turmoil when you were turned into a vampire in the first place, suddenly undead after being tortured in Garway church."

He tipped his head. "Undead is quite a potent term for vampire. I prefer transformed. My flesh died, but I didn't. Call it a transition that takes over. It didn't change who I was, just gave me a lot longer to explore it."

"And a lot longer to think about it too?"

"Well, when you put it like that. Yes."

He got me a glass of water and placed it down in front of me.

"Make sure you keep hydrated."

I loved the way he was so attentive, with care in his eyes. It was quite an intense combination of authority and almost parental care, mixed with the unmistakable buzz of sexual attraction. How did that work? And that wasn't the entirety of it, either. What other subtle dynamics were playing on different frequencies between us?

"Like I said, feeling not thinking," Hans said. "Don't try to fathom the unfathomable. Life is complicated. Souls are both too simple and too complex to understand all at once."

I held my hands up. "Busted! I'll try to keep my brain spinning to a minimum. Not sure how well I'll succeed, though."

I failed miserably in a heartbeat, since another question came out of nowhere.

"What happened to the people around you when you became a vampire? Did you have friends? A family? There must have been so much that changed."

"That's a deep one to answer at 5 a.m." He yawned but I'm sure it was faked.

"Maybe give me a condensed version?"

"Hmm."

He looked wistful as his mind turned inwards, no doubt looking back a long, long time.

"I was devoted to the Church and my role in the Templars. One of the vows was celibacy, so I didn't have a family. My parents were in Normandy. I wrote letters but hadn't seen them in years. I had grief for the people I lost, yes, but that grief was mainly for the brothers being interrogated to death all around me. Plenty of us got taken down."

I felt like I'd overstepped the mark by probing so deep into his past, but he took my hand.

"You can ask questions. As I said, I'm happy to answer them. Just make sure you want to know the answers before you voice them aloud."

"Why wouldn't I?" I squeezed his fingers. "Your life is fascinating."

He looked straight into my eyes, and something in his expression made it clear once more that he knew an awful lot I didn't. It made sense that he would do, clearly, since he'd been alive seven hundred years to my measly eighteen, but it didn't feel like it was purely historical knowledge he had over me. It felt like extra knowledge about *me*.

The trapdoor.

"And there we go with the thoughts again." He let go of my hand and patted it. "Be careful."

I wanted to ask him straight out just what the hell I was sensing in my subconscious that was scaring the shit out of me, but I kept my mouth shut this time.

I'd figured that the trapdoor had only appeared since meeting Hans, but had it? Didn't I have a sense of it from a long, long time ago, when I was a kid asking Mum and Grandma questions? It was just a whisper of the past, but whispers often tell more truth than shouting.

I'd always been shouted down and told to stop living in fairy tales. My questions about the depths of my dreams had always been met with nothing.

Did I want to know now? Did I want to know the answers from Hans?

The idea gave me an eerie tickle up my spine.

No. I didn't. Not yet.

I stretched my arms and yawned, finally accepting my exhaustion.

"Time for bed," Hans said.

We headed up the stairs hand in hand. My vampire guided me to an armchair in his bedroom and sat me down while he went to the fridge and poured a fresh glass of water for me.

Again, I felt like a little girl, so looked after it was beautiful. Safety in the care of a vampire, who'd have even considered it? I'd have expected to be either dead or a vampire myself by now.

I hadn't voiced that to myself before...

Dead or a vampire?

I drank my water while Hans bolted us into the bedroom, and my mind kept going through those same two outcomes.

Dead or a vampire?

Well, I certainly wasn't dead yet, and didn't think Hans was going to suck my blood completely dry anytime soon, but what about the other option? What about being a vampire myself?

"I can hear your thoughts, you know," Hans commented as he hung his robe up on a hanger. Of course my eyes went straight to his naked butt… and then to his beautiful cock when he turned to face me.

"Yes, I do know you can hear my thoughts," I said, my gaze eventually meeting his. "So, are you going to make me a vampire one day?"

I wasn't really asking the question seriously, not right then. I was still so heady from a bloodthirsty fucking and a huge steak.

"That would be a massive commitment," he told me, his eyes so serious.

I felt like an idiot for asking. Yes, it would be a massive commitment, he'd likely be stuck with me clinging onto him for all time…

"No, that's not what I meant," he said. "Not a massive commitment for *me*, but for *you*."

I played it light.

"I can decide now, if you like? I'll happily be a vampire with you, Hans. Convert me now."

His eyes were still serious

"Steady, and be careful what you wish for. You're blood-play drunk. You haven't even tasted vampire blood yet. Only your own, and that of a rapist."

My mouth must have dropped open, not quite understanding.

"You mean I could taste vampire blood without turning into a vampire?"

"Yes," he answered simply.

It reinforced in an instant just how little I knew about his life, and his experiences, and the true nature of being a vampire. I knew sweet FA. My knowledge all came from novels and movies.

"There are many different beliefs about our lifestyle," Hans said as he began to change the bedsheets. "Don't criticise yourself for ignorance."

"Yes, but I should've asked before assuming."

"You've had more than enough questions on your mind lately."

"There are some questions that are totally obvious, though. I just figured…"

My naked vampire started fluffing up the pillows. What a sight. And how surreal.

"Yes, you figured vampires take victims, and create more of their own kind by offering their own blood in return, and that is true. As I said to you, that's what dear Edwin offered me. But as with everything else in this world, there are levels."

"Levels?"

"It takes a fair amount of vampire blood to convert a human body to fully vampiric. Call it a beautiful poison. A lethal dose of rat poison will kill a rat, yes, but a token dose likely won't. The rat will feel it, most certainly, but it won't take its life away."

I nodded, following his words. I kept on listening, totally consumed.

"You'll see this for yourself in the blood house." He stepped on over to me. This time my eyes stayed on his. "Rat poison is a poor parallel, you'll observe that clearly when you see the blood games at work."

I got a shiver. *The blood house.* It would be so intriguing that I'd be tingling in private places like a dirty bystander. *It would be so much fun. Forbidden. Filthy.*

"No more questions now. Let's get ready for bed." His hand met mine and I was pulled lightly to my feet.

I threw off my blood-stained sweater and followed him into the bathroom, for hair brushing and teeth cleaning. All I could think about was the blood house, wondering just what blood games would be happening with experienced *victims. Players.*

"They are players, yes? That's what people are called?" I asked and Hans sighed as we slipped under the bedcovers together.

"What did we say about questions?" He switched the light off. "Yes, they are blood players. As are you now."

He pulled me close, so my head was on his chest and his arms were wrapped tight around me. We were locked up safe in the steel box again, and I loved it. It was beginning to feel like home.

His voice was a whisper.

"When do you want to see the blood house? How strong is the pull in your veins?"

I sighed, comfortable in his arms.

"Your turn for questions now, is it?"

"I think the scales are very lopsided on the question score, don't you? I'm owed some answers."

"Yes, but you're also a mind reader. You know when I want to see the blood house. You know about the pull in my veins."

He kissed my forehead, his full lips so deliciously warm.

"Yes, but some things need to be spoken aloud." He tipped my face to his in the darkness. "So, I'm asking you. When do you want to see the blood house?"

I let my instincts guide me, common sense left behind. I was thrilled at the idea of seeing a blood house in action, meeting blood players who were going as crazy as I was. I needed the sense of solidarity in my brand new world.

"As soon as possible," I admitted. "I want to see it all."

He stroked my hair. "You really are the curious little soul I believed you'd be. I can't wait to see how the years unfold for us."

Years...

Us.

Feeling... I felt him in my heart right then.

"We can go tomorrow night," he said.

I would have clapped my hands in gratitude if I hadn't felt the swell of his huge vampire cock against my thigh.

Seems I wasn't the only one keen to visit a blood house tomorrow night...

I was definitely growing in confidence. It was me who slipped further underneath the covers and took his cock in my mouth as deep as it would go. Trusting my initiative. *Feeling, not thinking.*

It worked.

This time I got a full-blown taste of vampire cum, without even a hint of blood along with it.

He bucked and grunted, and held my hair in the heat of passion as he unloaded straight into my mouth. I felt like a porn star in the making as I smacked my lips with pride and took my place back in his arms.

"Well done, and thank you very much," he said to me. "You really are a fast learner."

"You're welcome," I said.

"Your turn next," he told me, and flipped me onto my back in one fast motion.

Oh wow. Here it came again. Here *I* came again – hard and fast, gripping his gorgeous dark vampire hair as he ate my pussy.

"Bite me, please!" I begged again, but no.

"Patience," he said. "You've had your fair share of bites tonight. You will have to make do with pure, bloodless kisses and hard, deep cock instead."

"I think I'll manage," I said with a dirty grin on my face.

17

My confidence wasn't nearly so bright when I woke up. My bites were sore, and my body was still exhausted, even though my soul was glowing beneath the surface.

My vampire lover was already awake. He landed a kiss on my lips as soon as I opened my eyes.

"Good morning," I said, and he laughed.

"I think it's termed good *evening*, little one."

"Yeah, I forgot, the good mornings are long gone."

"Yes, I haven't seen a good morning in a long, long time."

I wondered if I'd be joining him in that one day. If I too would become a creature of the night. Now wasn't the time to be thinking about that, though.

"What time is it?" I asked him.

"Late enough to be dark outside. Eight p.m. Time to go soon."

Of course. The blood house.

"Yes," he said. "That's if you still want to go, of course."

Even through the flutter of nerves, I knew I wanted it. My fascination was too strong to ignore.

"Let's get you a wholesome evening breakfast first," Hans said, and helped me out of bed.

He wrapped me in one of his sumptuous dressing gowns. A classic robe in burgundy.

"Is it another steak for me?" I asked when we reached the kitchen, but he grinned at me proudly and showed me a jar of strawberry jam from the cupboard.

"Frederick was a kind gentleman and delivered this earlier."

He pulled out a bag of bat-shaped candy to follow, and I laughed.

"I'm spoiled!"

Hans' beautiful smile was glorious.

"You deserve it. I wouldn't say you've had all that much spoiling this lifetime. There's a lot to make up for."

The contrast jabbed me pretty deeply. He was right. I wouldn't say I'd ever been all that spoiled my Mum or Grandma. They'd usually been criticising me every chance they got.

"Don't worry," I told Hans, stepping up to him. "I can get my own toast. You don't have to keep looking after me."

He didn't hand over the butter knife, just kept on watching the bread in the toaster.

"No, you're right. I don't *have* to," he said. "I *want* to. Now, get your tender butt over to the breakfast bar and sit yourself down. You need some sugar to get your blood levels up."

"Thanks," I said and did as I was told, grabbing myself a glass of water on the way.

"Good call," Hans said. "You'll need plenty of hydration for later."

My stomach was fluttering at the thought of later. My confidence from last night still evading me.

"There's nothing to worry about," Hans said. "Any moment you feel uncomfortable, we can turn around and walk away. Your pace, your choice."

I nodded. "Thank you."

He delivered me a very generous helping of jam on toast and sat opposite me as I ate.

"What will the blood house be like?" I quizzed.

"Probably not quite like you're imagining it. It's not like a brothel, or a scene from a horror movie. It's a lot more upmarket than that."

"Yeah?" I pushed, but he shook his head.

"No spoilers. I want you to enjoy the experience through fresh eyes. No preconceptions."

"Exciting."

"Yes. It will be. At least, I hope so."

I wondered how many times he had been to the blood house himself. What he'd done in there before, and what he'd seen. Who would be there, and what kind of games would they be playing... maybe things I'd never even thought of.

"No preconceptions," Hans repeated, and I rolled my eyes.

"Are you going to be reading my thoughts for ever?"

He smirked. "Yes. Unless you block me."

"Block you?"

He nodded. "Yes. There are skills you can learn in order to be more *selective* in what I get to hear from your mind. They are not suited to everyone, but I'm sure you would be quite adept in no time."

"Really?" I asked between mouthfuls of toast. "Are you going to teach me? Can I be a *selective* mind-blocking student of yours?"

"It's really not my forte. That's in the realm of witches and wizards, not mine."

I giggled. "Witches and wizards? Wow. Are you going to introduce me to some? Can I book in for a magic course?"

He didn't laugh along with me.

"I'm sure it's possible. They might be closer than you think."

I got a shiver. Weird.

"Anyway," Hans said, clearly changing the subject. "I thought we could do something fun on the run up to the blood house. Get you nice and relaxed with a few glasses of wine."

"A bar?" I asked. "Do you have one in mind?"

The thought of being at his side in public again was very attractive. I'd be buzzing through every second to be on his arm.

"I do have one in mind," he replied. "Shall we avoid the spoilers on that topic as well? How about that? A night full of surprises?"

"Sounds amazing. I'll stop with the quizzing."

I glugged down another large glass of water when I was done with my toast and candies, then picked out another of my dresses from the drawing room. I went for a classic black number this time. This one was fitted tight, with a high neck and long sleeves. It was definitely the best choice for hiding bite marks.

I gestured to my shoe collection when Hans appeared in the doorway.

"Will I need to run across London again?" I joked. "If so, I'll go in sneakers."

He laughed back. "We'll give you a break from the chase this evening. There will be more than enough to thrill you."

I went for a pair of black heels, nicely high but not towering enough to risk tumbling on cobblestones. Not tonight.

Hans got ready in another stunning tailored suit as I did my hair and makeup in the ensuite. We looked each other up and down before we left the bedroom, and the heat was there between us in full force as we descended the stairs. It was so intense, it felt like I was plugged into him, together as one. It uplifted me, made me feel proud as well as horny.

"Time to go, which is lucky," he said, offering me his arm as we neared the front door. "If we hang around here much longer, I'm going to have to tear that dress off you and sink my teeth in."

"Don't tempt me," I said. "If we hang around here much longer, I'll be doing it for you."

There was a cab ready for us outside. Hans helped me into the back seat before he got in alongside me, and I waited with bated breath for him to reveal the destination. Maybe another Westminster trip, or somewhere gothic in Camden, or one of the bustling bars in Soho…

I did a double take when he gave the driver our destination.

"Regency Gentlemen's Club. Southall."

"But, wait," I said. "I'm not a member."

"Pah," Hans scoffed. "They can call it a gentlemen's club all they like, but it's so outdated it's ridiculous and they know it. You'll be most welcome there at my side. The regulars all think you are incredible, even though you were only working there a few short weeks."

It made me feel so good to hear that. I'd seen them as clients, not contemplating for a second that they'd have seen me as anything more than a girl pouring drinks for them.

"No," Hans said. "You definitely made an impression."

I squeezed his knee in silent thanks for his revelation.

"I hope they recognise me with my hair out of a bun."

"Oh, they will. You're a very distinctive girl."

It was odd when the cab dropped us outside the main entrance of Regency. I'd only ever used the staff door around the back.

"Ready?" Hans took my hand in his.

I thought I was prepared for it until I saw the eyes fix on us as we walked through the club. There was so much shock and surprise on people's faces as Hans offered me a stool alongside Frederick at the bar and sat right next to me.

"Katherine," Frederick greeted with a nod, as though we were great friends. "Lovely to see you."

I grinned at him, as though I was living in a conspiracy movie.

"Thanks for my things, and for the jam, too," I whispered. "Oh, and the bat sweets."

He winked and raised his glass of merlot.

"You're very welcome."

Eliza stared at me when she saw us there, open mouthed as she approached.

"Hey," I said, with my fingers twisting in my lap, expecting a confrontation at my sudden departure. But none came.

"Wow, you look incredible," she told me. "And congratulations! The management told me you'd be moving on to a great opportunity."

Hans took my hand visibly, squeezing my fingers on the bar top.

"Katherine is a superstar," he told Eliza. "Both personally and professionally. It's an honour to steal her from Regency, but my apologies for taking an such asset from you."

I swear she sighed as she smiled at him. "She deserves it."

I got another lovely glow at the flattery. This emerging self-worth was a world away from how I'd felt about myself through my years back home.

"A merlot for both of you?" she asked, and Hans looked at me.

"Yes, please," I said.

A look passed between Frederick and Hans before Frederick excused himself for a bathroom break.

"I'll be back in a moment," he told me, and for once, up close, I realised he was taking his glass with him.

Empty.

I got another strange tickle of a sensation, and it still took me aback, despite the fact I should be getting used to them by now.

"Is Frederick really taking that empty glass to the bathroom with him?" I whispered to Hans.

"Yes," he whispered back. "Trust your instincts. Feelings not thoughts, remember?"

I let the tickle spin around inside me. *Trust your instincts.*

"What do you think is happening here?" Hans queried. "You wouldn't have seen it before. We were very careful to hide it from view, and even the most observant people aren't all that observant. But your instincts are heightening. View this as a tester of instincts. Say what comes into your head."

"Is he, umm..."

I struggled to voice it out loud. In case I was wrong.

"You aren't wrong," Hans said. "Just speak it."

"Is he bleeding for you? Into the wine glass?"

Hans smiled like I'd just won a competition.

"Your senses are indeed heightening. Very good, Katherine. That's an excellent sign."

An excellent sign of what, exactly?

The trapdoor thumped into my mind.

Luckily, the thumping was interrupted when Frederick arrived back at the bar with a fresh glass of *merlot*. I couldn't believe I'd never noticed that before. It was plainly obvious that Eliza hadn't, either. She handed us our freshly poured glasses, completely unaware.

She didn't notice when Hans switched glasses with Frederick with a *cheers*. I joined in with them, amazed by the full scale of the association between them. Frederick was definitely a lot more than an accountant.

"Are you enjoying your new opportunity with the excellent Mr Weyer?" he asked me.

I nodded, with a genuine smile.

"Very much. It's been quite a shocker of an experience so far, but a very good one."

Hans squeezed my fingers again.

"She's a very, very astute learner, and very inquisitive," he told his friend. "We're going to be visiting the Manor later."

Frederick's brows shot up as he sipped his merlot.

"The Manor? Really? That's quite a sharp introduction."

Hans nodded, with a proud look on his face.

"Yes, but I'm certain she can handle it."

I wasn't so sure I agreed with him when I saw the look pass between them. I felt utterly out of my depth.

A merlot or two would definitely help me.

I finished my first one quickly, and Eliza refilled my glass in an instant. My second turned to a third, and conversation flowed steadily with both with Hans and Frederick, and also between me and the people I used to refer to as *sir* when I was pouring their drinks. They chatted to me easily when they arrived at the bar, as though me being there was most natural thing in the world.

Hans hadn't been lying when he said they liked me. I saw it in their eyes.

I *felt* it.

It went to show one thing, with crystal clarity. My life was definitely better suited to here than it was in Orcop. I didn't belong in Orcop at all.

Hans cleared his throat and leant in to whisper something, no doubt reading my thoughts, but he didn't get the chance.

I spun like I'd seen a ghost when the entrance door opened and the eccentric George Miller appeared.

"Oh my God," I said to Hans, my eyes wide on his. "I thought George was... gone!"

I clapped my hands together. It was such a relief to see George there, and wow, there was a woman alongside him as he stepped inside.

"Is this a bring your partner night or something?" I said when I saw her.

I was so grateful that George had survived his planned death that I smiled up at Frederick.

"Thanks," I whispered. "That's amazing. I'm sure you must have had something to do with the turnaround."

Only Frederick looked at me blankly.

"Thanks for what?" he asked, his gaze turning in the same direction as mine as George and his partner crossed the room.

There was no reaction from Frederick when he saw them. He shot a look at Hans and not at me.

"Is she seeing George?"

"I imagine so," Hans replied.

He put a hand on my shoulder firmly, turning me towards him.

"What's happening, Hans?" I whispered, my senses dawning.

Feeling, not thinking. Instincts. But no. No. It couldn't be...

Hans leant in closer than ever. His lips were a ghost against my ear.

Which was fitting, wasn't it? Given the words he was about to tell me...

Instincts. Instincts.

Feelings and whispers...

"George Miller is dead, Katherine. He died two nights ago. A terrible accident in his home. People will be so upset in here when they find out."

My stare shot straight back to George as he took a seat at the other end of the bar from us. He waved and pointed me out to the woman at his side, both of them smiling happily.

It was insane.

George Miller was THERE, in crystal clear vision, but nobody else so much as caught sight of him, bustling around him like he didn't exist.

"You can see him right there, can you?" Hans asked me, and I nodded.

"Yes, and the woman next to him."

"Fantastic! His wife Margaret, I imagine. How lovely. Do they look happy?"

"Yeah, they look happy. They're waving at me. George looks like he's won the lottery."

He did, as well. He looked like the happiest man in the world with his wife – Margaret – at his side.

"Excellent," Hans whispered, and raised his glass to me. "Congratulations on your emerging skills. You will make an amazing ghost whisperer. Well done."

"Yes, well done," said Frederick, and raised his glass too.

A ghost whisperer.

I was going to be a ghost whisperer?

I didn't know whether congratulations were truly in order, since I very nearly fainted out cold on the floor.

18

*I*t was my turn to take a bathroom break. I needed to get out of there. Fast.

"I'll be right back," I told Hans and Frederick, trying my best to seem like I was steady on my feet as I rushed away.

I don't know how I made it to the bathroom, but I did. I shunted my way into a cubicle and dropped myself down on the toilet with the room spinning.

It couldn't be true. There was no way I could be a *ghost whisperer*, whatever that even meant.

Once again, though, it all came flooding back to me… the countless times I'd told Mum and Grandma about the people I'd seen across the street in my *imagination* wearing vintage clothes. The countless times they'd told me I was daydreaming.

Stop lying! There's nobody there!

I'd heard the same response so many times that I'd stopped saying anything at all, giving myself the same message that they had. *Stop being a stupid little girl.*

Finally, I'd stopped questioning it, stopped talking about it. Stopped believing in it myself.

And now here I was, just turned eighteen, back in the midst of the fantasy confusion I'd had when I was eight.

I felt two different sides of myself battling, but there was no doubt which was going to win the war this time. For once in my life, the *stupid little girl* was going to stand up for herself and come up trumps. How could she not? Meeting a vampire named Hans and hearing him talk of witches, and wizards, and ghosts. There was no denying it. George and his wife were sitting at the bar.

Whatever the outcome of the inner battle, I had to get a grip of myself.

I couldn't break down in the Regency bathroom, rocking on the tiled floor like the world was ending. The world wasn't ending at all. My eyes were simply opening.

I moved from the cubicle to the basin and put my hands under the cold, running water, trying to slow down my heartrate. *I needed to calm down.* I thought that might be working a little until the bathroom door swung open.

There she was. *Margaret.* And she wasn't just a waving figure at the other end of the bar this time, she was right up close, standing beside me.

She was a frail old lady, but she carried herself so well, standing tall. The wrinkles around her eyes complemented her warm smile, and she was dressed so perfectly demure, in a cream blouse and dark green skirt, with an emerald broach at the collar. She looked like she belonged on George's arm. Most definitely.

"My husband has said lovely things about you," she told me. "He said you were an excellent barmaid, always very helpful. That's a massive compliment for an old grump like him."

I felt like a fool, out of my depth when I replied with a ridiculous *thank you, that's a lovely thing to hear.*

"It's really quite the novelty to be seen by someone after all this time," she said. "For over a decade I've been wandering around our house, trying to get George to see me, but it was like screeching at a wall. I only wish I'd accompanied him to the bar sooner, I may have been able to have a bit of chatter to fill my days."

She gave a little chuckle.

I knew I was staring, and my mouth was gaping. I was talking to a freaking ghost.

"Just as well George met his end and came to join me, wasn't it?" she went on. "I was about to give up and go haunt someone else, just to get them to notice me."

She was joking, but my laugh in return got stuck in my throat. I sounded like a coughing frog.

"Oh dear," she said. "Are you ill, my love? You look like you're burning up."

"I just can't believe this is really happening," I admitted.

"Can't believe what is happening?"

I gestured at her wildly. "This. Seeing you. Seeing George. Everything."

Her expression showed her confusion.

"Surely this can't be the first time? You are a witch, after all."

The room spun, my eyes trying to stay fixed on her.

"Sorry, what? What did you say?"

Her eyes sparkled along with her broach.

"A witch, sweetheart. You're a witch, yes?"

I shook my head. "No."

She looked as though I'd just told her the moon was made of cheese.

"You're not a witch? Really?"

I kept on shaking my head. "No. I'm not."

"Good Lord. What are you, then? A psychic, or full-blown ghost whisperer? You're not a vampire yet, clearly."

"I'm none of them," I blustered. "I don't think so, anyway. I'm just a girl from Orcop."

"I'm sure that can't be the case." Margaret put a hand to her chin, pondering. "Surely the vampire you're with must know what you are. Maybe you should ask him if you haven't already? I'm sure he'll be able to enlighten you."

It seemed I'd have the chance to ask Hans very soon. There was a knock on the door, and even though it was the ladies' bathroom, he stepped straight on inside.

He looked from me to Margaret.

"Ah, you're not alone?"

"How do you know that?" I asked him. "Can you see her? She really is here?"

"No, I can't see her, but I don't need to. I can tell from your expression. It's plainly obvious that you're speaking with her." He paused, then addressed the empty space beside me. "Hello, Margaret, sorry I can't see you in person, but I am pleased to hear you are well."

"Hello, Hans," she replied, then patted my arm. "Do thank him, please. For delivering my George to me. I know he was the one pulling the strings behind the scenes. George knows it, too. He was quite an angry sod when he first crossed over and saw his body at the bottom of the stairs, but he soon got over it when he saw me."

Alrighty then. I took a breath and looked at Hans. "She says thanks. For… for killing George."

He waved his hand. "I can't take all the credit, Margaret. I only gave the nod."

I couldn't believe this. I was in some kind of alternate reality, acting as an interpreter between a ghost and a vampire. Just what the hell was going on?

Of course, Hans read my mind.

"It's all right," he said. "You're bound to be a little bit disoriented. That's totally understandable."

"Understatement of the century," I managed to say.

I was still wobbly. I leant against the basin, then looked Hans right in his stunning green eyes.

"Is Margaret right? Am I a witch? Or a psychic, or a ghost whisperer thingy?"

He tipped his head from side to side, as though he was pondering.

"Oh, go on, tell him to hurry up," Margaret said with a chuckle. "I'm as curious now as you are."

I very much doubted that was the case.

"What am I, Hans?" I said. "What the hell is happening to me?"

He took my hands from the basin and gripped them tight. Then he spoke to the space beside me.

"Leave us alone, please, Margaret," he said. "I think this conversation should be a private one."

"Of course, sorry." She put her hand on my back before she walked away. "Good luck, darling. Enjoy the revelation. You'll have to let me know how it goes."

The bathroom door swung back open as she left, but Hans didn't seem convinced.

"Did she leave?" he asked me.

"Yes," was all I could say, staring blankly as the door closed up again behind her.

"Excellent." He paused, and his expression was a serious one. "I really didn't expect to be having this discussion in a club bathroom after you'd been talking to a ghost, so, my sincere apologies for that, Katherine, but I really didn't believe George would be here so soon. It usually takes a lot longer for souls to adjust to the fact they are dead, let alone take a jaunt out to their local, but I guess he has Margaret to thank for that."

I closed my eyes. "I don't give a shit about the location, Hans. Just answer me, please."

"Patience," he said, and I'd have wanted to give him an uppercut if my hands weren't so damn shaky and clutched in his.

My voice sounded so frantic when it launched from my throat.

"FUCK PATIENCE! What am I?! Am I a ghost whisperer, or a psychic, or a witch, or whatever else the hell is roaming around the place? Am I a werewolf? A human bat? A reincarnation of King Arthur?"

He sighed. "Well, now. That's the very opposite of patience, isn't it? Try not to lose your cool, little one."

"How can I not lose my fucking cool? I've just had a ghost asking me if I'm a witch in a fucking bathroom! I've gone mad, that's it, isn't it? I'm in a mental asylum somewhere, drugged up to the eyeballs."

Hans stayed so steady, shaking his head at me.

Then the thought really slammed me – I was in a coma! Maybe I'd been hit by a car on the way to work, and now I was in a coma, playing inside my mind.

"You're not insane and you're not in a coma," Hans said, "How about you go finish your merlot and we'll resume the conversation when you're a little calmer?"

I stared at him in shock, because he sounded like all this was the most natural thing in the world. Like it should be obvious that these entities existed and I should have known all about them.

"I *am* surprised you don't know about them, yes," he said.

His tone changed and he cursed under his breath.

"Your mother and grandmother did a very good job at hiding the truth from you, didn't they?"

Stupid girl.

Even now his eyes were so green they were mesmerising. I tried to focus on them and not the world that was twisting and warping around me.

I took a deep breath, and tried to still the inner whirlwind. There was no point in denying it. My rational beliefs were crumbling to nothing, and there was nothing I could do about it.

I sighed to myself, my hands still gripped in Hans'. He stayed as calm as ever while my mind lurched through my memories.

Maybe I should have fought an awful lot harder in the first place. Every time Mum and Grandma told me I was bloody insane...

"Don't beat yourself up," Hans said. "You were just a child. You're blossoming into a very skilled woman right now. You should be proud of yourself."

"What am I?" I asked again. "Seriously, just tell me, will you?"

His gaze was so intense it took my breath.

"I've said it before, but I'll say it again. Make sure you only ask questions when you're ready to hear the answers. Once you've heard them, you can't go back." He paused. "So, I'm asking you. Do you really want to know?"

Yes. That's what I thought in an instant. YES, OF COURSE I WANT TO KNOW.

Hans spoke again.

"Be sure, little one. Be very, very sure."

I could sense the trapdoor, thumping in my subconscious, and it gave me its usual shiver of *NO*.

NO.

DON'T DO IT!

Don't ask the question.

But I couldn't fight it anymore. I couldn't walk out of the bathroom with no idea what the fuck was happening to me, or who the fuck I really was…

I sounded surprisingly self-assured when I spoke next.

"Yes," I told him. "I want to know. So, I'm asking you again. What the hell am I? A psychic, a ghost whisper, or a goddamn witch, Hans?"

He sighed, and gave my hands another squeeze before he answered me.

"You're all three," he said.

19

*R*ational Katherine came back with a second wind, trying to bash *stupid fairy tale girl* into oblivion. A psychic, a ghost whisperer, and a witch? Just how? What? This was just plain crazy…

Hans interjected my thoughts.

"Feeling not thinking, remember? Throw the clockwork thoughts out of the window, and let your intuition guide you."

I must have been open-mouthed. The battle was still raging inside me.

Hans read it in an instant.

"It's interesting don't you think? How you are coping so well with the supernatural elements of the people around you, but not of the ones in yourself?"

"I'm not sure I'm coping so well with anything," I told him.

"That's not true, sweetheart. You're coping extremely well with everything. It's an awful lot to comprehend."

Sweetheart.

My *sweetheart* was a vampire. A bisexual, murdering, vampire. A stunningly handsome vampire with a monster cock. And I was his witch. I wasn't sure whether my cackling laugh was aloud or in my head.

He pulled me into his arms and kissed my forehead.

"I ask you again," Hans said. "Do you not think it's interesting how you can accept the supernatural elements *around* you, but not *within* you?"

I heard my grandma's screeching voice in my head. STUPID GIRL! STOP IT WITH THE DAYDREAMING!

Memories came back like a typhoon, running savage through my mind.

A teddy cat when I was a young girl, given to me by one of our neighbours. Me convinced he was a familiar called Goblin, and casting pretend spells with him, using one of Mum's big cooking pots as a cauldron. She'd gone ballistic and thrown him out with the trash. STOP IT, KATHERINE! NO GAMES ABOUT WITCHES!

Me telling Mum about my dream where Grandma had a nasty fall in church at the harvest festival, later that week. Please make sure she's safe, I said. I don't want her to hurt herself!

STOP IT, KATHERINE! I DON'T WANT TO HEAR ABOUT ANY MORE OF YOUR STUPID DREAMS! THEY AREN'T REAL!

I'd been right, though. Grandma had tumbled and knocked herself out on one of the pews.

"That's why you haven't realised," Hans said softly against my ear. "You've been told you're crazy for feeling the truth of things, ever since the day you were born."

"But how can it be like this?" I asked.

"It doesn't matter *how*. All that matters is that you *are*. Embrace it, Katherine. Let go of the fight and accept who you truly are."

"How can I embrace it? How can I accept who I am? I don't know what I'm supposed to do, or who I'm supposed to be. I don't know what being a psychic, or a ghost whisperer, or a damn witch even means."

Or do I?

The thoughts tickled and prickled inside me.

"I promise you, sweetheart," Hans said. "You have a huge number of skills you can learn to use. Spellcraft, divination, and communicating with the spirits of the dead. Reading astrology, channelling energy, tuning into psychic waves. They are all there ready and waiting inside you."

The truth in Hans' words was beginning to hit my heart. My guts were churning, senses on alert to the max. The trapdoor was rattling.

Hans rocked me gently in his arms. "Let yourself run with it. Allow your intuition to guide you, not your mind."

I took a breath and let myself sink into the sensations, the spinning of the bathroom disappearing. I listened to the trapdoor rattling in the distance, but this time I didn't run away from the sound.

I was on a woodland path, in the cool breeze of day, not drowning underwater, desperate to swim to the surface. The trapdoor was ahead of me, with its dark lid of wood sunk into the earth.

Red light started to glow around the edges, then came the THUMP, THUMP, THUMP like a pounding drum echoing through the woodland.

My skin prickled with fear, but it didn't stop me.

The THUMP, THUMP, THUMP got louder the closer I stepped.

What was under there? Monsters? Demons? Ghouls?

The undead? Zombies about to claw their way out...

The terror kept rising, but it didn't matter. I forced my steps steadily, in time with the thumps. My feet kept on moving in tiny little steps, and I knew I was sinking deeper inside my subconscious. I looked behind and the path was growing misty, taking me further and further away from the places I knew. The thought of turning around and running back to safety was so strong I could barely take it. But still I inched forward.

THUMP, THUMP, THUMP.

I wished I had a weapon for when the demons burst out. Even a pathetic little tree branch to put up a tiny bit of a fight. The glow of red around the edge of the wooden lid grew brighter, the thumps getting louder. The trapdoor rattling.

What the hell was in there? What was trying to get out?

It didn't make any difference what was waiting under there, I had to keep walking and face it. For once, finally, I had to face it. I was going to do it, whatever the cost.

THUMP.

I moved closer.

THUMP, THUMP.

The beats were in line with my heart.

Then I heard something else underneath the thumps. Something I'd never heard before...

Screams.

Screams coming out from underneath the wooden slats, and they were frantic. The thumps were the fists of something – *someone* – desperate to escape.

I froze, glanced behind, the path had gone, nothing but a wall of mist.

Another high-pitched scream and the trapdoor rattled.

THUMP. THUMP.

I'd never felt so terrified. Once I opened that door and whatever was in there ran free, I knew there was no way I'd ever get it closed again. It would be open for all time.

THUMP. THUMP. THUMP.

I arrived at the trapdoor and crouched down, reached out for the round iron handle and I wasn't sure I could do it. I wanted to bolt and run.

But that's what I'd been doing my whole life, wasn't it? Bolting and running instead of facing up to whatever was going on underneath.

I was going to open the trapdoor and face whatever was inside.

Do or die!

I turned the handle and it clanked. The light around the edges was no longer red, it was white. The screams were from a solitary voice in need of saving, rather than a chorus of demons baying for blood.

"HELP ME! PLEASE! HELP ME!"

"I'm coming!" I yelled. "Don't worry! I'll get you out!"

I struggled because it was so damn heavy. I had to get to my feet and brace myself hard, wrenching up that door with everything I had.

I gritted my teeth and strained, every muscle taut in my body until I managed to pull it up and push it back where it landed on the grass with a thud.

And there she was. A little girl.

She tugged herself up from the deep, wearing a white nightdress, with my teddy cat, Goblin, clutched under her arm, crying so hard her tears were streaming.

She had dark hair, and blue eyes, and the shock on her face matched the shock on mine.

Of course, I should have known it. *Feeling, not thinking.* The trapped girl was *me*.

She stared up at me with huge, wide eyes and I pulled her to her feet and held her tight.

"It's ok," I whispered. "You're going to be ok now. You're free."

I could barely hear her words through her sobs.

"Why didn't you save me sooner? I was so scared!"

The answer was obvious to me. I was crying along with her as I answered her question.

"Because I was too scared myself. But I'm not now. I'm not scared anymore."

I opened my eyes and took a huge gulp of air. The creature in my arms wasn't the little girl me, it was the vampire who'd led me to the trapdoor.

His stare said it all.

"Yes," he said. "You were trapped inside and cut off from the light. Bolted in so deeply that you couldn't hear your own cries."

The room spun afresh, but I didn't try to steady myself this time, I let it swirl and swirl, and I trusted Hans to keep me steady. Keep me safe. Keep me warm.

The sobs ate me up, just like the little girl crying with Goblin under her arm. I saw Mum wrenching him away from me in my nightdress, as I screamed and cried and begged her to let me keep him.

NO WITCHES, KATHERINE! NEVER ANY WITCHES!

"I can't believe they did this to me," I sobbed to Hans. "They did this to me, didn't they? Mum and Grandma. Why?"

He held me tighter and his silence said it all. He didn't need to speak the words, I was already beginning to know them.

Feeling not thinking.

I saw Mum and Grandma in church, praying. I saw them scowling and whispering, trapped in the world on the surface, just as I was trapped in the world underneath. Because they didn't want to face it either, did they? They didn't want to open their own trapdoors…

"That's it," Hans said. "Keep on feeling."

The years rewound themself in flickers, my own deep past, where they would hold my hand and lead me into church for prayers every weekend, before I even knew what prayers meant.

Please, our Saviour. Save Katherine from the path of darkness. Hold her in your arms and keep her from sin.

Please, Lord Above, take our child into your embrace, and forgive her the chains of our past.

Our past.

The chains of OUR past.

What past did they mean?

Now was the time to use my skills… I had to trust them. Trust myself…

The flickers of the past kept on coming.

Witches being burnt on stakes and drowned in lakes. A chain of women hiding who they were throughout my whole family line. The fear. The torment. The shame.

Mum and Grandma ignoring the screams from their own trapdoors.

I was the one who was freeing myself from the shackles.

I was the woman who would connect us back to our roots.

The little girl stepped back inside me, and my soul came home. My tears stopped, and the room stilled, and I pulled free from Hans' arms, because I didn't need his strength anymore. I had more than enough of my own.

His smile was magnificent as I stood before him. He nodded, sharing the secrets of my mind.

"Welcome home, little one," he said. "See the world through your brand new eyes."

The joy was incredible as I looked around me. There were sparkles of life and energy glistening through everything I could see. My senses were heightened, but they weren't intimidating. I held up a hand and felt the energy coursing through my fingers, free to burst out in whichever direction I chose.

Yes.

I was a psychic and a ghost whisperer, but most importantly of all. I was a witch.

"What do you want to do now?" Hans asked me. "Would you like to go back home? Take some time out?"

But I shook my head, touched my hands to his handsome face and kissed him. Kissed him deeply and tugged on his lip before I looked him in his gorgeous eyes.

"No, thank you," I told him. "I want to go to the blood house. Just like we planned."

20

I waved goodbye to Margaret and George. She looked so happy for me as I walked through Regency with my vampire lover, and I'm sure I looked very happy for her in return. It was wonderful to see them reunited. A couple still in love after a lifetime, despite what George might have been up to in this world.

"Will I get to speak to her again?" I asked Hans as we reached the exit.

"Quite possibly. It depends when they take the road into the light. Some couples prefer to live out the ghost of their past for as long as they possibly can. Margaret will be well aware of their options. She's been waiting for George a long time."

"Margaret seems a really nice woman, it would be great to get to know her."

Hans looked at me as he took my hand. "She'd make a great start to your circle of ghostly acquaintances."

I saw our taxi waiting on the road outside the club and squeezed his fingers.

"Hopefully I'll be better friends with ghosts than I've been with people. The bar isn't all that high."

He opened the taxi door for me.

"Orcop is a small village. Your options were limited there."

"They probably always will be in Orcop. I'm sure glad I moved to London."

"Perhaps you felt compelled to move here," he said as he slid into the seat beside me.

"Yeah, you could say that," I said, and then it clicked. Hans had always been in the shadows, beckoning me. London sure was a beguiling place, even more so when a vampire wants you there.

The driver turned to face us before I could ask Hans to elaborate.

"Where are you heading?"

"Ashwell," Hans told him. "Hertfordshire. The Manor of St Louis."

All thoughts of Margaret and George were pushed aside at the mention of our destination. I'd heard of Ashwell before. I'd seen it in online searches when I was dreaming up my perfect future. It was one of the posh quaint villages outside London. It gave me a buzz just thinking about it. A posh little village hiding a blood house. I couldn't wait to get there.

"Sounds exciting," I said.

"Excitement is guaranteed," Hans assured me.

The world outside the cab windows was alive with a new sense of life for me as we pulled away. I was fascinated by every streetlamp, and every single figure we passed on the roadside, transfixed by the dance of energy I'd never seen before. It was crazy, wild. Otherworldly in the most fantastical of ways.

"It will take some adjusting to," Hans said. "Don't worry. You will get used to it."

I didn't need his assurances. I was filled with a sense of confidence – stemming from a side of myself I'd never been able to know.

"Did you know I was blocked from myself?" I asked Hans. "Right from a little girl, I mean."

"I knew your mother and grandmother were trying to block you from yourself, yes."

"Did you know they were succeeding?"

"I knew they wouldn't succeed for ever, and that's all that mattered."

I felt a horrible wave of sickness at the thought of Mum and Grandma. I didn't want them to die in chains, running into death with their own souls still hidden away under trapdoors, just like mine had been.

"Very noble of you, I'm sure, But you can't fight their battles for them," Hans whispered. "Their road to their soul is their own road to walk. You can help them, but you can't force their paths."

"They tried to force mine."

"Yes," he said. "But they didn't succeed, did they? Look at who you are tonight. Look at who you are becoming."

I wished I could see exactly who I was tonight. I'd love to see myself in a full-length mirror and check out the full scale of my transformation. There must have been as many waves of energy in my own aura as there were in other people's. Maybe even more so.

"Definitely more so," Hans said. "Your soul has been unleashed, sweetheart."

I traced my fingers up his arm, adoring the fresh burst of static as I sensed his aura merging with mine. I had no idea what situation we'd be walking into with the blood house, but no matter what, I knew my heart would be ready for it and I belonged there. I'd follow Hans into Hell itself to see his true living culture.

"It's not Hell." He squeezed my knee. "It will most definitely be an experience, though. Expect the unexpected."

I relaxed into his warmth. "I'm getting used to expecting the unexpected, don't worry about that."

I absorbed the new me in the bursts, sparks and jangles of life around me, comfortable in the silence between us as we left London city and set off towards Hertfordshire. I could have asked more questions about the Manor of St Louis and what lay ahead there, but I didn't want to. I wanted to feel the whole, true shock of it in my veins.

The radio was loud enough that the driver wouldn't hear Hans' whisper.

"How do you feel about taking other people's fangs in your flesh? Is that what you want? Do you want to sample blood play with the other vampires we'll be joining?"

His eyes were bright in the dark of the cab. I stared right into them as I answered.

"Not yet."

"Not yet?"

"No, not yet, but maybe one day."

He smirked. "Sooner rather than later, I imagine."

"I guess we'll have to wait and see."

"Not for all that much longer, little one. Here comes Ashwell."

We'd reached the quaint little village I'd seen in pictures. The streets were filled with fourteenth century houses with beautiful timbered walls. Gorgeous.

"Wait until you see the Manor," Hans said, and the driver swung up to the left.

It didn't take long before a huge building appeared on the top of a hill, at the end of a large sweeping driveway. It was surrounded by fields, in the middle of nowhere. A halo of a glow burning loud on the skyline.

It definitely didn't look like a brothel when the driver reached the main courtyard and dropped us outside. It was a huge stone mansion, with ivy sweeping the walls.

Hans took my hand in his to help me from my seat. He didn't need to knock at the huge wooden entrance to the manor as the cab pulled away, as a butler was already there to bid us entry.

"This is Katherine," Hans said. "She'll be new to the establishment, firmly accompanied by me."

"Of course, Mr Weyer," the butler replied. "Please, do inform me if you need any assistance. Welcome to St Louis, Katherine. Very pleased to meet you."

"And you," I said, then spotted the clotted wounds on his neck above his shirt collar.

So, the butler was a blood player too.

"Only occasionally," Hans said as we walked away. "Devon is one of the least addicted players here, which is a good job, considering he's the one who manages entry."

"He's still an addict, though?"

I looked up at the huge sweep of a hallway around us, with open staircases ascending on both sides. There were huge, sparkling chandeliers and a plush, deep-red rug over the mosaic floor tiles. It felt like we'd stepped back in time.

Hans answered my question about the butler.

"I've never known anyone not become a player once they've received a decent bite. People are generally addicted as soon as they feel the force of the fangs. Devon was one of them."

I remembered the intense feeling of pleasure from my own experience. It gave me a fresh round of tingles, right where they fluttered the most. I knew my thighs were already clammy under my dress.

Hans read my body as well as my mind.

"I can't wait to feel how desperate your pussy is," he said and one fang glinted when he smirked. My pussy clenched for him. Talk about needy. "But first, let's get started on the formalities. Let me introduce you to some of my acquaintances. I'm sure you'll be very pleased to meet them."

Best be quick or I'll be coming on the spot in front of them, I thought.

Very funny, his thought came back.

He led me into a huge drawing room off to the side of the hallway. The far walls were lined with bookshelves filled with leather bound books, and clusters of antique chairs graced the room. I'd pictured a scene from a movie where a club full of vampires were dancing around together covered in blood, but instead there were just a few small groups of people.

They turned to face us and Hans greeted them with a raised hand before leading me over to the nearest group.

It took me aback when he introduced me to the first of the figures. A beautiful guy with long dark hair, dressed in a tux with a ruffled white shirt. He shook Hans' hand firmly, and their smiles for each other were warm and genuine.

"Katherine, this is Edwin," Hans told me. "Edwin, this is Katherine."

Edwin, the aristocrat who'd made Hans a vampire?

I don't know why I was so surprised that he looked like a man in his late twenties, tops. I'd expected him to be a grand old Lord in his seventies or something.

Again. *Expect the unexpected.*

Edwin took my hand and kissed my knuckles and I swear my whole body fluttered and my heels lifted from the floor. I couldn't stop the sigh that left my open mouth when he let go.

The man was… powerful. Hot and powerful. I could imagine Hans kissing him. Fucking him.

"Lovely to meet you, Katherine," Edwin said, "and yes. I've known Hans for a long, long time. I'm very honoured to have enabled his transition."

Could he read my mind, too? Could I read his, if I tried?

"I'm forever in your debt," Hans said, then introduced me to a woman to the side of Edwin.

She was a stunning creature in a dazzling white dress, who looked to be in her fifties, with her hair up in a bun highlighted by a sapphire hair clip.

"Lady Jane," Hans said. "Lovely to see you."

"Same to you, Hans. Pleased to meet you, Katherine."

"Pleased to meet you," I replied, but didn't get the chance to say more before Hans gestured to another aristocratic man off to the right.

"This is Joseph."

Joseph looked younger and had gorgeous shoulder-length red hair. I would have placed him as in his early twenties.

"I wish." Joseph laughed and gave me a flash of perfect white teeth as he kissed my hand. "I'm four hundred and seventy three years old."

"You don't quite act like it, though." Hans smirked and Joseph raised his hands.

"I like to play young."

With that I heard some raucous laughter from another cluster of chairs in the room.

"Just not as young as those rascals," Joseph added with a chuckle.

I looked across at the group responsible for the laughter, and it looked as though the guys there were even younger than him. They weren't in tuxedos, just tight black jeans and shirts, several of them with leather jackets over the top.

"We call them the blood boys," Hans told me. "They're a little more rowdy than the most of us. Characters, all of them."

I felt quite drawn to their energy. I could smell the leather of their jackets from here. One of them flashed me a grin, and nudged one of his friends to look in my direction. Both of them were blond.

"The twins," Hans said. "And those two guys behind them are kids they knew from school. They were in a rock band when they were younger. Groupies were easy prey."

The four of them were like magnets to me. I had to force my gaze away from them and give my attention back to the vampires closer.

"Have you had any experience of blood play?" Edwin asked me, and I knew my cheeks were burning.

"Only with Hans."

"She's a very new player," Hans told him, and a look passed between them.

Lady Jane seemed to catch sight of it.

"I'm guessing she's going to be a spectator, then?"

Hans tipped his head. His smile was divine.

"We'll see. Certainly initially."

"That's a shame," she said, and switched her gaze to me. Her eyes were just as bright as Hans' were. "I'd love to sink my teeth right into you, you pretty little thing."

She put a hand on Hans' arm.

"Have you introduced her to the dirty bite, yet?"

"Not quite," he said, and she tutted.

"Shame on you. If you don't do it tonight, please give me the honour."

"Or me." Edwin grinned. "Get in there, Hans, before the blood boys beat you to it. You know they'll be slinking in there before any of us."

With so many vampire eyes fixed on me, I felt like a true victim, but it was a good thing. I could have torn my dress from my body and offered them my flesh right there and then. That's what I wanted. What I *needed*.

I needed bites and heady pain. And the stretch of Hans' veiny cock…

"Steady," Hans whispered. "You're getting pain drunk before we've even started. At least let us get you to a room upstairs before we begin the games."

With that, he took my arm firmly and gave an *excuse us* to his friends. He led me away from the drawing room and directed me straight to the nearest staircase. My legs were wobbly as I walked, my breaths quickening.

I knew we were walking into the darkness.

The energy was very different upstairs, much more reminiscent of a gothic horror movie – despite Hans saying it wouldn't be.

He scoffed a playful scoff. "This isn't a psycho horror, Katherine. It's a blood den. There aren't people with axes waiting up here, only fangs, and flesh that is desperate for them."

The doors were tall along the landing, and most were closed. I heard hot, heated screams sounding out from one of them.

"That's Veronica," Hans said. "You can recognise her orgasmic cries from a mile away. I imagine she's with Francois and Xan."

One of the doors was open and the sight inside had me stopping in my tracks, Hans' arm still in mine. There was a woman spread naked on a bed, bathed in bright light. She had a vampire on each breast, arching her back and begging for more as they sucked at her. One of the vampires was an old looking gentleman, and the other was a woman in a ballgown. My heart was racing. My thighs were definitely wet. I wanted to be that woman.

"Vivian and Marlon," Hans whispered. "They are a couple. They always bite together."

I couldn't help but stare at the scene in front of me, watching the couple work the girl's pussy as they sucked. Her blood trickling down the pale flesh of her tits.

Hans was smirking as I broke my fascination long enough to glance up at him.

"Strip yourself bare and go join them if you'd like to," he said. "I'm sure they would very much enjoy your company. Be warned, though, they like to stretch their victims wide. You're still getting used to taking vampire cock on its own."

I backed away at that.

"Too soon," I said. "I'm still getting used to your bites and cock. I'm not sure I want anyone else's right now."

He led me further along the landing.

"You might be a dirtier little blood player than you're giving yourself credit for. I can smell how excited you are, as will everyone else in this building. They'll all be hoping for a taste of you."

I burned up as though I'd been caught out committing a crime, but Hans was still smirking.

"There is nothing to feel guilty about. As I said, blood play is addictive, and vampiric lust is ripe in the air. What we have between us is a lot deeper than games in a blood house. Feel free to act as you desire."

"Won't that bother you?" I asked him.

"Maybe I'm not quite the gentleman you think I am. I most definitely believe there is a lot more to a soul connection than blood play bites, but I come to blood houses for a reason. I'm not intimidated by you enjoying games of the flesh with other people's fangs."

I could see the lust in his eyes. I could feel the burn of his excitement. It took me to the filthy side of him in his bedroom, heightened by tenfold in this place.

Feeling not thinking.

And this time feeling felt an awful lot easier to access. I let my thoughts run free.

"You're one of the primary players here, aren't you?" I said to Hans, trusting my intuition.

His smile was glorious as he pinned me to the wall and pressed his mouth right up to my ear.

"Oh, little one, you have no idea. I'm one of the primary blood players in all the world."

21

My senses were heightened tenfold when Hans pressed his lips against mine. His body was fierce as he pinned me there, his hands running up my thighs.

I could hear the heated cries of the woman called Veronica so loudly it was like she was standing beside us, and I could feel the flood of pure energy from the woman taking vampires' teeth in her tits next door. It gave me tingles in mine.

I sank further into the pleasure of the people around me, parting my legs as Hans swept his hand underneath my skirt. I moaned when his fingers traced my pussy lips through my panties.

"You're considerably wetter than I thought you'd be," he told me. "That's a very impressive thing."

One thought above all others was making me even wetter...

"You said you're one of the primary blood players in the world," I said. "Tell me more, please. I want to know everything."

"Talking would be cheating you out of pleasure," he replied. "How about I give you a taster of my experiences instead?"

I didn't know what he meant until he took his hand away from my pussy and pressed his fingers to my temples on either side.

"Don't fight the sensations," he said. "Let the memories sink in as yours."

My God, how the flash of scenes from his past took hold of me...

Hans sinking his teeth into a sea of necks with people crying out for him, his cock ploughing into them like they were ragdolls of flesh. Men, women, it didn't matter. He was hungry for them all.

Hans and Edwin double fucking a hot young woman as she struggled to take them. I saw the trails of blood right the way down her body, from the pattern of bites they'd marked into her skin.

A group of vampires all using one guy at once, working his cock in their hands as they drank from him. Hans owning the guy's ass as he lapped blood from his neck, fucking him so hard that the guy was grunting in pain.

Holy hell, I struggled to believe it.

This was the vampire I was besotted with, committed to, his to use however he wanted.

More scenes of horny blood play flooded through my mind as he kept his fingers pressed tight to my temples. I saw so many people he'd bitten, and fucked, and stretched to their limits. Sometimes the memories were of him alone, sometimes him with other vampires, sometimes him spectating other people's filthy games like he was watching a sport.

"I think it's time you saw some games through your own eyes now," Hans said as he pulled his fingers away.

I did nothing but nod, mute, taking guidance as he led me further along the landing. My pussy was throbbing so bad that every step had me panting. I didn't know how much longer I could stand it.

"Patience, remember?" Hans said.

"Screw patience," I said and tried to calm myself.

I focused on his eyes and not on the needs inside me, trying my best to do what he said.

He stopped at the next doorway and pulled down the handle. He gestured me ahead of him, and I almost leapt back into him at the shock of the scene inside.

Three huge vampire guys were fucking one desperate woman at once. The pretty blonde was curvy and gorgeous, with big tits that bounced every time she moved. She was sandwiched between two of the vampires as they ploughed her with their cocks, and she was choking around the third vampire's dick as he fucked her throat, and fuck, she was covered in smears of blood from her neck right down to her toes.

"That's Sarah," Hans told me. "She'll take vampire cock and teeth all night long. We have to be careful with her. She gets so caught up in the fervour that she'd let us bleed her to death just to feel more fangs."

I could hardly breathe as I stared at the scene. The two cocks stretching Sarah's ass and pussy were as swollen red as I'd seen Hans' cock. I had no idea how the fuck she could take them.

"Practice," Hans answered. "Practice and craving the thrill enough to take whatever's being given."

The vampire fucking Sarah's pussy looked over at me and licked his blood-soaked lips. His eyes were bright blue, and his dark hair was cropped short. He must have been well over six feet tall, and he was huge with it – a massive wall of muscle as he slammed her deep.

"These gentlemen are Petre, Giles and Marcus," Hans whispered in my ear. "The one you're looking at is Petre, and yes, he's six foot seven. Quite a monster."

I whispered back at Hans, still staring at Petre.

"Have you fucked someone along with him? Like he's doing with those two other guys?"

"Yes," Hans answered me. "Many, many times."

I was sinking deeper into the blood house now, and it was all becoming clear. The sensations were like huge sea waves engulfing me. My pussy was so desperate I could have cried for the release.

Luckily, Hans wasn't going to make me wait any longer. I heard the words in my head before he spoke them aloud.

"Take your dress off," he told me. "I'll fuck you hard and rough while you watch Sarah take it."

My arms were trembling nervous when I raised them over my head, but it didn't stop me doing it. The four pairs of eyes from the bed made my skin burn as Hans tugged my dress up and off me. I still had bite marks showing, and I was glad I did. It made me feel like a marked victim amongst friends, even though we'd never shared a word. I slipped my panties down without being told, kicking them aside while still standing in my heels, then looked at Hans for my next instruction.

"On all fours," he said, and I dropped down for him, my hands and knees nicely cushioned on the plush red carpet underneath.

I heard him loosen his belt from behind.

"Keep watching," he told me. "Imagine that's you up there on the bed."

All three vampires smirked at his words, but Sarah was too desperate by now to acknowledge me. She was moaning like an utter slut, letting them use her like a toy.

I was transfixed as Hans joined them on the bed. He took hold of Sarah's throat, making her retch as the vampire named Giles pulled away.

"Make me nice and slick for my little one," my vampire lover told her.

He freed his massive cock from his suit trousers, but he didn't give it to Sarah's mouth. Instead, he held out his hand. She coughed up some thick blood and spat into his palm, and he rubbed it up and down the length of his cock as he looked at me.

Part of me wanted to retch. But a bigger part of me wanted to swallow his bloodied cock whole.

"Thank you," he said, and left the bed.

The fucking scene resumed. Sarah took Giles' cock back into her throat, all of them still pounding together in a deep, brutal rhythm. It was darkly comforting, making both perfect sense to me and no sense at all.

Hans stepped up with his cock standing tall, glistening with Sarah's spit and blood and throbbing with deep blue veins.

"Tell me how much you want me inside you," he said, and fuck, how I wanted to touch myself. The tingle in my clit was too strong to ignore.

"Please," I whispered. "I want you inside me, Hans."

He gripped his cock, the glistening head so close it made my mouth water.

"Don't hold back," he said. "Show the guys what a beautiful little blood player you want to be. Give me the sweet, dirty talk that drives me wild."

All three of the vampires were staring at me, even though they were still fucking Sarah so hard she was squealing.

Time for my instincts to take over. I wanted to show them what a beautiful little blood player I could be.

Feeling not thinking.

I looked up at Hans like he was my saviour.

"Please, Hans, fuck me as hard as you can. Tear me open, I don't care, just fuck me."

He worked his cock in his hand.

"That's good. Really good. And what else do you want?"

"Your teeth," I said. "Please, Hans, bite me. Make me bleed!"

"Tell me more. Tell me the truth from the depths."

Feeling…

My clit was crying. My voice was a moan.

"Please, Hans, I want them to see me. I want to be seen taking your cock and your teeth. I want people to see how good I am."

"You want to be a good girl, don't you?"

I nodded. "I want to be the very best good girl I can be."

"I hope you hold true to your word," he said, and stepped around me, trailing his fingertips down my spine. His touch made me shudder. Made my nipples prickle.

I heard the soft thump on the plush carpet as he dropped down on the floor behind me and I spread my legs for him.

I expected him to fuck me like a slut on all fours, but no. He grabbed my hips and hitched me back on top of him, held me tight against his strong body, my ass resting on his thighs, his cock looming between my legs. He spread my thighs wide enough that the people on the bed could see my needy splayed pussy. I must have been so wet they could smell me.

"Don't worry about that." Hans breathed against my ear. "They can taste you, too."

He grazed his teeth against my neck and I braced myself with a *yesss*, but it only made him smirk against my skin.

"You are an impatient little minx tonight. Good job we got some of Sarah's blood and spit to help you take me, isn't it?"

My God, how my vampire lover slammed me down onto him and speared me in one. Sarah's blood and spit made barely any difference. It felt like a rod of molten steel was stretching me open, setting my pussy on fire.

"It's all right," Hans said, bringing his hands to my tits and squeezing them hard. "You can cry out however loudly you need to. Don't be shy of the pain."

I whimpered, trying to keep it to myself, but Hans didn't let me. He squeezed my tits and thrust so hard and fast, and I bounced up and down on his rock hard cock so fiercely that it was more than I could contain.

"It hurts…" I cried out. "It really, really hurts."

"Yes, I know," Hans growled. "Your voice is so fucking beautiful when you're hurting. I think it's time I made you take a whole lot more."

He splayed my legs wider and fucked me harder, and I knew I must be trailing my own blood from my pussy as well as Sarah's. Hans was stretching me too fucking hard to take him without his cock tearing me up inside. He played with my clit as he kept on fucking me.

"Keep your eyes on the filth on the bed," he told me, and I watched the other players, just as they were watching us.

Even Sarah was staring over now that I was bouncing on Hans' cock like a horny slut. It felt like we were sisters of solidarity, so I let myself free and ate up the pain like the horny girl she was, begging Hans for more and slamming down to meet his thrusts. I cried out for everything I could get, even though my pussy was bleeding raw, and Hans worked my clit like a piano master, playing those cursed, faint high notes.

"Please," I groaned. "Please… I need to come now."

Hans stopped thrusting and grabbed me tight, locked me in his arms with his cock buried deep.

"No, you don't," he whispered in my ear. "What you *need* is my fucking teeth in your throat."

He didn't hold back when he sank his fangs into my neck. Pain spiked through my head, my vision split in two. It felt... amazing. Incredible as Hans continued fucking me and sucking me with a deep feral hunger as I kept my eyes on Sarah. The room turned hazy with need as the endorphins struck and consumed me. Hans' painful thrusts were a perfect agony as he drank my blood.

I saw another flash of solidarity in Sarah's eyes and smiled back at her as Hans took his fill.

The rhythms between us all grew more frantic – Hans' cock slamming inside me in sync with the three thick cocks slamming inside her. The vampires kept nipping at her as Hans kept sucking me, and the energy tensed, and tensed, and tensed, until finally it exploded. Six desperate bodies crested at once, and it was absolutely fucking beautifully insane.

"Fuck," I said as Hans pulled his teeth free from my neck.

My pussy was in agony, but I was grinning. *Pain drunk*, as Hans would call it, to a crazy high degree. The four on the bed handled the post orgasm with a lot more familiarity than I did. My breaths were still running ragged as they made small talk together, chatting in good humour about the horny, hot time they'd just had.

I was still perched loosely on Hans' lap when Sarah got up from the mattress and stepped over to me. She offered me a hand so she could pull me to my feet, and I took hold of it.

"How about I show you to the bathroom?" she asked me. "I'll introduce you to getting a little cleaned up."

She wrapped an arm around my shoulder like we were besties in high school, as Hans stared up at me with a smirk.

"Thanks," I said, and Hans was still smirking as she led me away.

She showed me into the bathroom a few doors down the landing and stood next to me at the basin, looking me up and down in the mirror. She really was a stunning opposite of me. Her curves were incredible next to the skinny slopes of mine, and we complemented each other just brilliantly.

"So, yes, I'm Sarah," she told me. "It's really nice to meet you."

"I'm Katherine. It's nice to meet you too," I replied, which seemed a ridiculous conversation considering what just happened.

She laughed out loud at that.

"Oh, don't worry, I know who you are, *sweet Katherine*," she said. "I've been hearing about you for years."

She looked at me like I was a celebrity she'd been expecting, but I stared back at her with nothing but confusion on my face.

"You've heard of me?"

She giggled, like I was stating the obvious.

"You'd sure hope so, wouldn't you? You are the long fated mate of Hans Weyer, after all."

22

I thought the trapdoor had revealed all its secrets, but I was wrong. The heavy wooden door was open wide, but the depths were still in shadow, even though I'd freed the crying child.

Sarah's voice was upbeat as she carried on talking.

"I've been praying for years that I'll be a fated mate myself one day, but I doubt it. I'm just a player holding on to a fantasy of true, vampire love."

I was looking at her, dumbstruck. The trapdoor inside me was rumbling.

"Has Hans not told you yet?" Sarah said, reading my expression. "Shit, sorry! I might have just ruined a big revelation."

Our conversation was another humbling experience. For a self-proclaimed vampire addict, I knew absolutely sweet fuck all.

"What are fated mates?" I asked her. "I guess it must mean an intense connection."

"Add an intense connection to a serious slice of destiny and souls entwining, and I think you'd be pretty close. I don't know anyone who's been a fated mate of one of the vampires around here, not before you showed up tonight." She checked out one of her shoulder wounds in the mirror, then met my eyes in the reflection. "You're so lucky to be Hans' long-term love. Like everyone else here, I've heard whispers about Mary, but he's as certain as it gets that you'll be the one to right the wrongs."

Wrongs?

The trapdoor kept on rumbling.

Mary. She sounded familiar to me in the strangest of ways. Like a ghost of a whisper.

Like a ghost...

The idea of Hans being in love with anyone else made my stomach turn. I didn't want to imagine him looking at anyone else the way he looked at me.

"Who is Mary?" I asked. "An ex of his?"

She looked horrified.

"You don't know who Mary is? Fuck! I've got to stop putting my foot in it. It's up to Hans to tell you this stuff, not me."

"No, please tell me."

She looked wary of sticking her foot further in the mud.

"There's not all that much I can say. I think Mary is some kind of ex of his. From a serious amount of time ago from what I can gather. People don't really share vampire secrets. All I know is that she was a woman he was very, very in love with. Someone who left him heartbroken for hundreds of years and took him off the path of everything he knew in his old life. The older vampires know all about her, and I've heard her name plenty of times. She must have been really special."

Mary.

Some distant part of me felt like I should know her.

"Are you ok?" Sarah asked. "You look a bit sick. Did you lose too much blood back there? It happens when you're a newbie. I can get you some help, if you like."

She began to step away, but I didn't want her to. It wasn't blood loss that was making me sickly, it was the thought of Hans being in love with a woman called Mary. There was something deep, dark and scary about it, but also deep, dark and beautiful.

Feeling, not thinking.

Mary was a woman I should know.

A part of my soul wanted to dig all the way into it, but the rest of me really didn't. It wasn't the time. Not in the aftermath of a blood house session with a brand new friend beside me.

I was still pain drunk and floating high enough to smile at Sarah and assure her I'd be fine.

"It was crazy back there," I said. "I've barely ever seen any movies about vampire sex, let alone watch it in its full glory. It was amazing. You were taking it so, so well."

"Thanks. You, too."

She brushed some of the drying blood from the wounds on my neck. Her touch helped me shunt the eerie *Mary* and *fated mates* thoughts away.

"He really got you good there, didn't he?" she said. "Hans' teeth sure are brutal."

It felt strangely good to watch her checking me out, as though it was totally normal for us to be here together, comparing vampire bite marks naked in a bathroom.

I looked at her wounds in return, pointing to a particularly savage looking bite on her hip. It was still dripping blood down her leg.

"Who did this one?"

"Petre."

It was obvious how much she liked him. I saw her burning up in front of me.

"He's huge," I said, pointing out the obvious. "I know the vampire guys are mainly huge, but he is *huge* huge."

"Yeah, he's a giant, but apparently there's a an even bigger guy. Down on the coast of Brazil."

The full scope of the global vampire scene still felt alien to me.

"Have you ever been to any of the other blood houses?"

"I've been to one in Germany, but none of the others. Who knows? Maybe I'll get a fated mate of my own one day and they can whisk me away to show me the world."

She turned me towards her, checking out the healing bite marks on my tits.

"They're really nice. Has Hans shown you the dirty bite yet?"

I remembered Lady Jane mentioning that downstairs.

"I don't think so. What is it?"

She spread her legs with no self-consciousness whatsoever, pointing out two places on her pussy, on either side of her clit. Yep. I got it. I gave her a nod.

"Ah, yeah. I remember Hans telling me about it, but no, he hasn't bitten me there yet."

She looked so pleased for me.

"You've got so much great stuff to look forward to. Girls in here go crazy for the dirty bite, but the vampires play the long game. They hold it back for special occasions, leaving us hanging like puppets on a string. It's so addictive, it's ridiculous. It feels like your clit is wound up to another dimension, and when that orgasm starts to blow, it's a mad combination. Pain and pleasure, at the same time beyond words." The expression on her face said so much, she was glowing.

She reached out and stroked the bite marks around my nipple. It felt so natural just to let her.

"I'm not kidding," she went on, "You've had some great tit bites from the looks, but times that by about a hundred. Imagine a vamp on each tit and a third between your legs, giving you the dirty bite. When you come, you really do come."

I wondered if I'd be experiencing anything like that myself one day.

"We should get cleaned up." She picked up a towel, dampened it under the tap, then started dabbing at her tits.

My tits were tingling and so was my sore pussy. A vamp on each tit and a dirty bite. I wanted that.

"How long did it take you to handle three vampires fucking you at once?" I asked her.

"About six months. That was over five years ago now though. It's like a rite of initiation, giving your ass and your pussy at the same time. Would you want that? To take two vampire cocks at once?"

I lifted a leg to show her the smears of blood between my thighs.

"I'm still struggling to take one of them. I feel like I've been torn to pieces."

Her grin was filled with life.

"My blood and spit lube didn't help all that much, then? Hardly surprising, since Hans is as rough as they come. Literally."

There were so many questions I wanted to ask her. How she learnt about vampires, and how she ended up here. What games she'd played, and which were her favourites. I'd have loved to quiz her on everything about this place, and the vampires who came here. The blood boys, and Edwin, and Lady Jane. And Hans, of course. I wanted to know everything she knew about my *fated mate*.

"Let's get you cleaned up," she said.

She showed me the best technique for clearing away blood without disturbing the wounds. A simple dabbing motion mixed with gentle sweeps. She did my neck for me as she talked me through it.

"Here," she said when she was done, and gave me the towel. "Have a go on mine."

I started with the bite on her shoulder, fascinated by the way her teeth marks looked as I washed them clean. I swept the wet towel down to the bites on her tits, loving the way they moved as I dabbed at them and how her nipples went hard before my eyes.

She angled herself so I could clean up the bites on her hips, then hitched her leg up for me, happy for me to clean her pussy. I was fixated as she spread herself wide.

She was still bleeding from the invasion of two huge vampire cocks, blood dribbling from both her pussy and her ass in dainty red trickles down her thighs.

I ran the towel so gently between her legs, my eyes fixed on what I was doing. I'd never seen another girl's pussy like this. I loved the way she moved as the cloth stroked against her.

"Damn," she whispered. "I'm already so horny again. Maybe Edwin will take me next, if I ask him nicely."

Part of me hoped I could watch them, like I'd watched her take the others.

"Your turn," she said, and gestured me to spread myself in return.

She took the towel back and cleaned me up as I'd cleaned her. I felt a shudder of pleasure at the brush of her touch. It was such a shame I didn't have more blood for her to clean from me, I'd have loved it to go on for hours.

With Hans watching.

"All done," she said, and dropped the towel in the washing bin. "At least for now."

She took my arm in hers and led me out of the bathroom. I almost jumped in shock when I saw Hans leant back against the wall opposite, staring at us.

Had he been hearing my thoughts, and could he hear them now?

About my fantasies of Sarah and Edwin, and how I'd liked her touch.

And about Mary. Fated mates, and the woman called Mary.

I didn't want him to hear my thoughts on that. Not here and not yet, with Sarah still on my arm.

"How did it go with the clean up?" he asked us both, but his eyes dug into mine.

I knew he was about to read my mind, but I didn't want it. I had to try for some new skills, and let my instincts guide me.

Feeling, not thinking.

I pictured those walls of mist in the woodlands by the trapdoor, fogging up the air all around me. Blocking out the world outside.

Hans must have known what I was doing. He lowered his eyebrows.

Sarah sensed that something was going down between us. She excused herself, waving goodbye as she trotted off down the landing.

"You're learning quickly, little one," Hans whispered when she was out of sight.

I felt the power in my imagination, the walls of mist growing thicker.

"The question is," Hans stepped up close enough to sweep my hair from the bites on my neck. "What thoughts are you so desperate to hide?"

He kissed my wounds. Gently.

"Has Sarah been sharing any secrets?" he whispered. "People can get very loose tongued when they're pain drunk. Believe me, I've seen it plenty of times."

"She showed me how to clean up my wounds," I shared. "And she let me clean up hers."

"You cleaned her pussy for her? And how about that? Did you like it?"

I moaned as he ran his tongue across my bite.

"Yes, I liked it."

"I thought you would."

He slammed me back against the wall. His kiss was gentle but fierce.

"She told me some more about the dirty bite," I panted between kisses. "When are you going to do that to me? What other dirty games do you have to show me? What things will I come to know?"

"Patience," he said. "Everything will come in its own time."

Patience. Yes. Always patience.

But I didn't want patience right then.

There was something tingling in me along with his kisses, and I couldn't fight it. It wasn't all about dirty bites, or what I wanted to see of Sarah, and Edwin, or the huge beast called Petre.

The depths of the trapdoor called me, the mists wearing thin.

"What is it?" Hans asked. "What did Sarah tell you?"

I didn't know how best to express it, but the mists were fading fast.

"Tell me," Hans said. "If there are questions you want to ask, then please do ask them. I'll give you the answers, so long as you are sure you truly want to hear them."

Did I really want to hear the answers?

The depths of the trapdoor kept calling, whispers coming out of the shadows. Something I couldn't place, couldn't fight, couldn't deny any longer.

I *did* want to know the answers. I couldn't stop myself.

"What is a fated mate, Hans?" I asked him. "And who the hell is Mary?"

23

"That's quite a pair of questions," Hans said. "I'm surprised Sarah managed to do such a thorough job on the secret revelations. You weren't in the bathroom all that long."

He didn't look angry, but I felt a flash of guilt, worried I'd dropped her in the shit.

"Yes, there is a code of conduct here," he said, and it was obvious the mists around my thoughts had faded away. "Players *and* vampires are expected to keep their confidences."

"How about Mary, then? Is she one of your confidences?"

"Mary *was* one of my confidences, yes. A long time ago."

I felt like I was digging in places I shouldn't, because I had no business there.

I felt like crap when Hans stepped away from me, wishing I hadn't said anything, but he shook his head.

"Don't ever give yourself over to regrets. I lived with that mistake for over three hundred years before I learned my lesson." His eyes were so beautiful. "You asked some questions. That isn't a crime."

"I shouldn't have been so demanding. It wasn't my place to ask so soon."

"You're a girl trying to make sense of a very unusual world, curious and overwhelmed, battling with whispers in both your ears and your head. It's hardly a surprise you are searching out answers."

I was trying to keep up with his words.

"So, what are fated mates, Hans? Sarah seems to think I'm one of yours."

"The *only* one of mine, yes."

"What about Mary? Who was she? Was she a fated mate of yours too?"

He paused, and I realised my legs were trembling, scared of the answer. I saw the trapdoor shaft and peered inside, just a little. There was a flash of movement down deep.

"We need to get home," Hans said. "Conversations like these aren't for a place like this."

There was no sign of Sarah or the guys as we collected my dress and panties from the floor of the bedroom. I slipped them back on without a word, still well aware of Veronica's screams sounding out from the room opposite. I was on mute autopilot as we descended the stairs. The atmosphere was different down here now, and the drawing room was a lot busier. I'd have loved to have met some more vampires.

If only I hadn't been such an idiot for blurting out questions.

"Stop it now," Hans said. "I've already told you, your questions deserve answers, they just can't be delivered here in this place."

"Why not in this place? Why can't you just tell me? I'm a big girl, I can take it."

"Trust me," Hans said, "You'll be glad you are at home when you learn the truth."

Things went by in a blur as we prepared to make our exit. I was smiling, but it felt distant, as though I was standing back from myself. I saw Sarah standing next to Edwin, pressing against his side as he placed a hand on the small of her naked back.

I was happy for her enough that my smile was genuine.

"People love Sarah," Hans whispered when he saw it. "You'll be such good friends in here. People are going to love you, too."

"Will she find a *fated mate*?" I asked.

"That's for destiny to decide, not me."

Hans was quick and warm with the farewells, and I said my goodbyes along with him, but Edwin was by far the main focus of Hans' attention as we bid goodnight.

Lady Jane interrupted their goodbyes. "When will you be back next? Will you be joining us for Samhain?"

"No," Hans' replied. "Not this year."

"Really? How come?"

Everyone around us looked puzzled.

"We have some prior engagements," Hans told them.

"They must be important ones," Lady Jane chuckled. "You'll be sorely missed."

"Indeed, they are," my lover confirmed, and I got another fresh prickle up my spine. "Ladies, gentlemen, we'll be seeing you soon."

"Bye," I said, dumbstruck like a fool.

Devon the butler provided a car for us, and we travelled back to Hans' place in the back of a limo this time, rather than a cab from London. It would have been crazily exciting if my nerves weren't interfering with the experience. My feet were tapping, my heart was thumping wild, as though I was about to attend a court of law hearing. The trapdoor shaft was calling me louder now we were away from the bustle of the blood house.

Hans placed a hand on my thigh, so steadily. I took strength and calm from the power in his touch, because I believed in him, even if my nerves were cut to pieces.

It was into the early hours when the limo arrived back at home. My eyes were fixed on Hans once we were inside the hallway as he took off his jacket and hung it on the rack.

I wished I could scream at him, beg him to tell me who the hell Mary was, but my voice would have been weak.

I should know her.

Prickles, so many prickles.

Hans led me into the kitchen, sat me at the breakfast bar and brought me a glass of water. I took a long drink and braced myself for what was coming.

Hans took the stool by my side, waiting until I looked him in the eyes before he spoke.

"Understand that it's not just vampires who have fated mates. The phenomenon has been around since the beginning of human existence. Soulmates, true love at first sight, the love of someone's life, and happily ever afters. They all exist, even though people have grown cynical of them over time."

"Is that what fated mates are?" I asked him. "Soulmates?"

"Yes, but in the case of humans the waves of love can often come in and out over many lifetimes. In some of their lives people find it, in some they don't. Fated mates are often like passing ships in the night, so near but so far." He clicked his fingers. "One tiny movement can change the course of everything. One spilled cup of coffee delaying a meeting in a doorway can change the road for decades ahead."

"You said over many lifetimes. People live many lives, then? Reincarnation? One life after another?"

"I think of it as a cycle rather than a series, but I'm still learning. I'm by no means a master."

I tried to weigh it up.

"How about vampires? Are you excluded from the cycle? You must be, right? Since you don't die."

He shrugged. "I don't know. Our cycle is certainly a lot… longer, if we have one at all. As I said, I'm still learning. I may never find the answer."

I loved the humility in Hans. The way he seemed to know so much, but didn't associate it with ego.

"Have you heard of the butterfly effect?" he asked me.

"Where one small thing that happens changes the course of everything around it, bigger and bigger, like a ripple effect?"

"Yes. That's the case with destiny, too."

He took my hand and positioned us so his upturned palm was just a small distance from mine, and I could feel the heat, the pull, the electric charge.

"Fated mates are two magnets with perfect polarity," he told me.

"They call and crave each other, and when they merge, it is the most wholesome feeling in the world, but if they miss the pull, even just slightly."

He pulled his hand away sharply and I winced. It hurt. He nodded in acknowledgement.

"Our two souls have been calling from the moment you were a spark of conception. I just kept away as best I could until you were ready." I saw the hurt in his eyes. "It was hard, yes, but it is an awful lot harder when someone is snatched away before you so much as get the chance to hold them tight."

I felt the ghost of a whisper.

Mary.

"Yes," Hans said. "Mary was my fated mate, back before I knew what such a thing was."

I felt sick to see the sorrowful look on his face. My eyes welled up for him. I felt as though I was going to throw up on the floor, because there was something else going on down in my guts. Something scary.

"Mary was twenty-nine years old when I last saw her," he said. "She begged for her life to be spared, and the life of the young daughter beside her, and they granted one wish, but not the other."

The room spun for me, alive with whispers.

"The wish they granted. They kept her daughter alive?"

"Yes. They did. Her name was Lillian."

Lillian.

I saw a sobbing child's face, arms reaching out as she cried for her mother. I knew her face. I knew the way her hair fell around her cheeks. I knew the touch of her tiny little hand.

She was so real.

As real as the girl under the trapdoor, screaming to be heard.

"Don't fight it," Hans told me. "Let it come, but take it slowly. Soul trauma is a difficult one to bear. Yes. You're thinking of Lillian. The girl you are seeing is Lillian."

I felt like a deer smashed by a car, waiting in pieces at the side of the road to be put out of its misery. I was done with coaxing. I didn't want an easy road to the truth, I wanted it short, sharp and fast, no matter how dangerous.

"Just tell me, please," I managed to whisper, holding back the retches. "What happened?"

His eyes were piercing. "You know what happened. You were there."

I shook my head on instinct, the trapdoor crying out. Was I also the girl with the tiny little hands, trying to keep hold of her mother?

No. I didn't want to be!

I didn't want to see her. And I didn't want to feel her pain. And I didn't want to feel the devastation in her fragile little body as her whole world got torn into pieces.

Hans gave me a moment, staring at me but not demanding. I was on the edge of a cliff of understanding, but all I wanted to do was back away.

Be sure you want to know the answers to questions before you ask them.

I'd messed the fuck up on this one.

"Was I Lillian?" I asked him. "I was, wasn't I? Just tell me. I was Lillian, wasn't I? Oh fuck, Hans. So much pain."

My lip trembled. The memories crept in from deep, strumming my heart with their pain, and they were going to suck me up, suck me in, leave me in pieces…

The side of a lake surrounded by people. Ropes and jeers and splashing.

And Lillian, the little girl crying out for her mother.

I hated the hurt in her eyes. It was so real, I could reach out and touch her, but my hands were locked. Bound together.

I wanted to make it better.

I struggled against imaginary bonds at the breakfast bar, battling so hard that I knocked my water glass over to smash on the floor. I got trembles from my feet, shuddering all the way up my body, and I could feel Lillian's screams piercing through my heart.

I kept struggling against my bound wrists, and the trapdoor was pulsing so loud that it hurt my skull.

"Don't fight it," Hans whispered, but I was still shaking my head.

The side of a lake surrounded by people. Ropes and jeers and splashing. Jeers...
WITCH!
DROWN THE WITCH!
Lillian crying, arms reaching out in desperation for her mother.
I heard a woman's voice, begging.
"*Don't kill her, please! She isn't a witch! She's just a little girl! Take me, not her! Because I'm the witch. I'M THE WITCH! I'M THE WITCH, NOT LILLIAN!*"

I slammed my hands down on the breakfast bar and pressed my forehead to the counter. My mouth wide open in a silent scream.

Don't kill her! Don't kill Lillian!
I'M THE WITCH, NOT HER!
A woman with her hair across her face as arms grasped at her, tugging and binding. So many arms and so much strength. Too much to fight them all.
I'M THE WITCH, NOT HER!

The cold of the marble against my forehead shot into my senses enough to realise that the screams were coming from my throat, right now in the present. I heard the desperation in my own voice, just like the woman in my memory.

"I'M THE WITCH, NOT HER! NOT LILLIAN!"

I sucked in a big breath, my eyes wide as I sat bolt upright and stared over at Hans with a new sense of recognition. The tears streamed like rivers down my face.

"It's true, isn't it?" I asked Hans through the sobs. "I'm the witch, not Lillian."

He reached out to take my hands. They were as pale as his.

"Yes, Katherine, that's true. You were the witch, not Lillian." He smiled like he hadn't seen me in centuries. So full of love it broke through my pain.

I felt the splash as I was dunked into the lake, the jeering of the crowd muffled underwater as I fought for breath. Lillian's screams fading in and out with my consciousness.

Hans was nodding, gripping my hands so tight.

"It's true. Believe the memories," he whispered. "You weren't Lillian, you were Lillian's mother."

I knew before he said it.

His smile burst in and ate my whole soul in one, two magnets slamming together after centuries apart.

"Yes, my beautiful little one," he told me. "You were Mary."

24

The feelings I'd had for Hans over the past few days were nothing compared to the longing that screamed inside me as I looked upon my vampire lover through long-lost eyes.

I was a trembling wreck when he held me tight in his arms. The memories were still coming through strongly enough to have my insides twisting.

I saw a younger Hans as a Templar at Garway church, sitting next to me by the spring as we talked about life and love and our faith.

Hans had been such a pure soul, so devout and full of strong, powerful hope, and I'd been Mary, a sweet simple girl from Orcop village. Two people who loved each other's smiles, and laughs, and friendship. And so many hints of the passion that was to come between them...

But then the world around us took it away.

The darkness kept coming for me. Memories whipping like a hurricane on a stormy sea.

"Let them flow," Hans whispered. "Don't worry, sweetheart. I'm not going to let you go. Not again."

Not again.

My body lurched at the next slam of pain, but this one wasn't of me fighting for breath as I was drowned in the lake for witchcraft. This one was all about Hans, the man I loved.

I saw the men with swords and burning torches descending on Garway church when Hans and his friends were in prayer. They'd rounded up the men of the Church like beasts, trying to force confessions of heinous sins, and my sweet love had been amongst them. I'd been dragged back to the village, wracked with sobs, praying that God would have mercy, and I'd see my love again.

I did see him again. Once.

I'd found him hanging limp from a cross a few days later, beaten, broken and destroyed. He was dead, his head bent forward and lifeless. Gone from me for ever.

Or so I thought.

But Edwin had saved him.

"I hid in the tombs under the chapel for a long, long time," Hans told me. "Edwin told me I should run, but I wouldn't leave Garway. Instead, he showed me the path to the vault under the chapel and told me to stay away from the world until the torture had passed. So that's what I did. I stayed hidden in the vault, venturing out in the still of the night and spending the days in silent prayer. Edwin was the only person I spoke to for decades."

I struggled to comprehend Hans being there so close to me, hiding under the chapel.

"Why didn't you tell me you were still alive?" I sobbed. "You could have told me you were a vampire, and I'd have been there. Hans, I'd have been there!"

"I know." He rocked me in his arms at the breakfast counter. "But I didn't want to take your life from you, to pull you into the pit of my own. I didn't want to drag you away from your family and your heritage to live in darkness with a vampire, condemned by the Church."

I couldn't hold the pain back. My voice was wracked with hurt.

"I WOULDN'T HAVE CARED, HANS! I'D HAVE BEEN WITH YOU!"

"I know, sweetheart, and believe me, if I could've known what was coming for you, I'd have pulled you into the Garway vault alongside me and protected you from the torture." He paused. "But then you wouldn't have had Lillian…"

Lillian.

The memories kept on flowing, as real as life.

I was Mary in my visions, kneeling at the altar at Garway, crying for the man I'd lost. How could I have ever known he'd been underneath me, living out his undead existence while I carried on, oblivious?

It made me tremble as I realised he must have been under there while I married Mark a few years later – my beautiful Lillian's father. Hans must have been under there as I had Lillian christened, looking at my baby and her bright blue eyes.

Then more…

He must have been lying in a coffin under the floor during the funeral procession, when Mark passed away from sickness. Lillian was just eight years old when she lost her father. And just a few months older when she lost me.

A fresh rush of whispers coursed through my mind…

Mary the witch, from a line of witches. Evil sinners of witchcraft. In league with the devil.

She killed him! She killed her husband with her evil magic!

What?!

No!

NO!

"Yes," Hans whispered. "It's painful, little one, but you have to let the past come back."

I wanted to block out the memories, but they wouldn't stop.

People had blamed my witchcraft for Mark's death, convinced that such a strong local farmer, a man in his prime had been taken because of my deals with demons. But I hadn't, of course. I loved Mark. I always loved Mark. I always would love Mark.

Just not as much as I'd loved Hans…

My world was shaking all around me. There had been so much pain for all of us. So much hurt left unhealed.

"I know," Hans whispered. "Believe me, the hurt sent me into a turmoil of broken faith for lifetimes. I'm still amazed I ever came through it."

My emotions were nothing but a jumbled mass of panic, pain and revelation as the spirit of Mary in me came to life in the present. I felt her rising in me, like a phoenix from the ashes, hurt but strong. Delicate but fierce.

She'd have died for anyone she loved. Fought for anyone she loved. Sacrificed everything she had for anyone she loved.

SHE.

But SHE was I.

SHE was ME.

My mind came alive with rational questions. *Why, what, how, when, where...*

I knew what Hans was going to say before he said it.

"Feelings not thoughts, remember?"

I tried to heed his words as the memories slowed. I felt the years of love for Hans, and my darling Lillian and for Mark, the devout man who loved me after Hans was gone.

I was a widow twice over, even though the Church only ever formally recognised me as the wife of Mark. I'd been the emotional widow of Hans Weyer, too. And maybe on some weird level, that was why my grandmother had been so vicious with her dismissal of everything my soul had remembered. If she felt her own calling deep within, maybe her deeper self was protecting me from the pain she knew herself. She'd watched my grandfather die in an accident. She was a widow herself.

"Yes, there are many layers to people's pasts and soul memories," Hans said.

"And so many choices make along the way. Maybe not all conscious ones, I guess."

"Indeed." Hans squeezed me tighter, and then he smiled. "You never knew this, but I was going to relinquish my knighthood and vow of celibacy for you. I was going to ask you to be my bride, but I didn't get the chance. I was captured on the day I spoke with the priest."

I got a fresh rush of pain in my heart.

"I'd have said yes!"

"I know you would."

I looked up at my beautiful Hans' face through my tears, sobbing fresh at the recognition of the eyes I knew so well. They were greener now, yes, but they still had the same love in them. *Love for ME.*

He stroked my hair with a pained smile.

"The torture I endured was brutal beyond all words, but it was nothing compared to the loss I felt at watching you live your life without me."

"You could have come for me!"

He shook his head. "Selflessness is the greatest gift of all. I chose my torment over yours, hoping you'd find a new love and a sweet Orcop life to keep you happy."

"I didn't have a happy ending though, did I? They drowned me as my daughter watched, with Mark's body fresh in the ground! Why didn't you save me? Why didn't you save me and Lillian?"

Hans tensed as though I'd stabbed him.

"I swear to God, I'd have charged out into the sunlight a thousand times over and met my own doom to forego you yours, Katherine. But I was trapped in the tomb, locked in tight by Edwin. I felt your pain, but I couldn't get to you. *That* was my biggest pain, little one. That will be the worst sin I'll ever live with. The shame will never go away. I should have known it was coming. I should have been tuned in enough to feel it."

I tried to collect my thoughts, feeling sick to my stomach.

I was scared to ask the next question. I wasn't sure I'd be able to speak it aloud, but Hans heard it anyway.

What happened to Lillian when I was gone?

"Your beautiful daughter lived a long life. She married a young man called Matthew and they had three children. Luke, George, and Elaine."

I smiled through a fresh set of tears.

"She was very happy," Hans told me. "She died a sweet old woman with her children and grandchildren around her. Luke and George had moved away to Wales, but they came back at word of her sickness. Elaine was at her side all through her life, with two girls of her own."

The thought gave me a wave of sad relief.

"What were the girls called?"

"I think it's time I showed you," Hans said, and chanced pulling me to my feet. "Come. Let me show you the beautiful road of your past."

He led me through a doorway at the back of the kitchen. It opened into a study with rich green decor, but there was barely any furniture in there besides one desk.

It was all about the walls. Pictures, and paintings. Framed embroidery, and pressed flowers. Hans pointed to the family tree painted in beautiful italics, framed high and proud on the wall.

It began at the top, with Mary, then showed generations of children, leading to children, and grandchildren and great grandchildren. My gaze flitted over them – so many relatives, all from me.

"You should be very proud of yourself," Hans told me, with his arm around my waist. "You left a great legacy."

I attempted to soak in all the names but it was pointless. There were too many. Tiny pieces of italic script, each one symbolising a soul. A whole life in one tiny scribble of text. It blew my mind to think about all those lives living out their journey. All of the people they'd known, and the love, loss and life they must have all experienced.

And then – right at the bottom – was me.

Katherine Jane Blakely.

Seven hundred years of a family tree, and there I was again, born anew.

"I don't understand it," I said. "With reincarnation and being in the same family line, why did it take me so long to come back?"

"I don't know the answer to that, little one. All I can tell you is that time means both nothing and everything, so far as I've learnt. Souls come back when they're ready. There are hints and whispers in the family chain, but a soul is its own beautiful thing on its own beautiful journey. I've been waiting for yours to come back for centuries."

"You've been watching my family for all these years? Really?"

"Yes," he admitted. "Very, very closely. They just never saw me doing it. I was waiting for you, sweetheart."

"How did you know for sure that I'd ever come back? That was quite a risk, wasn't it?"

He kissed my head before he answered me.

"Even through all my suffering and doubt, and through the turmoil of trying to reconcile my faith with my experience of life, I still believed in destiny and the benevolence of the great unknown. I trusted you'd be back, and I trusted your soul would pick the same beautiful family line to come back into. Your chain was too strong to let go."

My brain rattled at the thought. I felt like a tiny little speck of life in a very bright sky.

"I knew you were returning the very second it happened," he continued, and I looked up at him, adoring his happy smile. "I felt it at the moment of your conception. It made no sense, but it awoke me from my slumber. I rushed out to find Edwin and spun him around in my arms, whooping with cheers."

"Really?"

"Yes. I didn't find out your mother was pregnant for certain until a few months later, but I didn't need to. I already knew."

"I don't know what to say," I whispered.

He squeezed my waist as I turned my attention back to my vast family tree.

"You don't need to say a word. Your soul already has the answers it needs, your mind is yet to catch up with them. But it will. Don't worry about that. It will."

I scanned through the names, still trying to comprehend it. There were so many girls in our family chain, mapping out a river from me back to Mary. *Ruby, Georgina, Margaret. Jane, Deborah, Kerry-May.* So many distant relatives, all on the path from me to her.

Were we really all witches?

"You were all good witches," Hans said. "Some of you used your skills more than others. Some were a lot more reserved in their approaches, others dived in all the way."

He pointed to Kerry-May.

"She was quite a character. You'd have liked her. She lived the legend with everything she had. The head of the Garway group for over forty years."

I got a serious prickle right then.

"Wait. What group? What legend?"

He stared at me.

"What?" I said.

"You already know the answer. You just don't know that you know it."

I managed a laugh. "Another thing I'll add to the pile, then."

He took a few steps to the side and I moved with him, and there, on the wall was a framed piece of embroidery. It must have been hundreds of years old.

I recognised it from childhood. It was one of the myths and legends I'd learnt about in school. I'd written it in my school book and drawn some pictures around it, but Grandma had torn it up and told me it was rubbish. Like she had about so many things in my life.

I heard it as a whisper. The words dancing and glowing with life as I stared.

There will be nine witches from the bottom of Orcop to the end of Garway Hill as long as water flows.

I'd sung the line in the grounds of Garway church when I was dancing around the gravestones. I used to make daisy chains up by the old spring, to my own little song.

Of course. It was all making sense now.

I was one of the nine witches from the bottom of Orcop to Garway Hill. Just like the witches before me.

The question was, just who were the others?

"You'll find out soon enough," Hans told me. "They're waiting for you. Just as they have been for years."

25

My mind danced through so many of the women I knew from Orcop and Garway. Who were the other eight witches in the legend? Who would be in the Garway coven? Had I passed them every day without even knowing about it? Was it old Edna who walked her old Labrador every morning through Orcop village, or the goth girl who lived at the old pub in Garway, with the faded sun tarot card as a tavern sign? What about Amy, who everyone knew as the *crystal healing lady*?

"You'll find out soon enough," Hans said.

I stared up at him with a raised eyebrow.

"You already know, don't you?"

He didn't answer, just turned his attention back to the embroidered phrase.

There'll be nine witches from the bottom of Orcop to the end of Garway Hill as long as water flows.

"Come on, Hans," I pushed. "Who are the other eight witches? Do I know them?"

"That's a surprise for you to uncover yourself. Not one to be handed out to you. It would be cheating you out of a revelation."

I could have laughed out loud. I didn't need any more revelations this lifetime. I'd had more than enough to last for centuries. Still, despite the carnage I had a strange sense of euphoria. It was bursting through the chaos and pain of memories long gone like a phoenix rising. A weird excitement, as though my true self was peeking her head above the turrets for the very first time.

Seeing life through Mary's eyes seemed different to mine. They were like mine – *Katherine's* – with an extra magical shine on them. Mary's magic and mine combined.

"Yes, your hearts and souls are two as one," Hans said. "And the others will be pleased to see it. The ninth witch coming home."

My heart sped up.

"I'm going back to Herefordshire? To live in Orcop? Is that what's supposed to happen?"

His eyes were so steady on mine.

"No, Katherine. *We're* going back to Herefordshire." He looked so happy, it was beautiful. "Don't worry, I've got my eye very tightly on the clock. Events are unfolding, just as they should be."

I didn't know what he meant. I narrowed my eyes, trying to read him the way he read me. He must have sensed it, because he kept the stare locked between us, as though he was giving me the chance.

"I can't do it," I said. "I'm not a mind reader."

"Stop digging so hard. Rather than searching for answers, listen for them. Let the instincts come."

I looked at him again, trying. But nothing came.

"I can't hear anything."

He didn't give up, even though I had.

"Tell me the first words that come into your head, right now."

"Halloween," I replied. "Halloween and… Garway."

I thought I was stating some obvious guesses, but he gave me a nod of acknowledgement.

"Good. Keep going."

"Keep going?" I took a breath, trying to clear my mind.

Instincts.

I let myself sink into my subconscious until I was back in the woodland, staring at the trapdoor, no longer afraid of what I might find in there. I looked into the depths and focused on nothing. Quiet.

Instincts.

My voice sounded distant when I spoke again.

"Halloween night… Garway church. Moonlight on the gravestones, and you, and me. Running. Dancing." I kept my eyes closed. "The ritual. That's what I hear, Hans. Ritual."

"That's good," he said. "Let it flow."

His encouragement kept me there, staring into the darkness in my imagination, and this time I saw images there like motion paintings in the depths. Like an overlay of instincts on instincts that didn't make any sense. Imagination within my imagination.

I saw Garway church, and I saw us there, me and Hans. I felt my bare feet on the grass as I spun in the grounds like I used to do when I was a little girl, but I wasn't young anymore. It wasn't just Hans' legs I bumped into when he appeared in front of me this time. My whole body pressed against his, and his lips met mine.

And then it ended. The motion paintings stilled and disappeared. *But they left something.*

I opened my eyes.

"I'm going to taste your blood," I said, with crystal clarity.

He nodded gently.

"Yes. I'm certainly going to give you your first taste."

"Am I going to be a vampire?"

"That will be your choice, Katherine, not mine."

It was an easy choice to make.

"I want to be a vampire with you. I'm not going to lose you this time."

He took my hand and kissed it.

"That's a beautiful statement, but it needs to be the right time. You're still a youngster in the world. You still have early sunrises, and afternoons with your friends, and twilights in the meadows to enjoy."

The idea of having friends still felt alien to me, let alone having friends back in Orcop. I'd been an outsider my whole life.

"Do you mean the other witches?" I asked him. "Are they going to be my friends?"

"The witches and the blood players, as well as all the people you'll meet now you're allowed to become who you truly are."

The thoughts were exciting, but that didn't change anything. I wanted to be a vampire with Hans. I'd known that in my soul from the very second he'd chased me along the cobblestones. My soul was just singing a lot louder with Mary's voice along with mine.

Hans was still an awful lot better at reading thoughts than I was. He was still holding my hand as he gestured further along the wall.

"Do you want to look in the mirror of old times? Do you want to see yourself as you used to be?"

He led me further into the room until we were standing beside the window, and there, up on the wall was a painting. A portrait of a woman that made me gasp.

It was me, in times gone by. Her eyes were like mine and her smile had the same quirk as mine, with one side raised slightly higher, and she even had the same dusting of freckles on her forehead. But Mary's hair was longer and lighter. She was wearing a simple dress in white, sitting by Garway spring. I recognised the low walls on either side.

But there was something else behind her smile and her simple white dress. A tiny tickle of want in her that most people wouldn't have seen, just like the one in me.

She wanted to explore the pleasures of the flesh with Hans. Like I did.

"I didn't know you'd look so much like her," Hans told me. "I knew you were going to be her soul reborn, but I didn't foresee that your family chain would be strong enough to give you the same beautiful eyes and smile and grace."

There was something so eerily stunning about seeing myself like that, in ancestor form. I'd sat in her position many times as a younger girl, oblivious to the fact I'd been there in a life gone by. Mary had been lucky enough to see the spring in its gorgeous flowing glory. She looked as transfixed by the spot as I'd always been.

"It's an artist's interpretation," Hans said. "But it's very accurate."

"Who painted it?"

His eyes spoke louder than his mouth did. I didn't need to be a mind reader to know the answer.

"Yes," he said. "I painted it. This must have been at least my fiftieth effort. The image was imprinted in my mind for a long time before my paintbrush could do it justice."

"I didn't know you were a painter."

"I'm not. I'm just well-practised in many things. I can play five different instruments at orchestral level and speak almost every language in the world." His eyes were mischievous. "Who knows, little one. You may well be an awful lot better than I am at any of them in a few hundred years."

He fascinated me more and more every second, if that was even possible.

We both stood looking at the portrait of me on the wall, and it was a stunning silence. I felt so assured in myself standing there, as though I'd truly come home to life. My thoughts sounded more wistful in my head, my intuition speaking at a deeper depth, and I was confident in my own heart. No longer just a girl running away from Orcop, afraid of being myself.

"We're heading back to Garway for Halloween, are we?" I asked Hans. "That's what the ritual is about."

"That is my plan, yes."

I was coming to know him so well.

Hans was a brooder. A planner. A thinker.

He'd been planning this for years.

"You knew how things were going to go, didn't you?" I pushed. "You had the timings mapped out from the start."

He was so perfectly honest and simple in his answers.

"Yes. I did."

"That night when you chased me along the cobblestones, you knew we'd be in Garway a week later."

"Fate can never be predicted fully, but yes, I had high… expectations, but the choice has always been yours to make. It still is."

My questions kept coming.

"Did you always know you'd come for me at eighteen?"

He hesitated for a few seconds before he answered.

"I hoped I'd be able to hold back and let you live your life a little more fully without me invading your reality, but it's one of the few times I've failed in my selflessness." He looked at me and not Mary. "I couldn't risk losing you again. I'm sorry, but I had to take the earliest opportunity."

I squeezed his hand.

"I'm glad you did. I wouldn't want to live my life without you. It wouldn't be full without you in it. I didn't even know what living meant until I met you."

I looked at Mary in the painting.

"Is that how I looked at you in real life?"

"Yes. It's exactly how you looked at me in real life." He paused. "Just like you do now."

"We didn't get the chance to consummate our passion then though, did we?"

"No. We didn't."

The needs in me were rising, looking at Mary looking at Hans that way, even in oil paint. Yes, I was right. She was as hungry for him as I was. The attraction between us really did run between lifetimes.

"We need to remedy that," I said. "Mary will be in me now. She'll be able to have what she couldn't have then. I need it more than ever and I know that she does too."

"What do you need?" he asked. "Say it."

I couldn't imagine Mary speaking filthily to Hans. It seemed almost perverse.

He shook his head.

"Mary may have had a pure outlook, but her heart was as dirtily beautiful as yours. Speak for both of you."

A sudden burst of hot tingles surged down through my chest and swirled around my stomach, intense enough to take my breath away. I swear... the girl in the painting... her cheeks appeared redder than before.

The words came unbidden. "I need you to fuck me, Hans."

He liked that. I could see it in his eyes.

"Keep going."

I looked up at Mary again, trying to sense her spirit inside me, and those tingles pulsed in the pit of me. She was as desperate as I was. She wanted his vampire cock as much as I did.

Maybe even more.

"She wanted you so badly," I whispered. "She would have been desperate to feel your teeth in her."

He pulled me close, his huge dick pressing into my stomach.

He stroked the hair back from my brow. "She's here in the present. In you. Where does she want my teeth now?"

"Where I do," I said, and took hold of his ass to pull him closer. "I want you to give me the dirty bite. I want to know what it feels like."

He raised an eyebrow.

"Sarah has made quite an impact, hasn't she?"

It felt like years since Sarah's filthy scene, despite it being a few short hours. My mind was able to switch between moods like lightning.

"I wanted your teeth in my pussy anyway. She just gave me a little teaser."

"Hmm. But, Katherine..." He gazed into my eyes. His green eyes so... different. As if he was seeing deeper into me. "...the dirty bite is quite something. I'm not sure if –"

"If I can handle multiple orgasms all at once?"

I was buzzing so much at the thought of his fangs either side of my clit that I could feel the wetness on my thighs.

Hans smirked, showing just the points of his fangs. I moved against his hard cock, and he licked his full lips. His mouth was watering at the thought.

"Mary's soul is in mine," I said, still pressing against him. "I think she deserves it along with me, don't you? You'll be biting both of us now."

"Steady," Hans whispered. "Keep talking like that and I'll be biting your pussy right here in front of her picture."

Confidence bloomed in my chest like never before.

"Why don't you? Isn't that what you want? To bite my pussy and drink my blood until I come like the most desperate girl in the world?" I smiled a smile like Mary's. *Like mine.* "Come on, Hans. Give her spirit what she wants along with mine."

He hitched me tighter against his cock this time, then grunted to let me know the feeling was entirely mutual, and I really thought he was going to do it. I thought he was going to pin me down on the rug in front of Mary's portrait and suck the blood from my pussy as I came for him.

But he shook his head no and looked at the window.

"Now isn't the time to be fucking you until you're screaming on the rug. The sun's about to rise."

"Oh dear, is it bedtime, then?" I asked, teasing.

"You already know the answer to that."

I slid a hand between us, grabbed his hard-on through his pants.

His hand grabbed mine.

"If you want to earn your reward, little one, you'd better get your sweet little ass upstairs and spread yourself wide. I'm sure we'll be at it all day long."

There was a lightness to my feet when I turned tail and raced away from him with a laugh. It wasn't just me bounding up the stairs. It was Mary, too. She'd have been as adventurous as me.

She deserved it a hell of a lot more than I did. The poor girl had been waiting centuries. When I heard the force of Hans' steps pounding after me, there was no doubt about it.

All those years of waiting would be very, very worth it indeed.

26

*H*ans caught me from behind in the bedroom doorway and scooped me up in his arms. I squealed like a naughty little girl, loving the game as he carried me across the room and threw me down onto the bed.

I watched the gorgeous creature as he walked back to the huge, heavy door, admiring him as he bolted us in.

"Get ready for me," he said, then shot me a sly smile as he bolted up the windows to follow.

I did as I was told, tugging off my dress and panties as quickly as I could. I fell back on the mattress and spread my legs as wide as they could go, hitched up high so he could see how wet my pussy was. He was looking at me as I ran my fingers over my bruised bites on my tits, loving how tender his teeth marks were.

Now I'd truly seen the depths beneath the trapdoor and recognised myself hanging proudly on Hans' study wall, I was a different girl. So much more confident in my own skin.

It made my heart soar that such a beautiful man as Hans had been waiting for me for centuries. It was pure bliss to have the incredible man I'd missed out on in my last incarnation. I'd never let that happen again.

I'd have circled my clit myself if Hans would let me, and I'd have come in a heartbeat. There was no way I'd be able to hold it back.

I moaned for him as he joined me on the bed and I caught my

breath at the touch of his hand on my thigh, his eyes burning my pussy as he stared at me.

"It's going to hurt so much," he told me. "You're still bloody from the club earlier."

I clenched my sore pussy. "I know, but I can take it."

He leant over me, face to face.

"I suspect there's more to it than taking it, little one. I think you want my cock to stretch you open so wide you're screaming."

He was right on that. My body responded by arching for him.

His fangs were incredible when he smiled.

"Just imagine how much it's going to hurt when I take your ass for the first time."

The thought of him thrusting his cock into my virgin ass made me shiver.

"Are you going to do it tonight? Is that how you're going to make me take it? While I'm still hurting, raw?"

"You'll have to wait and see."

I loved the way he made me feel so powerless to his will. On one hand I was his perfect princess, seated high on a glorious throne, and on the other I was a little slut, craving his body in any way he was willing to give it to me. I'd have begged him however he wanted me to. I'd have dropped onto my knees in front of him and kissed his feet just to feel his touch on my skin, but I didn't need to.

His mouth was as hungry as mine when he claimed my tongue with his. I knew what was coming by now and lifted my arms above my head for him, loving the way his grip took hold of my wrists.

I was his perfect princess and his horny little girl, both at once.

He didn't move quickly, even though my whole body was crying out for him. I was bucking against nothing but air, muscles clenching with need, but he didn't give me anything but deep, hot kisses. Not even a nip on my lip to make me bleed.

I squirmed and I bucked, and I moaned against his mouth, but it didn't make any difference. He kept me hanging until I was lost to the need, my pussy in a frenzy when he finally kissed his way down my neck.

I smiled at the ceiling and braced myself when I felt his breath against my nipple. My wounds were burning, and they made it feel even better. Nervous tingles were like heaven on my skin.

"You want my teeth right here, don't you?" he asked, deliberately running his fangs across the marks.

Yes, please, I thought and I saw his smirk in my mind.

"You know what hurts more than a fast hard bite?" he whispered. "Being pierced really, really slowly."

I knew what he meant when he pressed his teeth in the wounds, just hard enough to freshly break the skin. There was no sharp stab and then sucking, more like a poised torture of the flesh.

I gritted my teeth as he pinched just a little bit harder. I felt blood trickling around my nipple, but he didn't suck, just lapped it up with his tongue.

My breaths quickened because it hurt so much. I cried out as he clenched just a little bit harder, still bucking up with my hips, even though there was nothing to greet me. He gripped my wrists tighter as he sank his fangs in further, but the endorphins were flooding through me now. My cries turned to moans.

His lips were bloody as he pulled his teasing fangs free and looked up at me.

"Can you even begin to imagine how much it's going to hurt if I pierce your pussy this slowly? That's how I like it, little one. I like to draw out the pain as long as possible to make the contrast so... *desperate.*"

"Show me," I said. "I don't want to imagine it, I want to feel it."

"What have I told you before about patience?"

I smiled up at the ceiling, heady on lust.

"I don't have a lot of patience left. You're driving me insane."

"There's a lot more left yet, sweetheart. Your impatience is going to have to shut up and take it."

He bit me again, harder and quicker this time, with no warning as he sank his teeth into a part of my breast without any marks. Fresh wounds. Fresh pain that spiked through me.

"Fuck!" I arched my back, pushed against the pain. "More," I said, whining. "I need it."

"Yes, but you also need plenty of blood left," he said when he finished sucking. "I'll be taking a lot more before we're done."

He sunk his fangs into my other tit in one stabbing bite. My head flew back and I cried out, soon moaning as he sucked and drank from me.

I hissed with pleasure as he withdrew his fangs.

He was so pleased with me. I could feel his pleasure coming from his very soul.

"You love being pain drunk, don't you?"

I let out a breath. "God yes. It drives me crazy."

"Yet another reason we're fated mates. I'm desperate to bite, you're desperate to bleed."

I was heady enough to grin.

He licked up a trail of blood that was running down my tit. "You're the sweetest thing I've ever tasted."

A strange thought came into my head.

"What about when I'm a vampire myself? Will we still be able to play like this?"

His eyes were so green. Like bright emeralds in the lamplight.

"We'll still be able to play, but it'll be different. The sensations will be a lot more even."

"Maybe I should hold back a little while, then. I want to experience everything there is to know."

"I'll milk you dry of sweet human blood as long as you want me to," he said. "Don't worry about that."

I could've spent years right there on his bed while he played with me. I could've been pain drunk for months at a time and adored every second, coasting on waves of hurt and need.

I moaned again as his bloody lips kissed a hot path down my stomach and my clit sizzled, his mouth so close, his hot breath on my pussy. I braced myself once again, but no. He ran his tongue over the bites on my thighs and I cried out when he sunk his teeth in afresh. Cried out and tried to clench my thighs together.

"Stay spread," he growled with a bloody mouth.

My skin was awash with smears of red when he sank his teeth back in, and I felt so free as I bled. It felt so liberating as he sucked at me, leaving all the pain behind.

"You look so beautiful," he said when he pushed from the bed.

I watched him undress and he watched me smear blood over my tits, keeping my legs spread for him as he kicked his pants away and climbed back on the bed with his hard-on raging.

"You're not looking so bad yourself," I said, barely able to take my eyes from his cock.

"How about you show me what a good girl you can be, and I'll show you what the dirty bite is?"

"I'll be a good girl, don't you worry," I told him with a naughty grin.

I really was pain drunk. I hitched myself so my pussy was spread wet and wide, ready without him so much as laying a finger on my clit to get the sparks flying. I didn't need them.

It was a different kind of pain this time when he eased the head of his cock inside me.

I couldn't stop whimpering.

"Take it," he hissed, but he didn't need to. I'd take it at whatever cost.

I was being speared by a huge rod of vampire flesh an inch at a time, but I still kept my legs spread wide, offering myself to the hurt as he stretched me.

He held my legs back and I gripped the sheets as he pushed slowly, all the way deep until skin met skin.

Fuck, it felt like I was being split in two.

"Good girl," he said, *"feel* it."

My pussy was clenching him so tightly as he slowly withdrew, it felt like he was drawing my soul right out of me. Felt even better when he pushed back in, filled me up.

I gripped the sheets above my head and moved to meet his hips like a wanton little whore. I wanted to prove myself. I wanted to feel the dirty bite and I'd do whatever it took to earn it.

"That's nice, Katherine. That's really nice," he said and his pace was steady, his thrusts were deep. "I could fuck you like this for days. I could keep up this rhythm and fuck you until you're so sore you'll be begging me to stop."

I shook my head. "I'll never beg you to stop."

His eyes were so filthy, dripping with lust.

"We'll see about that when I'm fucking you along with another huge dick at the same time."

The thought made me moan.

"When did you start liking this?" I whispered. "When did you go from the devout, holy knight to the dirty vampire who wants blood house filth?"

"A long time ago," he answered. "Filth is addictive, sweetheart, but so are you."

I kept on moving against him as he picked up the pace. His eyes were adoring along with dirty when he looked at me this time.

"I mean it, Katherine," he said. "*You're* my addiction, not the filth. If you want to be a pure little girl for the rest of time, I'll happily go along with you. I wouldn't touch another soul as long as I lived."

His words made me grin, but there was no doubt about it. Mary could have looked as sweet as she wanted sitting by the spring, but beneath the surface she'd have been a horny, needy girl for the games with Hans. Just like I was.

"I don't want to be a pure girl for the rest of time," I said to my fated mate. "I want to experience everything there is to experience, along with you."

"I've got an awful lot to show you, then," he said, sinking his cock deep and holding it there.

I reached up to stroke his face, hoping my eyes displayed the depth of my truth.

"You'd better start showing me now, then."

He grinned a bloody grin.

My pleasure, little one.

His hips were brutal, and his cock was tearing me apart, but I was craving it all. I cursed out loud as he pulled away, then moaned like a slut when he lowered his face between my legs – lapping at my clit with his tongue.

Was this it? The time for the dirty bite?

"Please!" I begged him. "PLEASE! Show me, Hans! I need to feel it!"

He sucked at my clit and I took hold of his hair, silently urging him on.

Please, please, please!

He glanced up at me one more time, fangs looking lethal as he spread my pussy.

"Get ready," he said, and I braced myself.

His tongue flicked out at my clit, and then he smiled, fangs revealed. I could only watch, transfixed, as the points of his fangs touched to my tender flesh.

And then…

Any ideas I'd had about the dirty bite disappeared to nothing in a heartbeat. The sudden stab of his teeth was like a lightning bolt exploding in my head, so intense it made my vision turn white.

I was rolling in blindness, caught in nothing but exhilarating pain, but it was mind-blowing. The suck of his mouth as I bled streams from my pierced pussy was heaven itself. The way my clit pulsed strong and hard along with my heartbeat was more than I could take.

I don't know if I whimpered, or screamed, or cried. I don't know if I bucked, or squirmed, or fought him. All I knew was the sensation of a lifetime.

And then he speared me with his fingers and twisted them inside me.

I heard the sucking of his lips, and the wetness as he ploughed me, and I was as bare in my soul as it's possible to be. Me, Mary, and lifetimes apart all disappeared to nothing. There was just the sublime bliss pulsing between my legs. Me and him. Two bodies, one spirit.

Connected.

Oh how the pleasure rose.

Sarah was right. It wasn't like one climax – it was like a whole decade of them all at once. The force was a tidal wave crashing into the shore, and so was I.

I knew I was a squirming mess, spurting and bleeding for him. I knew the bed must be soaked wet underneath me as the need erupted, and my toes must have been clenched so tight they were cramping.

So, this was it. The dirty bite. Everything Sarah promised it would be.

And more.

It was a dirty bite from my fated mate. The creature whose body was meant for mine.

My heartbeat was ripping through me when the waves started easing away. I was disoriented as I struggled to pull myself together, my hands reaching out for the man who'd driven me insane.

But he wasn't done with me yet. Not even close.

"Let's test you out," he said, and I realised he was positioning himself back up to fuck me. "Let's ride those shooting stars and give your sweet ass the pounding it deserves."

Hans didn't take it steady. No easing and no inching. Nothing but pure, raw pain in one hard thrust that tore a scream from my throat as he slammed into me. He didn't wait. Didn't hesitate. Just fucked my ass hard and fast and it felt like I was being ripped to pieces.

I probably was.

"You can tell me to stop," he whispered, clearly reading the agony on my face. "I've been waiting centuries to claim you and you've been waiting centuries to be claimed, but even the dirtiest souls have limits."

I shook my head.

No limits. Nothing but us.

"Harder! I want everything!"

"As you wish…"

Hans pushed my knees right up to my chest and gave me everything there was to give. I felt tears flowing through a blissful, agonised smile, but I took my gift from him, because that's what it was. His filth, and his lust, and his cock, and his passion were all beautiful gifts.

My clit was still throbbing, and my wounds were still bleeding, and my heart was crying out for it all when he spoke next.

"I'm going to come inside your tight little ass, little one. You want that, don't you? You want to be dripping vampire cum from your asshole."

I let out a moan. "Yes, I want it!"

It was divine when he reached his own climax. It felt like his dick was impaling me, and I couldn't even begin to picture how big he was with all of that blood inside him. He cursed like a demon as he lost himself to the pleasure, and we were in sync as one, two souls gripping each other in the mist of carnal desire, and there we stayed.

Bliss.

Pure bliss.

He collapsed onto me when he was done, his breaths heaving in time with mine. I wrapped him in my arms, and hooked my ankles together around his waist, praying this connection would never leave us.

"It won't," he said. "Fated mates last an eternity, and so will we."

My love raised himself enough to kiss me, with the blood from my pussy still wet on his lips.

I was a mess of cum, blood, and wetness as he pulled out and left my stretched ass behind.

"That was insane," I whispered. "Absolutely insane."

He pressed his forehead to mine.

"Don't talk in past tense." He smirked. "We're not ready for sleep yet. Not even close."

My body was trembling, petrified I wouldn't be able to take

another round, but the moment Hans ground against me again I knew the nerves had no meaning. They meant nothing.

My soul was already crying out for more.

And so was I.

Fuck me, Hans. Just fuck me!

27

*I*t's hard to tell days from night when you're living in darkness, but my body didn't care. Night turned to day again, and day must've turned to night, then morning anew. We fucked and kissed and played through the hours, and I ate steak on loop as I glugged back glasses of water and feasted on strawberry jam.

My dreams and fantasies around Hans were crazy. Images flowing free.

It wasn't just Mary's pain from the past that transfixed me, it was her excitement at knowing that this was it. Her life finally living out through mine.

I woke with a smile on my face to find my vampire love still asleep by my side after the longest session of them all. I listened to his breathing, letting my senses run riot. I didn't need light to see him. I could see his gorgeous form in the darkness, and it didn't matter how pained and battered my body was, I'd have sacrificed my flesh in a heartbeat, just to feel him inside me again.

"I can hear you, you know," he said and turned to face me.

I let my fingers run down his chest. His body was so ripped. So toned.

I knew what was waiting for me as my hand moved lower. His cock was hard and ready for me. I could barely wrap my fingers around him, but my pussy was already hungry at the thought of more.

"That feels good, little one," Hans said, "it's been some time since I've had anyone to share my evening glory with."

That made me smile.

I stroked the thick veins on his cock.

"Take what you need," Hans said. "My body is yours, just as yours is mine."

The offer was magical. The sentiment so real it set my heart alight.

I knew what I needed before I was ready to take him inside me again, though. I needed help to get me ready. I needed his mouth…

"As I said," he whispered. "Your pleasure is all that counts right now. I'll take mine through yours."

The invitation gave me a thrill. Inexperience meant nothing in my new adventure. I was growing in confidence. I could sense right through me just how much he was craving me, just as much as I wanted him.

"More than that," he told me. "I've been waiting for you for centuries, remember?"

He guided me up and onto him, and I felt so raw as I positioned my knees on either side of his face, but fuck, it was blissful. He groaned as his mouth worked me, his tongue flicking at my clit so perfectly that I was moving to a rhythm within seconds. He gripped my ass cheeks and urged me on, and I let myself free.

Damn. It was insanely hot.

I was riding Hans' beautiful face, and he was as crazy for it as I was. I opened my thighs wider, offering my pussy spread bare and he moaned along with me, Fuck, he made me so wet. I knew I his face must be soaked, and it only spurred me on.

I waited for the pain, but it didn't come. He teased my wounds with his teeth but didn't bite me.

For once, it was a relief. I was sore enough without it. I just hoped I would be good enough for him without blood.

His thoughts came loud and clear.

Your body doesn't need more bites right now, and neither do I. Your body needs more sex. Take what you want, exactly how you want it.

He was right. My pussy needed to take his cock, and I needed to be ready for it.

I moaned, moving in sync with him as he lapped and played and sucked my clit. I braced myself on the pillows and my back arched, and my hips circled, and Hans kept on giving. His mouth was divine.

I felt like an utter goddess as I took my pleasure from him.

The bite marks on my pussy were stinging, and it hurt as I built up to orgasm, clenching and hungry, but it was primal in its calling. I couldn't hold back.

That's it, little one. Set yourself free.

His hands left my ass and snaked up to my tits, cupping them gently and squeezing my nipples and he was a master with his tongue, setting off the sparks that danced through me until I was a bucking mess. He was there, giving, and I was riding, taking.

That wasn't all I wanted, though.

I wanted to ride a whole lot more.

I was still panting from coming when I edged myself down the bed, still straddling him.

"Steady," he whispered as I rubbed my pussy against his cock, but I didn't want steady. I wanted him inside me all the way.

I eased myself as gently as I could, whimpering against the stretch, but nothing could have stopped me, and the hiss that came from my lover's mouth as I sunk my pussy onto him had me hissing right back.

"Fuck me," he said and I was riding my vampire lover in no time, letting feral nature take its course.

Our bodies were made for this, but this time it was at my command.

"You really are a pain hungry little beauty," Hans said, with a glorious tone of pride.

It made me ride him even harder, with a huge grin on my face. Circling and slamming, circling and slamming. He was so deep it was like he was buried in my stomach, but that's where he was meant to be. All the way inside me.

I found the angle myself, shifted to hit the spot inside me, trusting my own motions.

"Good girl," he said. "That's right. Make yourself come."

I cried out, struggling to bear it as the waves hit. It was so painful and so fucking good, both at once. *Pain drunk.* But it wasn't from teeth and blood this time, it was from the way my pussy strained to take him, even though I wanted him so fucking bad.

So fucking bad that I braced myself on his thighs and rode him like a whimpering slut.

"Fuck," he groaned, and I grinned to myself again at the ultimate success.

He was going to come along with me. I was going to milk his cock as I took my thrill.

My little bruised tits bounced, and flesh slapped flesh, and I felt it building, and building and building… and then fuck. FUCK.

It was like our bodies were destined to be together. Our souls felt like they were exploding together along with our orgasms, and I knew what fated mates were. It was a feeling that made no sense, but pure sense both at once. Beyond comprehension, yet the most natural thing in the world.

So were the words that came out of my mouth as I struggled for breath after coming.

"I need to be with you for ever, Hans. I need you to make me a vampire."

He was quiet at first.

"I mean it," I told him, the confident goddess side of me still in control. "I need you to make me a vampire. Feed me your blood."

"Katherine–" he began, and I felt his hesitation.

"No," I said. "I mean it. I want to be your fated mate for ever. Not from lifetime to lifetime with centuries apart. Not anymore. I want to be a vampire along with you. Now."

I gasped as I rose from him but didn't hesitate in crawling across the bed to flick the bedside lamp on. I wanted to see his expression.

"Little one," he said, and his tone was firmer. "Becoming a vampire isn't an easy decision."

"It is," I countered, my tone firmer along with his. "Being with you is an easy decision. I don't care what that involves. Take all my blood right now, I couldn't give a shit. I just want us to be together."

"You're pain and sex drunk," he said, reaching out to stroke my face, but I gripped his wrist.

"I might be, yeah, but it doesn't make any difference. I won't feel any different when I'm not."

His eyes weighed me up, but they didn't need to. He could read my thoughts.

I WANT TO BE A VAMPIRE WITH YOU, HANS. I'M NOT LETTING YOU GO AGAIN!

"That was quite a yell."

"Yeah, and maybe it needs to be. Why won't you let me be a vampire with you?"

He looked so beautiful beside me, so full of love as he smiled.

"I didn't say that, sweetheart. I am more than willing for you to be a vampire with me, nothing would make be happier, but we need to make sure it would make *you* happier. Giving up your living flesh is a huge thing to consider. I'm not certain you're ready to make that call."

That pushed a button inside me, like a deep wounded trigger had been pulled. For so long I'd been told what I should and shouldn't want, and what I should and shouldn't think, and what I should and shouldn't be doing. I wasn't taking it anymore.

"I don't need to consider it," I told him. "I've known it since I was a little girl. I've been fascinated with vampires because it was my destiny to be one. With you."

He didn't respond to that, and I knew I'd nailed it.

"Argue it," I challenged. "Tell me I'm wrong."

He tried.

"You haven't even tasted vampire blood yet. Let alone fully comprehended the reality of being a blood seeker for all time, losing the love of sunlit mornings and seeing the world in the light of the day."

"So? Who cares? It's destiny, isn't it? *Our* destiny."

He was silent. I knew I was right.

"So what's the problem?" I asked. "Why can't you just bite me and suck me to death and let me drink from you to make my transition? That's what's we're destined for, isn't it? If you weren't going to make me a vampire why would you have introduced yourself in the first place?"

He sighed. "Us being together is destined, Katherine, yes. But when and how you choose to become a vampire is something your body and soul both need to be ready for."

"And they are!"

"Really?"

With that he leapt up and pinned me down on the bed. It was so rough, so forceful, and his eyes were burning fierce, teeth looking savage as he hissed in my face. My body responded before I could stop it, I flinched and screamed with terror. I thrashed with crazy panic, breaths ragged, and he let me go as I was still struggling.

"There we go," he said, and took himself off me. "You're not ready yet. It's a progression that will happen when it's time."

Fuck it.

I felt so angry with myself as I raised myself up. I was staring down at him, and I felt frustration like I'd never known it.

"Let me guess. Patience, right?" I asked. "Is that going to be your answer to everything, Hans? Patience, patience, patience? I'm sick of fucking patience."

His eyes weren't angry back at me. Not at all.

I kept on speaking, the passion spilling over.

"You're not the only one who's been waiting centuries. I have too. I may not have been conscious of it, but I lost you, just as you lost me. And fuck that, Hans. Fuck it!"

"Sweetheart, it'll be all right," he said, but I didn't want to do it anymore.

I don't know what possessed me as I got up and wrapped myself in a robe on my way to the huge, bolted door, hauling it open with all my strength before I marched out onto the landing.

"Katherine!" Hans called. "Katherine, come back here. We aren't finished talking. There's plenty more to say."

I didn't look behind, just gave it everything I had. I dashed downstairs as quickly as I could, and fuck knows how I did it, but I reached the kitchen before he caught me. I tugged the kitchen drawers open one after another, looking for blades, because if he wasn't going to bleed me to death, I was going to do it myself, and it would be his choice then. Lose me or give me his blood.

I had a blade in my hand when he stormed in and snatched it from me, lifting me up from behind as it clattered onto the floor.

It was like I was possessed, screaming and kicking out at the frustration.

And the pain.

"STOP!" I said. "I'M NOT DOING THIS AGAIN, HANS! I'M NOT! I'LL DO IT MYSELF IF YOU WON'T DO IT FOR ME!"

"Shh," he soothed, and dropped to the floor, holding me tight on his lap as the sobs hit me. "This is impulse running wild. It's natural. It's fear. It's all right."

The trapdoor was well and truly open now, as was the grief. I screamed in his arms as the full force hit me. I was there, watching him hanging, butchered, hating every second like it was a lifetime. Broken myself along with him.

"Let it out," Hans whispered, and rocked me, and I felt insane, but it didn't matter. I spun on his lap to face him, barely able to see through my tears.

"Don't risk it again!" I told him. "I can't stand it. I don't want patience. I want to be with YOU. I don't give a shit about sunrises, or walking through sunny meadows, or how I'll be seeing everything in the fucking darkness. I don't fucking care!"

We sat in the quiet, him holding me as I struggled to get control of myself. It was hard. It was a war raging inside me, and I was on the edge of tumbling straight back under the trapdoor, but I wouldn't let it. I had to be here in the present.

"Oh, little one. Your commitment is divine. But–"

I shook my head, I wasn't interested in *buts*.

"I'm sure," I insisted again. "I don't give a shit how scared my body is, it can fuck off!"

He smiled a little at that. "Your soul really is shining through now. It's beautiful."

"Good," I said, somehow managing to control the sobs. "Make me a vampire then. Fuck my body, and fuck patience, too."

I expected him to fight me again, but this time his argument didn't come. He brushed my hair from my face, and then he said the words that would seal my destiny.

"All right, Katherine, I'll make you a vampire."

"Really?" I asked him. "You'll do it?"

He nodded and pulled me up with him as he got to his feet. I watched mutely as he headed to the other side of the kitchen and took down a phone from the wall.

"Time to call Edwin," he said.

28

"You'd have really slashed your wrists on the kitchen floor, wouldn't you?" Hans asked when we were in the back seat of the limo.

In any other universe it would have been a crazy statement, but the driver didn't so much as shoot us a glance.

"Yes," I replied.

Hans nodded. "That's quite something. It really is."

I chanced a smile, loving how his face looked in the orange glow of the passing streetlights through the window.

"Yeah, well. If I so much as hear the word *patience* one more time, I'll be doing it again."

He laughed a little. "I'll try to hold back from saying it."

"Please do. It drives me mad."

He squeezed my knee. "I've gathered that much."

So, here we were, on the journey. My journey into the realms of the *transition* as Hans called it. I was going to die a mortal death and become a vampire, and I had no idea how that would truly feel – losing the life in the body you've always known.

"Not fantastic," Hans said. "As I've told you, the body fights, even when the soul doesn't want it to."

"Mine can fight all it likes, I still want to be a vampire."

I got another smirk from him.

"We've most definitely ascertained that."

Even under the nerves and the tension of earlier, I was alive with excitement for what lay ahead. I felt the calling getting stronger with every mile we travelled. Who'd have ever thought that the place I'd run away from like a scared little puppy would be the place my soul would once again call home?

That's what it felt like as the limo passed the *Welcome to Herefordshire* sign. Home.

I was seeing the place through totally different eyes as we passed Ross on Wye and began the final stretch. I'd been avoiding the ocean of *where, what, why, how* questions throughout the journey, because right now I didn't want to talk in words, I wanted to talk in feelings. Hans' feelings were strong enough that they touched my spirit. He was giving me love, and support and commitment without speaking out loud.

The silence was becoming a lovely thing. Self-assured and unassuming. Natural.

"Nearly there," the driver told us as we hit the turning for Garway.

I looked up at the beautiful, huge stone manor at the top of Garway hill, and I should've known it. I'd looked at it plenty of times as a girl when I was in the church grounds, but I'd never stepped a foot on the private gravel lane that led up to it.

"Edwin lives there, doesn't he?" I asked Hans, but it was rhetorical. Now I was getting used to my new heightened instincts, things were becoming clear.

I could feel the essence of life at the top of the hill, and I recognised the same presence as I felt in the blood house. Yes, it was Edwin's house. Hans' silent nod just confirmed I was right.

Edwin opened the door to the manor himself, swinging it open wide. He was genuinely pleased to see us, I could tell that from the huge smile on his face. His long, dark hair was tied back this time, and he was in a plain back suit, but he still had a ruffled white shirt underneath. I guessed they were a staple of his. He looked fantastic for it.

He pulled Hans into his arms, and I got a taste of the familiarity between them.

"Good to see you!" he said, and then he turned his attention to me. "Hello, Katherine."

He kissed my hand, and invited us in with a sweep of an arm. I stepped inside and the décor was similar to the blood house. Almost identical. The huge, sparkling chandeliers and the plush, deep-red rug over mosaic floor tiles.

"Yes," he said. "I was the designer. The London blood house was a creation of mine."

"A great achievement," Hans said, casting his friend a smile.

"Why, thank you. I'd hope you would think so, given that you've enjoyed it plenty." Another familiar look passed between them, but I didn't feel threatened by their closeness. Not in the slightest.

"Come," Edwin said and led the way through to a dining room.

The table was huge but there was only one person sitting at it. He must have been two years older than me, max. And he was human. I could feel it. He was a lovely looking guy with a ruffle of dark brown hair, dressed casually in a long-sleeved t-shirt, quite at odds with the suits that Edwin and Hans were wearing.

"Hi," he said, and gave me a wave. His t-shirt slipped far enough up his arm that I could see the bite marks. "I'm Daniel."

"Hi, I'm Katherine," I said back.

"Edwin told me you were coming. Nice to see you. I've heard a lot."

I hadn't heard a thing about him, but didn't speak that aloud. I was still the newbie in a very tight knit crowd.

One I'd spend a long time getting to know. That was for sure.

Edwin put his hand on Daniel's shoulder, and holy fuck, I felt the connection between them sizzling across the table. Daniel was Edwin's lover. A serious one. The lust between them glowed like a furnace.

"I'm sure you two will have plenty of time to get to know each other," Edwin said.

Hans pulled out a seat for me on the opposite side of the table from them, taking his place beside me.

His friend didn't waste any time before getting down to business, addressing Hans the moment they were both seated.

"I wasn't expecting Katherine's transition so soon. I thought you'd hold back at least twelve months."

"You knew I intended to visit on Halloween, Edwin."

"Yes," Edwin replied. "But there's a big difference between showing your love the place you were transitioned, and taking their life on the same spot."

I didn't know what to say, so I didn't say a thing. I was definitely becoming more self-assured in my silence.

Hans wrapped his arm around my shoulders. "Katherine is very insistent, and very sure."

"I'd hope so," Edwin said, and wrapped his arm around Daniel's shoulder to mirror us. "Daniel has been very sure for nearly two years now, but I'm still not certain it's time."

"It's Katherine's time," Hans insisted, and they stared at each other for a few long seconds.

It was Edwin who broke the stare.

"Excellent. Then I guess this calls for a preliminary celebration." He paused. "ROBERT!"

With that another man came in from a door off to the side. A butler, clearly – but a much older one than the one at the blood house.

He gave Edwin a bow. "Yes, sir?"

"Steaks, please," Edwin said, before looking at me. "Assuming you like steak, of course, Katherine? I'd hope so. My apologies. I forget that not everyone may be accustomed to blood-player traditions."

My stomach was crying out for some actually.

"Don't worry," I said. "And yes please, I'd love some."

Robert the butler disappeared, then returned to present us with bottles of wine before our steaks. There were only two glasses on the tray he offered.

"Would you like some wine, madam?" he asked me, and I nodded with a *thank you* as I took my glass.

I felt like I was becoming initiated into traditions without even realising it.

"It's merlot, right?" I asked.

Robert smiled. "Yes. It is."

I looked over at Edwin and Daniel. "Merlot and steak. These must be the staples."

"Not for you much longer," Hans said. "Your days of steak and merlot are shortly coming to an end."

I looked at his expression. Another hint of humour.

"Ah, ok. Did Frederick change your merlot for blood in the bathroom every single time, or just some of them?" I asked, and he smirked at me.

"He's very good at it. Quite a professional. You're the only one to notice in quite some time."

"I'm hardly a detective. Not many people would be looking out for it, since they think vampires are nothing but fantasy."

"Quite," Hans said, and then Edwin cleared his throat from across the table.

"Are you truly ready to switch out merlot and steak for the immortal life of the undead?" he asked me. "I know the excitement of the transition can make people heady, but are you really certain? I'm sure the prospect of spending eternity with someone can seem irresistible, especially when they are a creature as divine as Hans, but honestly. He isn't playing it down when he says you need to be ready. Daniel has been telling me he's ready for two years now, but I'm still not so certain of it."

Daniel shifted in his seat, and I knew that he must be pissed off about it. I didn't blame him. I'd hate waiting two years for it. Fated mate, or not.

"I *am* ready," Daniel said, and rolled his eyes at Edwin.

"Yes, yes," Edwin said, and then he said the word that made my teeth grate. "*Patience.*"

Patience, patience, goddamn *patience.* I couldn't help it. I laughed out loud, and nudged Hans in the arm.

"It's not just you, then?" I smirked.

Hans grinned. "No. It's not just me. Patience is a term vampires use a lot with mortals."

"Yeah, too right," Daniel said. "I'm sick to death of it. It's annoying as fuck."

"But not quite so annoying when you're fucking." Edwin laughed and kissed his cheek. "There are plenty of times the term *patience* suits you very well."

It was there again, that furnace. The images flashed in my imagination, and I could see Daniel on his back with Edwin's cock in his ass, desperate to come himself. *Patience.*

The orgasm must be explosive.

"Well, well, well. You really are embracing your talents, aren't you?" Edwin grinned at me from across the table. I blushed at the knowledge he could read my mind. "That's very accurate. Maybe you'll get to see it for yourself in the flesh one day. We'd like that."

Hans shot him a glare. "Edwin!"

"What?!" Edwin was still grinning. "Oh come on, Hans. You brought her to the blood house already. She's hardly an innocent. Sarah said she loved watching the games. I'd have Daniel up on the table right now if you weren't being such a prick."

"Ignore him," Hans told me, with good humour. "My dear friend here is quite a character. You'll get to know that."

I hoped so. I already liked him a lot. He was funny.

"Come on, then," Edwin continued, looking at me. "What makes you so certain you want to be transitioned? Is it Hans? Have you tasted his blood? Are you already a vampire blood addict? Don't worry, we vampires still love it as much as mortals do, of course. I adore having a drink of vampire blood myself. It's delicious."

I must have looked blank. My thoughts were trying to catch up. Edwin laughed another light laugh, holding his hands up at Hans.

"She hasn't even tasted your blood yet, has she? Fucking hell, Hans."

"No, she hasn't."

"Extraordinary," Edwin replied, still grinning as Robert returned with two rare steaks with sides of vegetables.

I got started on my steak, keen to ease the hunger. Daniel was as hungry as I was, both of us eating happily as Edwin and Hans looked on.

"You're making me peckish myself," Edwin whispered to Daniel after a couple of mouthfuls, and Daniel's face lit up. He put down his cutlery and offered Edwin his arm. I paused with a forkful of steak, transfixed as Edwin tugged back Daniel's t-shirt sleeve and sank his teeth into his flesh with a moan.

Daniel moaned right back, tipping his head back, eyes closed. I instantly knew he had a hard-on, and I couldn't help it. I was thrilled by the sensations coming off them. I felt my nipples harden under my tight blue dress, and my thighs clenched under the table. Edwin knew it. He looked me right in the eye as he sucked on Daniel's arm.

"Ignore him," Hans said. "He's winding you up on purpose. He loves playing the fool."

"I'm mischievous, not a fool," Edwin corrected as he pulled his fangs out of Daniel's flesh and dabbed a napkin to his mouth. He had such a lovely grin. "Hans can be so bloody uptight sometimes. Finding one's fated mate doesn't always turn them into spoilsports."

Edwin stuck a bloody tongue out at Hans and it was obvious they'd been laughing for centuries. I was looking forward to being a part of it. I loved the humour between them.

I looked Edwin straight in the eye, using the opportunity to convey my truth.

"Yes, I'm ready to be a vampire," I told him. "It's what I want. I've known that for ever, I just hadn't realised it."

Edwin held the stare between us. I could feel his mind whirring, but I couldn't read his thoughts.

When his next words came, they knocked me sideways.

"And how about your father? Does he know about your transition yet? What was his reaction to it?"

What the fuck? My father?

I'd never even known my father. Mum and Grandma had never so much as told me his name. My blood ran cold, like someone had walked across my grave, and Hans slammed his fist on the table.

"Edwin! Stop being an utter fucking idiot!"

Edwin's gaze flicked from Hans' to mine and back again. He seemed genuinely surprised, and Hans seemed genuinely fucked off.

"Jesus Christ, Hans. You haven't told her yet?!"

"No!" Hans replied. "She's had more than enough to contend with already."

"What?" I asked, heart pounding. "You know my father? Both of you?!"

I hadn't heard a single thing about my father in years. Every time I'd asked Mum or Grandma about him they'd cussed and told me he was an evil nobody who'd left the village and deserted us. They were pleased about it. They said he was a sinner.

"Seriously?" I asked Edwin. "You know my father?!"

Edwin looked right at me. "Yes, of course I do. Everyone knows your father."

Everyone except me.

Yet again, I felt like I'd been raised blind and dumb, blinkered off from the whole world and everything in it.

Every*one* in it.

"You really don't know who he is, do you?" Edwin asked. He looked agitated at Hans. "Have you told her a damn thing yet?"

"Yes!" Hans snapped. "I've told her plenty."

"Hardly," Edwin snapped back, and I wished we could whip time back so I was still watching him sucking on Daniel's arm, not sitting with my heart pounding, scared of another trapdoor explosion.

Edwin took a breath, and put on a fake smile for my benefit, although he was still talking to Hans.

"How is he going to feel about it when he finds out you've transitioned his daughter without so much as courtesy visit?"

"I don't care," Hans told him. "This is between me and Katherine, it's got nothing to do with Thomas. Or her mother or grandmother for that matter."

Thomas.

I put my cutlery down and held my hands up.

"Will someone please tell me what the hell is happening here?"

The silence was deafening until Edwin moved. He tapped Daniel's shoulder as he got up from his seat.

"Come on, lover boy, bring your steak."

I stared in shock across the table.

"See you later," Daniel said, and did as he was told, following Edwin out of the dining room with his plate in his hand. Edwin closed the door behind them, and I turned to Hans.

"Don't bother with the *don't ask the questions unless you want the answers* stuff," I said. "I want the answers now, please. Who the fuck is my dad?"

"Edwin can be such an ignorant tosser at times." Hans sighed. "I was waiting to introduce you properly when the time was right. Your father doesn't even know you're back in the village yet."

"WHO IS HE?!" I shouted. "All I know is that he's some asshole who fucked off and left Mum and Grandma with me!"

Hans' eyes were piercing, but he didn't speak, just let my mind chew over my incoming thoughts.

"That's another load of bullshit they fed me, isn't it?!"

"Yes."

"Like everything else."

"Indeed."

I sighed to myself, trying to accept another house of cards tumbling down. I should be getting used to it by now.

"So, who is he then?" I asked. "Do I know him?"

"Not yet."

My eyes must have been as piercing as his.

"How come everyone else knows who he is? Is he some kind of vampire celebrity or something?"

Hans shook his head. "No. But everybody has two family chains behind them. Yours has a lot on your father's side, too. They will certainly help with your talents. As we said, you are a psychic, a ghost whisperer and a witch. You don't generally inherit all of those talents from one side of the tree."

My pulse was racing.

"My father's side isn't on your wall though, is it?"

"No, it's not."

"So WHY? Just tell me, will you? And if you say fucking PATIENCE I swear I'm going to–"

Hans sighed.

"Fine. He's the head of the Templar Masons," he told me. "A senior order of the Western Mystery Tradition."

I was confused.

"And what does that mean?"

Hans didn't hesitate.

"It means he's a high level initiate. The very highest in England, in fact." He paused as I stared at him. "He's an occultist, Katherine. An extremely good one."

I pictured an occultist as some kind of horror movie character, but Hans shook his head.

"No. Think of a wizard and you'd be much closer. Minus the starry sky robe and pointy hat, that is."

I couldn't quite picture it. "So, let me get this straight. My father is a head wizard in a group of wizards?"

Hans couldn't help but chuckle. "Something like that."

I didn't know whether to laugh along with him, or freak out, or cry.

"It's all right," Hans said. "He's quite renowned, and very, very well respected."

I pulled a face, still trying to get my head around it.

"If he's the leader of some kind of occult group, how the hell was my mum involved with him? She hates anything to do with magic, or weird stuff."

I loved the adoration in my vampire's eyes.

"Oh, sweetheart. She hates anything to do with magic, or *weird stuff* or anything that doesn't fit in to her brainwashed idea of *normal* and *holy*, but she definitely didn't hate your father. She fell in love with him, after all. She was devoted to him, just as he was to her. Love defies reason. Unfortunately, hate can dissolve it all."

I felt a lump in my throat. I'd always figured he was a nobody who'd cast her aside.

"It wasn't like that," Hans said, and ran a thumb down my cheek. "Your father didn't up and leave. Your mother turned her back on love, and on him, but that was because she had to. She wasn't given the choice."

"And my father let her, did he? He just walked away?"

"Your father didn't have any choice without waging a war. He wasn't the man he is now. He was a lot younger."

"Why didn't he have a choice? And what war?"

I was reeling so bad my heart was pounding. Another spin of unknown memories swirling around. I'd expected tonight to be a grand, mystical build-up to Hans giving me eternal commitment, not another slammer of revelations about my past, with an erotic kink on the side to go along with it.

Holy shit, what the fuck was happening to me? Maybe I should expect this from now on. Bombshells of revelations. Things I didn't know jumping out from the shadows wherever I looked.

Hans took my hands and gripped them tight, pulling me back to him.

"It will be all right. This is another part of your journey back to yourself."

I didn't care about that, though.

"Why didn't my father stay around?" I asked again. "What is the war you're talking about? Who the hell would want to fuck him off and push him away if he's all so good and brilliant?"

Hans' eyes were fierce and cold. I got shivers at the anger in them, but it wasn't directed at me.

His voice was full of venom when he answered me.

"Because of your fucking grandmother, Katherine. She's the biggest bitch of a witch I've ever known."

29

"Your grandmother turned her back on tradition before you were born," Hans told me, "but that didn't stop her using her skills. It never has done. She can deny them all she likes, but it makes no difference. She exploits them every day of her life."

"What skills?"

Hans was shaking his head as he spoke. His indignation obvious.

"She's a witch of the highest level, through and through. She's an expert mind reader and in tune with energies of all kinds, and believe me, she always takes advantage of them. She can put it down to *common sense* and *intuition* all she likes, but she fools no one. She knows far more than she should about everyone she meets. She's the epitome of *holier than thou*, in godawful form. It's tragic. Truly."

I thought of Grandma, and the way she glared at me when I was growing up, always whispering in Mum's ear and cussing me for being a *stupid girl*. She was judgmental and scathing, I'd always known that.

I was scared of her, like so many people were. She was a gossiper of *secrets* and seemed to know everything about everyone, whispering and sneering whenever she passed them in the street.

Georgina White is a slut whore who's been sleeping with David Lewis and Raymond Jones at the same time. Phillip Taylor is cheating everyone in the community with his fake car deals and worthless warranties. Penny

MacGregor is having lustful thoughts about Karen's husband, and he's fantasising about her.

Evil!

Disgusting!

Sinners!

I'd put her down as being in touch with everyone in a tiny village community, but maybe it was more than that.

"It's definitely more than that," Hans said. "She knows everything and uses it to her own self-inflated advantage. Her ego blew to sky high proportions from when she was tiny. She used her talents for manipulating the other children in the school playground, lording herself over them, and then she carried on. She calls it *Godly* and *knowing sinners*, I call it being cunning and self-important. Being a bully."

He was so angry as he spoke about her. *Ashamed.*

"Yes, I'm ashamed," he said. "She was from such a decent background of people using their talents and empathy for goodwill, but she dismissed them as belonging to the dark side, whereas she's the one who embraced the sins."

"What sins?"

He counted on his fingers. "Pride, greed, wrath, and envy. She hasn't done quite so well on sloth, lust or gluttony, admittedly, but there is still time."

"Grandma's a nasty cow, then. I always knew that much. But what has that got to do with my father?"

"Your mother fell in love with him," Hans said. "He was visiting Garway for the masonic traditions, and she saw him up on Garway hill. There was an instant connection. The kind that sweeps people off their feet, as you well know."

"Fated mates, but mortals?"

"Yes. Soulmates. The same thing, without the length of time of the undead. He knew who she was at heart. That's the woman he fell in love with."

"And they truly loved each other?"

He nodded. "For a short while, at least. It would have lasted an awful lot longer without the bitch of the Blakeleys cursing them from the off."

I could hardly imagine my mum being with anyone. The idea of her being in love with an occultist just didn't fit my idea of the puzzle.

"Your mother didn't want to fall in love with your father," Hans said. "Your grandmother has been in control of her since the day she pushed her from her womb, just as she likes to be in control of everything."

That made sense to me. Grandma was always waiting in the wings to whisper her opinions to Mum. And Mum would agree with her, always singing from the same hymn book.

"Yes," Hans continued. "Because that's how your grandmother wanted it. And your mother allowed it, until your father came along."

I felt a horrible rush of resentment at the thought of my father being so perfect when he hadn't been a part of my life.

"How come he left us if he's such an incredible *occultist*? Wouldn't he just tell Grandma to fuck off and take Mum away from her?"

"And then would come the war," Hans said. "The war of spirit, mind and body. And ultimate sacrifice. Your father wasn't as confident then. He wasn't as capable."

"I don't understand…"

"It's a sad one to understand, little one. People wage wars inside themselves all the time, it's a battle we all continually face. But your mother was a sensitive one, easily influenced by the grip of the woman who raised her. She's been on the losing side of the battle from the start. And the same would have been true of your father."

"She was in love with him, though," I countered. "Wouldn't that have been enough to fight any battle? I'd fight any battle for you."

"Another beautiful sentiment." Hans raised my hand and kissed it. "But your mother was already firmly in the grip of her influence. Your mother had *sinned* by then, by having sex with your father, and your grandmother told her so constantly. She believed you'd be born cursed and hellish, possessed by demons, and when you arrived as a tiny little child it was clear you had *gifts of the Devil,* as your grandmother called them. They could see the magic in your pretty blue eyes."

I remembered the way she'd judged me and told me off for everything I did. Every little fantasy I played out or story I made up. She'd tell me I was a *bad little girl.*

Mum had watched. Mum had listened. Mum had believed her, and agreed with her, and told me I was a stupid, bad little girl along with her.

But maybe Mum had been afraid to show that true side of herself her whole life, and scared for me to show it too?

"Your father tried to reason with your grandmother and keep it civil once he knew for certain your mum was expecting a baby," Hans said. "But he saw the heartbreak as your mother nursed you in her womb, praying she wasn't carrying a demon child. Standing up to your grandmother would have waged a war beyond all measure. She knew every one of his secrets. She knew about his traditions and connections with the occult, and she would have used them against him. She would have turned faction members against faction members, and stirred up lies and disgusting rumours, and your mother would have been at the heart of it, pulled in all directions and tearing her soul apart."

I flinched at the thought and Hans sighed.

"And she would have been tearing your soul apart along with it. Your grandmother would never have let your father take custody of you."

"Take custody of me?"

"Yes. Because that's what it would have come to. She'd have destroyed your mother's life for the sake of fighting your *demon* father."

"But how could she have taken custody of me? Why would she need to?"

Hans didn't answer me.

It all sounded so harsh and so tragic, like everything else in my family line. An instinctive lump of tears sprung up in my throat. I tried to imagine him. My father. I wondered what he would look like, sound like, *be* like. Would I like him? Was he a great man, like Hans said he was?

"Your father was great enough that your mother slept with him out of wedlock, because that's what her heart urged her to do," Hans said. "Despite your grandmother's influence."

I took a big slug of my merlot.

"Why did he let her push him away? I just don't get it. He loved her, she loved him. They had me! Wasn't that enough? What could have stood in their way apart from Grandma being a manipulative, callous bitch to them?"

"This isn't my place to say," Hans said, but I shook my head.

"Don't fob me off! What was he so afraid of? What could she have used against him that was so powerful? And what could she have used against Mum?!"

Hans got to his feet, pacing up and down and rubbing his temples.

"Your steak is getting cold," he said.

I pushed my plate away. "I don't want fucking steak, Hans. I want answers. What could the old bitch have used against my mother? Tell me!"

"Damnit," he said, glaring at me. "I shouldn't be the one doing this."

My voice got louder. "You need to! I need to know!"

"Fucking hell," Hans said, and cursed under his breath. "I have Edwin to thank for this lovely exchange, and putting you through another round of soul-battering."

"Tell me," I insisted. "Seriously, I've been *soul-battered* plenty enough. Another round of *what the fuck* isn't going to break me now."

He didn't look so sure. It gave me a fresh set of fucking shivers, and I felt myself tuning in to him.

What did my mother do? What could Grandma hold against her? What could she hold over my father?

Hans shook his head. "Stop."

But why should I stop? This was my family line, and my history, and the secrets of my past. *I* was a witch, and a psychic and a damn ghost whisperer from a long line of the same. My mother was a witch, under the thumb of my grandmother who was denying being one, and my father was an occultist wizard of wizards or some crazy shit, and I was spinning in all directions, trying to make fucking sense of it.

So I would do.

I would make sense of it.

I summoned all my strength and counted on all the skills I had in my subconscious, and I stared Hans right in the eye.

"Stop," he said again, his stare fierce.

"No," I said. "I won't stop. I want the answers. I won't be like my mother anymore and back down whenever I'm told to. I'm done with that shit."

"Fine, yes, that's all very well," Hans said. "But it's not *me* who should be giving you the answers. I'm not the one who's been waiting to share them for decades, sweetheart."

I must have looked puzzled.

"Who is, then? My father? Are you going to call him up and invite him over? *Hey, fancy a meet up with the daughter who didn't even know your name until a few minutes ago?*"

"Don't be sarcastic," my lover said, but there was a hint of affection in it. "You're really growing stronger, aren't you? It's lovely to see."

"I'm growing stronger thanks to you, Hans. Don't stop now. Tell me the truth."

"The truth," he said, resting his hands on the table, his eyes looking into my soul, "sometimes the truth can be too much to bear."

"Fuck that," I said, "just tell me."

He sighed. "Very well..."

I felt so self-assured and ready for it, but holy fuck, I wasn't.

"Your mother is a murderer," he said. "Or so your grandmother would have her believe."

My mouth dropped open.

"Just, what?! What the fuck? My mother is a *murderer*? No. Just NO."

"It's true, Katherine," Hans said. "The grand family showdown around your birth left someone else very much in the dirt. Literally."

"Who?!"

Hans offered me a hand. "Come. Let me show you. Visions speak louder than words."

My thoughts were rattling. *My mother was a murderer? How the hell could that be?*

I stepped along with Hans, following him out into the grand hallway and through a door at the side. We went through a long corridor, and he opened another door, and another to follow. We climbed down a set of stairs, and turned off into another. It was as though we were in a maze, getting dustier and mustier, heading down and down, until we were in a cellar.

Hans flicked on a low glowing light and pulled a lantern down from the shelf. He looked at the wick and the flame lit right up.

"Here we go," he said, and opened a heavy, battered door to reveal a dark tunnel. "This is the way to the church tomb. Even now, the archaeologists haven't been able to find it. It's hidden deep under the depths of the Garway spring."

My heart pounded as I stepped into the tunnel to join him. I remembered his tale of being stuck in the tomb when poor Mary was drowned up above him.

We had quite a long trek through the damp depths of the passageway before another bolted door appeared before us. It echoed when Hans opened it, and I leapt back as the glow of the lantern lit up the outlines of Knights Templar tombs. So many grand graves, covered in cobwebs. He pointed to one in the far corner, then gestured me along with him.

"This one was mine."

It looked so cold in there as he shunted the top stone to the side, even though it was lined with purple silk.

"You slept in here?"

"Yes. For a very long time. Until I could risk being at Edwin's. People were very suspicious."

It didn't matter how in awe I was of the surroundings and the snapshot of Hans' heritage – I couldn't let him distract me. He knew it.

"I'm coming to the truth of your past," he told me. "Don't worry."

He guided me to the opposite side of the chamber, and there was yet another door and another tunnel, but this one had tiny muddy steps leading upwards, not downwards. Sharp and steep.

"Be careful not to slip," Hans said, keeping a firm grip on my hand as he led the way.

All the years I'd been a girl spending time around Garway church felt like they meant nothing as we ascended. I didn't know this place at all.

But it wasn't the church itself we climbed up into via the staircase, it was the tower. Disused and abandoned, and now nothing more than a spectacle of times gone by.

Hans moved to the side so I could embrace the location as the cold night wind hit us. I could feel the open sky up above.

"Carry on," he told me. "There's someone up here you need to speak to."

"Up here? On the turrets of the tower in the middle of the night? Are you serious?"

He tipped my face to his and landed a kiss on my lips.

"Yes. They've been here for years. A permanent feature since you were just a tiny baby in your mother's arms."

I got a prickle of otherworldly senses, like I had done seeing George and Margaret appearing at Regency.

"A ghost?" I asked.

Hans nodded. "Yes, a ghost."

A round of palpitations hit me as I walked up the stone steps ahead of Hans. The stairs were broken, and crumbling. Mossy underfoot.

I felt someone's presence ahead of us as we reached the top. I heard them breathing before they came into view, and when I saw a man sitting there, lonely, I got a flood of sympathy. And recognition. Love.

But Hans couldn't see him. He looked around blankly.

"He's here, yes?" my lover asked me.

"There's a man here, yeah."

With that the man stared over at me. He was broken looking, with small, pained eyes and an expression of pure shock as he saw me there.

Hans stood next to me, still looking around for signs of the invisible person.

"He's over here," I said, pointing to the figure.

Hans turned to face the ghost.

"Ah, excellent," he said. "Katherine, meet your grandfather. And Joseph, hello to you. Your introduction has been long overdue."

30

"Katherine?" the ghost asked with a trembling voice, peering through the darkness. "Is that really you? My God, you've grown!"

He grew in colour as he got up and walked towards me, bathed in the moonlight. His ghostly presence was cold as he wrapped me in his arms, but his soul wasn't. I could hear his heart singing loud. I held him back as tight as I could.

My emotions came unbidden. My heart singing as loudly as his.

"What happened to you?" I asked, my thoughts whirring back through old snippets of unanswered questions from when I was a little girl.

What happened to Grandad, Grandma?
An accident.
What kind of accident?
He fell.
Fell from where?
From where the Devil wanted him to fall from...

I shuddered at the memory of her vicious face.

"She doesn't mean bad, my Rhona," my grandfather whispered. "She may seem like she does, but she doesn't."

I could see the love he had for her shining in his eyes.

"What happened to you?" I asked again. "Hans said that Mum... he said she..."

I had to take a breath.

"Did she murder you, Grandad? Did Mum murder you?"

My ghostly grandad pulled back from me, looked at me with sadness in his eyes. "She didn't mean to. Lord above, she really didn't. And believe me, it wasn't that simple."

I couldn't understand it.

"How did she do it, then? How did it happen?"

He beckoned me over to the side of the tower. The ground looked miles away, gravestones like little rocks in the grass.

"I fell, from here."

"She pushed you?"

"No, no!" he said, and clutched my hand in his cold fingers. "I was searching for her and your grandma. They'd been arguing for hours before your mother stormed out of the house, and I knew Rhona would be going crazy, threatening all sorts if your mother left with Thomas. She was convinced he was the Devil, and convinced you were the Devil's daughter, but I promise you, she truly believed you could be saved."

He sighed a sad sigh.

"She does love you, Katherine. Your grandma loves you very much, despite how she shows it."

It had never felt like it. She never seemed to think I could be *saved* of whatever madness she thought I was blessed with.

Hans must have seen my expression, talking to the man who was invisible to him.

"Listen to whatever he's telling you," he said. "He knows the true soul of everyone involved."

"I needed to see the grounds because I knew they were here somewhere," Grandad carried on. "It was dark when I got here, and I couldn't see them. I could hear them rowing but I couldn't see where they were."

He clutched his hands together, shaking his head in frustration.

"Their voices were going crazy, screaming, and I was shouting for them, but they didn't listen, and I thought it would come to serious blows. I really did. Otherwise I wouldn't have been such a fool and climbed up here. I was just trying to bloody see them. To stop them."

I could picture Grandma's cold face telling me he fell, and was there a hint of something else in her eyes I'd never noticed before?

Pain?

Grandad pointed over to the far side of the grounds, in the corner by one of the old graves.

"They were over there, arguing. Your mother was packed and ready to go, and you were crying in her arms. She was screeching, saying she was leaving, and she didn't care if Thomas was the Devil or not, she was going anyway. Rhona couldn't take it. She said she didn't raise your mother to be like that, and I was so angry with myself for not stepping in sooner, but Rhona was Rhona. Trying to argue with her is like raising a red rag to a bull."

I knew that well enough.

He waited a few moments before he continued. Hearing him speak was like hearing a confession. He seemed so relieved to be telling the story.

"I waved at them from here, trying to get their attention. I shouted for them to stop fighting, but they didn't hear me, they were too busy screaming at each other. I'd have gone down there if I could and tried to scream some sense into them myself, but I didn't have time. It was all happening so bloody fast. Thomas was on his way to get you and Serena, and Rhona went into a rage."

I could imagine that, too. I knew Grandma's rage when she lost her temper.

Grandad carried on.

"I yelled as loud as I could when she tried to tear you from your mother's arms, but she didn't mean harm, not really. She believed she was trying to protect you and Serena from the Devil. I just should've stepped in sooner... Damn it. DAMN IT!"

I braced myself. "How did you fall, Grandad?"

He shrugged. "I was leaning out, trying to get their attention, waving my arms around like a bloody madman, and your mother exploded and lost her temper along with your grandma. But with your mother it was much stronger, desperate. And the power... oh my life, the power. It all came out of her in one huge blast that shook the ground. I mean it, Katherine. It shook the earth of this whole churchyard," he told me. "The tower rumbled, and I was leaning out from the turrets like a fool, and your mother was screaming in the middle of the night. I should have backed off... I should've..."

I placed my hand on his shoulder.

"It's not your fault, Grandad."

"No," he said. "But it's not your mother's either. She didn't know what she was doing with her powers. Rhona never gave her the chance, and I can see that now."

He laughed a little.

"Hindsight is a great thing to have when you haven't got anything left to focus on. I've had a lot of time to think about it."

I turned around to see Hans looking at me. He looked so sad for both of us, even though he could only hear my side of the conversation.

"Your mother didn't mean it," Grandad told me again. "She's a lovely girl. Sorry, *woman* now. I see her here often, alongside Rhona, and I saw you too. I had to stay hidden, of course. Your grandma would have torn you apart if she knew you could see me. And me along with you, most likely. She's definitely a fiery one, my Rhona."

"How come you've been stuck up here on your own?" I asked him.

"Don't know quite how," he said. "Suddenly I was staring down at myself as your mother and grandma came rushing over. Your mother was screaming, and you were crying, and Rhona was bellowing, and I was stuck up here, not knowing quite what to make of it."

He pointed to the ground.

"I was down there, flat on my back. Glad I wasn't closer. I'd have looked a right bloody mess, I'm sure."

I could see his thoughts in my mind. I saw my mum and grandma down at the foot of the tower through his vision, shaking my grandad's dead body as they tried to wake him. I saw myself screaming in Mum's arms.

And then I saw my father's car pull up at the gateway at just gone midnight.

I saw his powerful figure, even in the moonlight. I watched him run from the gate towards the screams to see Grandad's dead body on the floor.

I sucked in a breath as the images grew stronger. I didn't want to see them, but I couldn't push them away.

"Don't try to hold back from whatever hits you," Hans told me, breaking into my thoughts from the other side of the tower. "Your soul won't listen."

I kept tuned in to the memories.

Grandma had got up and met Thomas – my father – on the path. She'd shoved him out of the way before he could reach the carnage, while Mum was still wailing in shock along with me. I saw Grandma's hate in her eyes as though I was there next to them. I saw the way she jabbed a finger at his chest while Mum was oblivious to everything going on around her.

Leave now, and I'll make sure Serena doesn't know the truth, my grandma had told him. *Otherwise, I swear to the Lord Almighty, I'll make sure she knows she's a murdering sinner who killed her own father with her witchcraft, and I'll let her know she deserves to meet the Devil in Hell.*

Mum would have listened.

My father had known it.

Mum would have thrown herself off the turrets to make amends.

"You won't be able to hide the truth for ever, Rhona," my father had said to her, but she was smug. She knew her own power. Not power over my father – Thomas – but over her daughter. Over her own flesh and blood.

"I won't NEED to hide the truth for ever," she said. "Serena deserves to die for what she's done, using her evil sinning witchcraft to kill her own father, and that's what she'll do. She'll kill herself by her own hand, and so she should. She's a murderer now."

"This is YOUR fault, Rhona, not Serena's. Let me get to her."

He'd gone to push past her, but she'd gripped his arms in bitter fingers.

"You know I'm right, you sinning demon," she'd hissed at him. "And then what will happen to her? What will happen to your daughter? Will she grow up knowing her mother killed herself as a murderer because of you, a demon of a sinner?"

He'd paused. Thinking. He'd watched his love crying, with a broken heart.

Why was Grandma such an evil witch to him, and to Mum, and to me?

I realised I'd spoken that question out loud when Grandad answered me.

"She was grieving, too," he said, as though he was trying to reason with my memories. "She was lost herself, she just didn't want to be. She was as upset as Serena was, I swear it. And after that she was even worse. She wanted to blame your mother because she couldn't face blaming herself."

It all felt like one horrible explosion of grief and carnage. Repressed power and truth. I felt sick.

"So, my father left to save my mother from her own self-hatred," I said aloud. "Is that what happened?"

It was Hans who replied.

"Yes, that's what happened. It was a sacrifice. It was the ultimate bargaining tool your grandmother could ever have, and she'd have used it. Plus, your mother would never have left with Thomas while your grandmother was grieving. Rhona would have been too selfish to let her go."

The ghost of my grandfather spun to face Hans, and he was angry.

"Tell him not to think about my wife that way! He doesn't know Rhona like I do. He never did!"

I cleared my throat before I spoke to Hans.

"Grandad says you don't know my grandma. He says she doesn't mean it."

"That doesn't excuse the inexcusable. It doesn't cleanse the *sins* as your grandmother likes to call them."

"That's why she goes to church every bloody weekend!" Grandad said. "I see how upset she is under the surface, even if you don't. She may gripe and moan like she always did, but she's carrying her own demons, just like we all are. She just can't stand the thought of facing them."

"What's he saying now?" Hans asked, and I repeated Grandad's words to him.

"Hmm. Maybe he's right, or maybe she doesn't want to face them because she's a nasty bitch who can't break her own ego. I can't say I'm all that convinced she's some little saint under the surface, if I'm honest."

"He doesn't need to be convinced," Grandad said. "She's my wife, not his, and she's your grandmother, not just some woman he can moan and whine about."

There was something so simplistically honourable in the way my grandad spoke. I wished he hadn't died when I was just a baby, because who knows… who knows how different life could have been for me. For all of us…

"The past is the past," Hans said. "Understanding it can help us make sense of ourselves and our destinies, yes, but we can only live the future through the present."

I didn't try to interpret his phrases through rational thought, just let them sink into me. I also didn't give a shit about the ins and outs of sinners, and witchcraft, and who'd done what to who. Not right then. Not with my long lost grandfather in front of me. I wanted to sit with him. Talk with him. Get to know him, even just a little.

"Yes, of course," Hans said, and approached me with open arms. "Take your time, little one. Enjoy some space with your grandfather and then do what you will. I'll be waiting at Edwin's. Send me a thought and I'll come for you."

"Thanks," I said and hugged him. "I know this was hard for you to do – to bring me here – and this must be shit, and this whole thing must be a crazy whirlwind, but thank you. For everything. Without you I'd be nothing. Just a girl running away from all this without a clue, trying to live a life I was never supposed to be living."

"*This* is the life you should be living," he said and laid a kiss on my forehead. "And you are more than welcome, little one. You always will be. From now on I'm not going to be a figure in the shadows. I'm going to be a part of your world."

I chanced a bit of humour.

"I can't wait to introduce you to the family. That'll be a fun one."

Hans laughed. "Hopefully nobody will fall off a turret to their death when they kick off next time around. At least I wouldn't die from a fall. I'm too immortal for that."

"Neither will I when I'm a vampire. Better hurry up and turn me into one, hadn't you? And if you even think of saying *patience*."

Hans grinned and stroked my face.

"Send me a thought when you're ready."

"Thank you."

There was going to be so much to do, and learn, and think about. My mother and grandmother, and how I was going to approach them about this. If at all. Trying to find out how much they knew about our family history, or if they'd even care.

If they could care about me when they knew the truth of it. That I really was a witch, a psychic and a *sinner*. Whether they'd ever accept Hans.

And what about my father? Would I ever get to meet him?

But now wasn't the time for it. Now was the time for my grandad.

I bid my vampire lover farewell for a short while, looking at him with love and pride as he left us, and then I sat down with the man I'd never had the chance to know.

One of them.

He told me about Orcop and growing up in this small village, and what a feisty girl my grandmother was. Stubborn and proud, but a tender soul in the heart of her, even if nobody could see it.

He shared stories about their life that made me laugh, and tales about my mother that had me grinning, and slowly he was coming back to life again. *As a ghost.* His pain was replaced with happiness as his memories returned in colour.

And then, when the dawn started to break, I knew it was time for him to go.

I felt heartbroken.

"I've never climbed down these steps," he admitted as he rose to his feet, indicating the spiral of steps that led to the ground below. "I've always been waiting."

"For what?" I asked.

He gave me a grin and ruffled my hair. "For someone to walk down with me, I guess. I always hoped it would be you. Give your vampire love my thanks, will you? It's time for me to step into the light. My time is done. Good timing, isn't it? Halloween morning, when the veils are the thinnest of them all. Anyone would think it was fated. Ha. I guess they'd be right."

Fated or Hans' careful planning.

I welled up as we made our way down the steps, the morning dawn giving a mist to the air.

"You're really going, aren't you?" I asked him.

"Yes," he said. "Now I've said my piece, it's time. I'm sick of this place, to be honest. I'll be waiting for your grandma on the other side. She'll be getting an earful, believe me, but no doubt I'll be getting one in return."

I didn't want to broach the obvious, but he did it for me.

"And as for you, sweetpea, I have no idea when I'll be seeing you next. Not now you're giving yourself to a vampire."

It felt shit, but I nodded.

"Hopefully quite a long time." I managed to smile. "I don't want to be burnt to cinders anytime soon."

He looked up at the breaking sun when we reached the bottom of the tower.

"Enjoy this dawn. You won't get to see many more of them."

Or any at all.

He was right. I was going to savour every second.

"Bye bye, then, my little kiddo," Grandad said, with another joyous bit of simplicity. I saw his full outfit in the light. His loose farmer trousers and the old green shirt he had on. He was in welly boots, and looked like he was off to work for the morning.

"Goodbye, Grandad," I said, and gave him a hug. "It was amazing to see you."

"You too, sweetpea. You too."

I was rooted to the spot as he walked away. His outline faded with every step, but he looked back at me just in time to raise his hand in a wave.

"Say hello to your mother and grandmother for me, And tell them both that I love them. I miss Rhona's cooking, even now. Though her omelettes always tasted of rotten eggs."

I laughed along with him.

"Don't worry, Grandad. I will."

I was still smiling as he disappeared from view, a tear running down my cheek as he stepped into the light.

I didn't realise I was crying until I looked up at the sun to take in the beautiful sunrise, savouring the pinks and reds of the heavens.

Then I thought of Hans. He couldn't come out here for me. I'd have to go back up the tower and into the tunnel. I turned to leave when his voice came into my mind…

No need for that, little one. The car is already at the gate for you, he told me, and I looked up. Sure enough, there was a car waiting.

I walked on over with my arms tight around myself, in a distant state between dreaming and waking, midway between pleasure and pain.

Love and loss, grief, and anger, and hate. And forgiveness, and joy and hope.

Too many feelings to balance all at once, so I didn't even attempt it.

I got into the car with a *hello* to the driver, and then I sank into the back seat, preparing for the ride. We were on the way when I got the urge to change direction.

I leant forward between the seats.

"Not back to the manor yet, please. I need to go home… to my mum's house."

31

I'll be back soon, my thoughts whispered to Hans. *I just have business to take care of first.*

His reply came straight into my head.

I'll be right here waiting. Just be careful to mind your grandma. She's not going to be a happy witch. And if you need me to help you–

I shook my head in my mind. *Thanks, but no.* This was something I needed to do for myself.

It felt like I'd been gone years not months when the car arrived at Orcop. We crossed Garren brook and before I knew it I was in Lyston Lane, pulling up outside Mum's place as the sun rose over the hill.

"Could you wait for me here, please?" I asked the driver.

"Of course, ma'am. I'll wait as long as you need."

The little red brick house seemed different. I could see the cloud of desperation for *holy* swirling inside like a heavy dark mist as I walked up the garden path.

I could feel it, too – a weight on the shoulders.

Mum's car was in the driveway, and I saw the curtains twitch upstairs. I knew it was Grandma peering out with suspicious eyes. I knew they were both in there. I felt it.

It seemed Mum didn't know it was me appearing on the doorstep, though. She jumped back in shock when she opened the door to find me there on the porch. Her eyes widened.

"Katherine! What are you doing back home?"

She looked smaller than I remembered, in her thick white dressing gown with her hair tied up on her head. I hadn't realised before just how much white my mother wore. *Trying to dress like an angel to please my grandmother.*

Grandma appeared behind her, wrapping her old grey dressing gown around herself as she came down the stairs, and Hans was right. She was a lot more attuned to her skills than Mum was. I could see it in her eyes as she glared at me.

"Ah," she said, stepping up behind Mum with her hands on her hips. "London life has been suiting you. Cavorting with sinners in the city."

I didn't rise to the bait, just kept my eyes on Mum.

"Can I come in?"

Mum stepped aside. "Of course you can. Have you had breakfast yet? Do you want some jam on toast? I have your favourite strawberry."

I brushed past Grandma on my way, but for once in my life I was immune to her judgmental sneers. My self-doubt had shrivelled away.

"I'm not hungry, thanks," I told Mum as I joined her in the kitchen.

I looked around the place as she put the kettle on, remembering all the times I'd been getting my biscuits from the cupboards late at night and pouring milk on my cereals before school.

"Why are you back?" Mum asked as she got the mugs out. "Is your bar job doing ok? It's great to see you."

It hurt a little to see how happy she was. I'd written her off as nothing but Grandma's accomplice, judging me just as much as Grandma did. But Mum was a puppet on Grandma's strings, strung up in her web of control.

"Answer your mother," Grandma said with venom. "Why *are* you back here? Aren't you too busy cavorting with dirty men?"

"I haven't been cavorting with dirty men," I replied, with no lowering of my head or pounding of my heart.

"Don't lie, Katherine," she said. "I know you have."

I shrugged like her words meant nothing as Mum offered me my tea with trembling hands.

"I've been with a lovely man called Hans, actually," I said. "I think you know him, don't you? He's been around Garway church quite a lot over the years. It was lovely to meet him. Finally."

"Hans?" Mum asked, then looked over at Grandma. "Who is Hans?"

Grandma knew who he was, it was obvious. She knew he was a *sinner*, yes. But did she know he was a vampire?

She answered that with a smug nod of her head.

"Don't worry, *little one*. I know bloodsuckers exist. They are demons. Hans isn't a *man*. He's a monster from Hell."

I took a sip of tea without rising to it, managing to keep calm. It was tempting to break out and curse and battle, but I wouldn't lower myself. There would be no shouting or screaming from me. It would frustrate her so much more if her nastiness didn't touch me.

"Bloodsuckers?" Mum raised her eyebrows. "Have you met demons, Katherine?! What the hell have you been doing?"

"This *little one* has been playing filthy games with dirty sinners," Grandma told her, but I took another sip of my tea and shrugged.

"You can say whatever you like, Grandma, but Hans isn't a dirty sinner. He's the opposite."

"All vampires are dirty sinners, Katherine."

Mum held her hands up, shocked.

"Hans is a vampire?! KATHERINE! What on earth are you doing messing around with vampires? Have you lost your mind?!"

It seemed that neither Mum or Grandma were quite so oblivious to the truths of my *imagination* as they had made out to be.

Mum dashed past me to stare out through the window, scoping out for other visitors along with me, no doubt afraid to see *dirty sinners* on the driveway. She let out a shriek when she saw the blacked-out limo, visible through the garden hedge.

"Is he in there?! My God! Is there a vampire in there?"

"The demon won't be out there," Grandma scoffed. "How could he be? He's confined to the darkness, right where he should be."

"No, he's not out there," I said. "That's a regular human driver waiting for me, not Hans, and definitely not a demon from Hell."

I couldn't be doing with any bullshit debating about vampires, or how much of a filthy sinner Hans was, or what I had or hadn't been doing down in London. I wanted to lay my cards on the table, and watch the lies face the light.

"But *I'm* not a regular human, am I? I'm a witch, and I know it," I said to both of them. "Apparently I'm a psychic and a ghost whisperer too. And my father, Thomas, is an occultist, isn't he?"

They both sucked in breaths.

"You could have just said so," I said, holding onto my calm as best as I could. "It would have been better than calling me *stupid* and telling me I was delusional every day of my life."

"Why in God's name would we do that?" Grandma said, and I could feel the anger in her as the kitchen units started shaking all around us. "Why would we want to lose you to Hell?!" she yelled and the cupboard door by her head flew open.

I addressed her with a steady tone, my eyes firm on hers.

"You already pushed me into Hell every day you punished me for being myself."

"Being yourself? A puppet of the devil? The good Lord Jesus will be weeping for you, stupid girl."

"Jesus can weep for me all he likes, but I think he's weeping for you more, Grandma. And he's definitely weeping for Mum, isn't he? You made sure of that."

"Jesus isn't weeping for me," Mum said, but there was a flash of fear in her eyes. "Why would he be? I'm not a sinner."

"No," I replied. "You're not. It's just a shame Grandma made you feel like one when you were young enough to believe her. And it's a shame you made me feel like one along with her."

Mum's eyes were like saucers, and I didn't blame her for the outburst when it came out loud.

"This is crazy! Are you on drugs or something?!"

She looked at Grandma, expecting her to step into the situation, just as she always had done. But Grandma didn't. Not this time. She read the strength in my stance and the pure truth in my soul, and for once in all the time I'd known her, she looked unsteady.

"Mum!" my mother pushed, gesturing at me. "Is Katherine on drugs? Is she lost to the Devil?"

Grandma was silent, staring at me as I stared back. She was raging, challenged, but I wasn't. I felt a lightness to my soul that raised me high, and it made sense.

She had no power over me anymore. Grandma's spite and judgement had no hold over my life.

"Katherine is well and truly lost to the Devil," Grandma whispered. "She needs to leave now, Serena. She's finished."

She turned her back as my mother looked on.

"But wait... wait! Surely she can't be damned after just a few months?"

"She's damned," Grandma said, already on the way into the hall. "See her out, Serena. She doesn't belong here anymore."

We'd see about that.

Time to play my first Ace card.

"Grandad says hello, Grandma."

She spun in an instant, eyes like hot coals. "Sorry? Excuse me? What the hell did you just say?"

"Grandad says hello," I repeated. "I've been up on the tower turrets with him through the night, chatting about his life. And his death. He says he loves you, by the way. He misses your cooking, but not your rotten egg omelettes."

"Your grandfather wouldn't be on the tower turrets," she hissed. "He's gone to the Lord."

"He has now," I told her. "But he's been waiting an awfully long time to leave. He's seen you trying to make up for your lies. He's been watching you attend church every weekend since he fell, trying to tell yourself that lighting a candle makes you a saint, when it doesn't."

Mum was white-faced, bracing herself against the sink. It was obvious I'd touched a guilty nerve at the mention of my grandad.

She truly was more of a fragile woman than I'd ever realised. I got a flood of sympathy I'd never expected to be feeling.

"It wasn't your fault, Mum," I said. "Grandad told me that himself. Grandma can hint at it all she likes, and tell you the world is made up of sinners who need to atone for their sins, but she's talking bullshit. If anyone's committed any sins in this house, it's her."

Mum shook her head. "Stop it! I don't know what you're talking about."

Grandma's eyes were simmering when they locked onto mine. It was a challenge. I felt her vicious soul squaring up to mine. But mine would win. I was sure of that now. She could spin the house up into the sky like the wicked witch of the west, but it wouldn't make any difference, I'd still be secure in my heart, ready to come out unscathed.

"Don't do this to your mother, it's vile," Grandma said, and I laughed, still holding my mug of tea.

"Don't do *what* to Mum? Don't tell her that you threatened to destroy her life unless my father walked away from Garway church that night? That you told my father she'd kill herself from the guilt of killing Grandad if he didn't drive away and leave us alone?"

"This is ridiculous!" Grandma yelled, but I kept going.

"How about I don't tell Mum you've been a vindictive witch reading into everyone's secrets and using them to spread hate? How about I don't tell her that Grandad sends his love and assures her she wasn't to blame for his fall?"

"STOP!" Grandma screamed and every cupboard door flew open, the cutlery drawer shunted to the floor, spilling cutlery in a clatter. Mum jumped back, cowering.

I didn't even flinch, just smiled at Grandma.

"You're disgusting," she went on. "You're a delusional liar, beyond redemption!" She turned to Mum. "Tell her, Serena! Tell her to get on her way and out of our house!"

I felt genuinely sorry for my grandmother's hatred of everything. The crucifixes on the walls meant nothing. Her soul was dark and hidden in bitterness, and it was lashing out at me.

"Tell her!" she yelled. "Tell her to get out of here, Serena. She has no place here anymore!"

But Mum didn't say a word. She was still white-faced, braced against the kitchen sink, eyes like saucers, but she didn't tell me to leave.

"I mean it, Mum," I said. "Grandad says you did nothing wrong. He knows Grandma has been controlling you since you were a baby, and he regrets not trying harder to stop her scheming."

Grandma jabbed a finger at me with a *get out*, but Mum shook her head, dismissing her.

"Is Katherine telling the truth? Did you tell Thomas to leave that night? Remember, lying is a sin. Don't lie to me!"

Grandma didn't speak, just folded her arms.

"Is it true?" Mum asked again. "Did you use Dad's death to threaten Thomas into leaving me?"

"Thomas is a *sinner*," Grandma said. "I was doing it for you."

"Lying is a sin actually," I said. "If you want to preach the virtues, maybe you should start practicing them. You threatened my father away and used it to keep Mum where you wanted her. Admit it."

My poor mum was staring at Grandma in shock, eyes silently begging her to deny it.

"You sent Thomas away from us?" she asked again.

"Like I said," Grandma answered. "Thomas is a sinner. A servant of the Devil. I did what I needed to."

"So you sent him away from Garway church when he came to collect me?"

Grandma's arms were still folded. Her chin was high.

"Yes, I did. And I'd do it again, because people of magic are destined to Hell. Thomas and Katherine will both face the gates of the unholy, don't join them there, Serena. I didn't raise you for that."

"BULLSHIT!" Mum snapped. "THAT'S BULLSHIT! Thomas isn't destined for Hell, and neither is Katherine."

"Oh, they are," Grandma said. "And if you turn your back on our holy life, you will face the wrath of our Lord. You will finally be punished for what you did to your father that night."

Mum was quiet, and Grandma nodded.

"Oh, Serena. Stop pretending. You know your witchcraft powers threw your father to the ground. I've been trying to help you redeem yourself, and I thought it was working, but now this little sinner has shown back up, determined to drag you down with her." Grandma looked at me. "We should have turned our backs on you when you were born. You are made of your father's blood."

"Yes," I said. "And I'm made of Mum's too, and yours, and Grandad's. And all of our family members before me. If I'm a demon child, then surely we all are? Aren't you just a demon sinner as well?"

"I've had enough of this!" my grandmother raged. "Serena, tell this godawful little witch to GET OUT of our home!"

I didn't even look at Grandma. I looked at Mum.

"Do you want me to leave?" I asked her calmly. "I can leave if you want me to."

Mum didn't answer, torn in two.

"TELL HER TO GO!" Grandma screamed.

"I can go, Mum." I said. "If you can't love me for who I am, then I'll walk away right now. I'd rather be alone than be with people who try to stop me being myself."

"TELL HER TO GO!" Grandma yelled again, but my mother shook her head. She stood her ground.

"I don't want to tell Katherine to go. I want to know the truth!"

"You already know the truth, Mum," I said gently as Grandma seethed with rage. "You know who I am, and you knew my father for who he was, and you know who you are yourself, down deep inside. The only one denying the truth here is Grandma, and that's because she can't face her own lies."

I sounded much more wise and confident than I felt, but that was

Mary inside me. It was my ancient past holding me strong – a beacon of calm in the storm.

When Mum smiled I knew it was at the memory of Thomas, my father. I could read it in her.

"I can't believe it," she whispered. "I really thought he'd abandoned us…"

"He didn't abandon us," I said. "Grandma sent him away."

"BECAUSE HE IS A FUCKING SINNER!" Grandma raged, and her fury made the whole room rumble. "GET THE FUCK AWAY FROM HERE!"

I tried to ignore the shudders of the house around us, but when Mum looked over at my grandmother there was a whole other level to the tremors.

"You lied to me! You've been lying to me my whole life."

"FOR YOUR OWN SAKE!" Grandma yelled. "Don't let this evil little witch turn you away from God, Serena. Don't!"

The tremors kept rumbling. Louder.

"You lied…" Mum whispered. "I thought Thomas left us…"

Grandma screeched in rage.

"I SENT HIM AWAY TO SAVE YOU, AND I SHOWED MERCY ON YOU! BECAUSE YOU KILLED YOUR FUCKING FATHER!"

Holy hell, how the walls shook, but it wasn't just from Grandma's anger anymore, it was from Mum's too. The plates rattled on the shelves, cupboard doors flew open and banged shut, and it was like Grandad's vision of them from the tower. Both of them waging a war.

But I was right there next to them, in the same room, not screaming with waving arms from a turret in the distance.

"Don't let Grandma win," I said to Mum. "Because the greatest power you have is forgiveness. Don't battle with her demons. There's way more strength in making peace with yours."

It wasn't me speaking, it was Mary. It was my past. It was my heritage.

"Honestly, Mum," I said. "Don't let her win. Your spells are stronger than hers. Have faith in them. Have faith in *yourself*, like she should have had right from the start."

I was silent, daring to hope my words would make a difference and speak to her soul, and it worked. My God, it worked.

Mum looked at me, and she nodded. She took a deep breath and let it out slowly, and just like that, the tremors in the walls turned to stillness.

It was incredible. In one heartbeat the air of the house lightened in a heartbeat. Fresh, and bright, and new. *Cleansed of bullshit lies.*

I smiled at my grandmother. Her spell was finally broken, and she knew it.

"Mum has better control over her skills than you do, doesn't she?" I said. "You should be proud not ashamed."

"Curse you both to Hell and eternal damnation," my grandmother spat, and stormed out of kitchen, out through the front door and down the garden path.

"Don't worry," I told Mum. "She'll be back. She's nothing without you."

Mum's eyes filled with tears. "I'm so sorry, Katherine. For all of this. I'm truly, truly sorry."

I shook my head. "You don't need to be. I'm fine now."

"Maybe. But it's because the man called Hans saved you, isn't it? Not me. *I'm* the one who should have saved you. *I'm* your mother."

"Hans isn't a man," I said. "He's a vampire, just like Grandma said."

Mum laughed a teary laugh.

"And you know what? I don't care anymore. Please, just don't make the mistake I did. If Hans is the one you're in love with, do whatever it takes to be at his side and don't let anyone stand in your way."

"I won't, don't worry," I assured her.

She nodded. "Good. I only wish I'd had the chance to do the same."

Her words hit me in the gut. I wondered if she'd ever see my father again.

I hoped so.

At least the storm was passing now. My grandmother's ultimate spell was breaking apart, and Mum was breaking her chains. Thank God, I could be part of it.

I looked up at the clock on the kitchen wall. One daytime of sunlight left before I did whatever it took to be with my vampire lover for ever.

I was going to enjoy every second before my transition. I was going to spend my final hours of sunshine with my mother, asking her about my father, and for once, finally, I knew I was going to get the truth and not the lies.

Mum smiled, and I knew she could read my thoughts. She had the same gifts I did. She'd just been denying them to herself for years.

"I have *some* of the same gifts you have," she told me. "But a lot of yours are from your father's side. And yes, I'll tell you all about him. So how about we get you your jam on toast and have our breakfast out in the sun?"

"I'd love that, Mum," I said.

32

"You're really going to do this?" Mum asked me. "Hans is going to turn you into a vampire tonight?"

I told her all about him. From how we met in the Regency bar, to how he'd pursued me in my dreams across the cobblestones. I recalled all the memories that had come back to me about the times I'd seen him in the grounds of Garway church when I was younger.

I shared with her how strongly I'd fallen for him, and how incredible it felt to be by his side. His fated mate across the centuries, returning to be his lover. This time for ever.

She finally listened to me without telling me I was a *stupid girl*.

It was as though a light had been flicked on inside her head, revealing her own truth to herself. But that shouldn't have been much of a surprise to me, since I'd experienced the same thing for myself. It was just a shame she was a little bit older when the truth hit her.

So long after my father walked away...

I smiled at her, loving the closeness.

"Yeah, I'm going to become a vampire tonight, at least I hope so. Happy Halloween to me."

I was looking through the clothes in my wardrobe for something suitable to wear. I came across one of my old white dresses – a really pretty one with a bow around the waist and a lace overskirt. I hadn't worn it in years.

"Do you think it will still fit?" I asked Mum as I held it up to myself in front of the mirror.

She came over and took hold of the hem, running her thumb over the lace at the bottom.

"Yes, almost definitely. It's a good choice. Quite fitting for someone being turned into an immortal on Samhain."

My heart raced at her words. Spoken out loud, it all felt so real.

I still had no idea quite what was in store for the transition. Hans was keeping his thoughts to himself besides the instructions of *head back to Edwin's manor when your soul feels the calling.*

Standing there, in my old family bedroom as the sky turned to dusk, there was no doubt about it. My soul was beginning to crave Hans.

Badly.

It wasn't just his teeth in my throat, or in my breasts, or his cock buried deep, and not just his body next to mine. There was more to it than that. *Longing for his blood in my mouth. Longing to feel what it felt like to be a vampire.*

"Try it on," Mum said, pulling my attention back to the dress I was holding. "Let's see how it fits you."

I was so relieved when I tugged the dress on in the bathroom. It fit like a glove in all the right places, albeit a little bit tighter. Maybe Hans had already seen me in it a few years ago. Maybe it wouldn't surprise him in the slightest to see me returning to Edwin's all in white.

One thing was for sure though, Mum would never have seen any vampire bites before. I flinched as I caught sight of my reflection. The wounds on me were fierce and deep. Definitely beyond a bit of a concealer to hide them from view.

Her voice was light when she knocked at the bathroom door. She sounded almost excited for me.

"Well? Does it fit?"

"Yeah," I shouted back. "It fits well."

I knew the inevitable would follow.

"Come on, then. Show me."

Fuck. I pulled a face at my reflection as I gave my wounds another onceover. The neckline was low, and the sleeves were puffy but short, and it was obvious I'd been the victim of some serious bites. I'd totally understand if she freaked out up to the rafters at the sight.

I mean, it's one thing someone explaining how amazing it feels to have blood sucked out of you by a vampire, but another thing altogether seeing the marks on their skin.

But. Here goes nothing…

I stepped out of the bathroom, giving her a little curtsy on the landing.

She clasped a hand to her mouth, her eyes wide as she looked me up and down.

"I know, I know," I said. "They look bad, but they felt fine, I promise. Hans wouldn't hurt me. I mean he hurt me, but not hurt me *hurt* me, you know?"

"No," she said, and shrugged. "I don't know, but I'll take your word for it."

I stared at her in shock, because that was probably the greatest thing she'd ever said to me in my life.

She'd *take my word for it*.

There was so much sentiment in those few words and in the calm expression she showed me.

She'd trust me and my judgement, and trust me to know myself and my own needs, and trust me to be making the decisions I wanted to be making – which was so much more than I'd ever been allowed as a child here at home.

Mum could read my mind – of course she could.

"You're not a child anymore, Katherine. If anything, you should be judging me, not me judging you."

I smiled at her. "Shame Grandma doesn't feel the same."

The wicked witch of Lyston Lane hadn't returned yet. I almost laughed out loud at the thought of her in Garway church right now, still in her dressing gown, praying for the atonement of my sins at the place I'd be giving up my mortal life in, to the man she condemned as a *sinner*.

Mum shrugged. "Maybe she'll be the next one to get her wake up call. She might be a little more entrenched in delusion than I was, but there is still a spark of her true self underneath, I'm sure."

I smirked. "I don't know, but I'll take your word for it. How about that?"

"How about you take the same words for it from Grandad? Seems he had the same words for it, too."

I remembered the love in his eyes as he'd talked about Grandma. His Rhona. His wife.

"Yeah. He did. He thinks she's got a lovely soul under the surface."

"Maybe one day she'll show it. The people in the village will think she's lost her mind."

I laughed. "You'll have to give me updates on the local post office gossip. It's not as though I'll be able to call in there myself anymore."

The laughter eased off as we looked at each other, and with the resentment gone from Mum's eyes she looked much more familiar to me. As though she was different. *Seen through the lens of a family line gone by.*

"Night's coming soon," Mum said, and gestured to the sun lowering into dusk outside the window. "No more sunshine for you."

"It's ok," I replied, trying to stop the inevitable burst of nerves. "Hans is worth a lot more to me than daylight."

I kept my white dress on as I brushed my hair in the bedroom. I put on a tiny bit of foundation, but kept my makeup minimal as usual. I wanted to be as bare for him as bare could be. Innocent and pure like the girl he'd watched grow up in front of him. A virgin whose love he'd taken as soon as it was morally right to take it, and a woman he was going to turn into an immortal partner on Halloween.

"What's it going to be?" Mum asked me. "Some kind of formal service or something?"

"I have no idea," I admitted. "Hans has been keeping his cards close to his chest on that score."

"Yes, and his ideas cloaked up in a cloud of mystery from the sounds of it."

He sure had. For hours now I'd been trying to hone in on his thoughts and visions, but he was still keeping me at arm's length.

Head back to Edwin's manor when your soul feels the calling.

Those are all the thoughts he'd had to say.

The calling was rising how, I could feel it. I could sense the rumble of the car outside, all set to deliver me to my fate.

"Go," Mum said, and put her hand on my arm. "If it's time, it's time. Just please make sure you keep in touch and let me know how it goes for you."

I got a lump in my throat at that, seeing the affection in her eyes. She mirrored me with a nod, and we both laughed to break the tension.

"I still can't believe you're such a big girl now," she told me. "It's crazy, just how fast time flies."

"I'll keep in touch, I promise. You'll need to invite me over the threshold next time, though, and it'll be a little bit later than a lunchtime eating jam sandwiches in the sun."

"I can do that."

I just hoped Grandma would let her.

"She will let me," Mum voiced. "She won't have any choice from now on. The secrets have come to light."

"How do you feel about that? Do you think she'll still be able to be your mum?"

"Yes," she said. "The bond between us is too strong to break. It will have to twist and turn and take a new road, but it won't be destroyed. I don't think either of us will be pushing the other off the turrets of Garway church, given what happened last time."

"Good," I said. "Maybe one day she'll be willing to speak to me again, too. Without cursing me for being a damned to Hell sinner."

I walked down the stairs as Mum followed me. She watched as I fastened up my high heeled shoes.

Her arms were folded as she looked at me, and her thoughts were somewhere else, skirting around memories of the past.

"I'd better go," I told her, because my soul was beginning to tingle. "I'm ready for my transition. I'm ready to be committed to Hans."

She opened the front door for me, and I stepped out, but I couldn't help turning back to face her, pulling her tight into my arms. Me and my mum. Close. Like I'd been crying out for since I was just a girl.

"Thanks," I said. "It's been amazing today."

"Same for me," she replied. "I'll be thinking of you tonight."

She put her hands on my cheeks as I pulled away, and planted a kiss on my forehead.

"Don't wait too long before you come and ask permission to cross this threshold, Katherine. And next time, maybe you can bring Hans along with you? I'm sure he could bicker with your grandma if it comes to it."

I was halfway down the garden path when she called after me. She was waving to get my attention.

"You said Hans knows of your father?" she asked.

"Yeah, he said so."

Even in the dimming light of dusk I could tell she was blushing.

"And, um, do you think you'll meet him one day? Will Hans be able to give you an introduction?"

I smiled. "I hope so, yeah."

She grinned, blushing harder.

"Well, um… if you do… then please say hello from me. I hope he's doing ok."

My heart bloomed at the thought.

"Don't worry," I said. "I will."

The driver didn't look frustrated in the slightest when I slipped into the back seat of the car.

"Thanks for waiting," I said.

He tipped his hat at me. "You're very welcome."

There was still no sign of Grandma as we made our way from Orcop back towards Garway. I was expecting her to jump out of the hedge at any minute with a pitchfork armed ready, but there was nothing, just the dimming road up ahead.

It was almost dark when I saw the glow of Edwin's manor in the distance.

My soul was screaming so hard for Hans that I could hardly bear it as we pulled up into the driveway. I was aching in my seat until the car parked up outside the main entrance and I dashed away with nothing more than a *thank you*.

It was Daniel who answered the door, still in an oversized long-sleeved t-shirt with an emo smile on his face.

"They're waiting for you," he told me, and closed the door behind us.

I nodded.

"This way," he said, leading me through to the drawing room.

And there he was. My Hans. My beautiful vampire lover in an incredible black tuxedo, waiting for me with a beautiful, fanged smile.

He held out open arms and I dashed for him, feeling like I was coming back home after a long time away.

"You look beautiful," he told me, easing me away by my shoulders.

"Yes, you do, sweet little Katherine," agreed Edwin and appeared in my view from the right.

There were candles everywhere, and the chandelier was glowing, and it was obvious from the way they looked at each other that this was a major ritual. I got butterflies so strong they nearly had my legs wobbling.

I took a long sip of merlot along with Daniel as the two vampires watched alongside us, and we made a short social of it as the clock ticked away. Tick, tock, tick, tock, tick. And then – as midnight grew near – Hans gestured to the hallway.

It was time to go.

"Good luck," Daniel said, and I felt sorry for him as I spotted the non-malicious envy in his eyes.

"Yes, indeed. Good luck and congratulations," Edwin added.

Hans took my hand and led me back through the house as he had the night previous. We descended the steps until we arrived at the tunnel to the tomb, and he gave me the illuminated lantern, flickering brightly.

He pointed at the darkness of the tunnel.

"You have a head start, little one," he whispered. "So use it. Let your body run free and your soul run free along with it, until it gives up the fight and lets me take you. I'll be following. Closely."

I nodded, taking a breath, his words prickling my skin.

"Go," he said.

And I went for it, as quickly as my giddy legs would carry me, and charged through the tunnel like a girl possessed.

33

The cold stone walls of the tunnel felt tiny around me. The lantern flickered, and my breaths sounded savage.

My body knew I was going to die.

I made it through the tunnel with my heart racing and threw myself through the door to the tomb under Garway church. I heard whispers sounding loud, as though I was in another world. Dead knights breathing secrets. Eerie lights shining from vaulted graves. Sacred, twisted, beautiful... almost beguiling. But I didn't have time to stop and listen. I saw Hans' coffin in the corner, and I knew the exit was somewhere on the opposite side, but no matter how frantically I searched, there was no door to be found. Did Hans create it? Was it imaginary? Was there no door at all and I was destined to die here in this tomb surrounded by the dead?

Be more careful amongst the dead, Katherine...

Hans' words came slamming back to me, loud and clear in my head.

It was enough to make me shiver, so I started pounding a fist against the wall, desperate. There had to be an exit somewhere...

Come on. COME ON!

It was when I heard Hans' slow, solid footsteps echoing through the tunnel that fear catapulted me to search faster, harder.

COME ON!

Open your eyes, little one!

I spun around to the tunnel, footsteps getting louder, echoing…

Open your eyes!

I spun back to the wall and there it was, a solid wood door with a big round handle. What the hell!?

I tugged it open to find steep stone steps leading up into the night. I bounded up them two at a time with the lantern still flickering, and found myself in the grounds of the church I'd come to know so well.

This couldn't be real, surely? There was no door from the church to the tomb. I'd have seen it hundreds of times. Was this imagination? Was this whole thing one crazy fantasy of my mind?

My heart said no. My heart told me this was as real as real could be. The limits of the rational were fake, and my eyes were open to a whole other world.

The lantern flickered and died as I stood there, mesmerised.

Luckily the moon was bright enough to light my way.

The familiar gravestones were all around me as I hurried up the path and past the old yew tree. I kicked my heels off and took the long route up the bank at the far side, and the moonlight lit up the church in a midnight glow.

It was absolutely beautiful.

I got flashes, like cards being dealt one after the other of all the things that had happened here. So many people finding faith in the Lord, so many ceremonies and powerful events. Weddings, christenings, funerals, over and over in a cycle. Sunday services, and candles being lit in reverence, and people praying to God. And now there would be me, taking my final breath at the hands of the man I loved. The *vampire* I loved.

The huge sense of fate was almost enough to sink my body into acceptance, *almost*. Until I saw the shadow of Hans approaching across the grounds.

No.

My body had a final surge of flight left in it. Just like on the cobblestones.

I kept stumbling further along the path, my bare feet soaked by the damp grass, until I broke from the familiar route and darted through the gravestones, just like I had as a little girl, and slammed straight into...

I fell back, landed on my ass. But I hadn't slammed into anything. There was nothing there...

Be more careful amongst the dead, Katherine.

Whispers rose up into the cold night air all around me. The voices of those long gone. The dead that had watched me – *watched over me.*

Suddenly, with a weird sense of knowing, I felt free, not chased.

Truly free for the first time in my life. My God. It was fantastical.

Surreal but real. So real I could touch it, feel it in my soul.

I was free like the winds in the grounds, and the clouds sailing up above, and the soil in its earthy depths all around.

Free like the waters underground, and the moon overhead, and the essence of life flooding through the world.

I rose to my feet as if I was being lifted by invisible hands and it was the was most natural thing to dance and twirl as my soul took over.

For all of my time in the church with Mum and Grandma, I'd never felt anything so close to God as I spun around with the greatest feeling of joy.

It made sense. The journey beyond the body wasn't just about transition, it was about transcendence. My body was a temple, but it was the flesh and blood of a human. It needed to give up the fight and sacrifice itself to for ever. That was the price to pay for lifetimes over with my fated mate. But that didn't mean I was a sinner, or damned. I was pure, and loved, and guided by the force of it all.

I knew Hans was watching me from the shadows. I could feel his joy, too – his joyous soul lighting up with mine.

It made me twirl faster.

I was dancing for us. Me and Hans. For ever.

My spins had my soul soaring. My twists and turns through the gravestones were magical, just as they should be. And then came the intuition. I knew where I needed to be and my dancing feet were taking me there, twirling all the way to the bench by the old spring.

Dressed in my pretty white dress, with the moonlight glow over me, I stood by the bench and waited for Hans. There was no pressure or force in his approach, just his strong powerful steadiness as he listened to my spirit. A strength and steadiness that felt so much more powerful than before.

"You look absolutely divine," he told me as he stepped from the shadows. "That was beautiful, little one. A display of pure, stunning soul."

Thanks wouldn't cut it, so I didn't say a word, just opened my arms and smiled at my gorgeous love.

"Are you ready?" he asked, and I nodded. "Truly ready?"

"Yes."

The heat of his presence was beyond comprehension, so I didn't try. I let the higher forces of love soar free, and offered him my neck. My heart was ready, and my body was too. Finally, I wasn't scared. Death of the flesh could take me, and I would go willingly.

Hans brushed the hair from my neck and his fingers gave me the finest tingles. He tipped my face up to his and brushed his lips against mine before he kissed me.

"Make me a vampire," I whispered. "I've never been more ready in my life."

"Or death," he whispered back. "I'll be right here for you. I'll be here on the journey with you."

I wrapped my arms around his neck and held him in celebration as he blessed me with his touch. His hands trailed down and hitched my dress up, and I silently thanked him as he slipped his fingers inside my panties. I wanted him so much it hurt.

"I'll be loving you as I kill you," he whispered and tugged my dress up and off.

The night was cold as he stripped me bare, and my skin prickled with goosebumps as I smiled at him with the greatest adoration. We would be two bodies together, and two souls meeting as one.

I adored him even more as he stripped himself bare in front of me, loving the way the moon lit up his flesh.

He guided me down onto the damp bench, and I sat with my back pressed tight against the wood, opening my legs wide for him as he dropped to his knees. His tongue was bliss as he spread and sucked and lapped at me. Gently enough to tease. *Fuck.* I held his head to my pussy and asked for more.

And of course, he replied with the word.

Patience.

This time it made me grin.

Hans looked up at me with a smirk.

He carried on working my pussy with his mouth as I arched my back and offered everything. He pushed three fingers inside me as he sucked and swirled his tongue around my clit, and he kept me on the edge for what felt like hours as the clouds ghosted over the moon, but I didn't rush him, or beg.

Patience.

He didn't make me come this time. He got up from his knees instead.

He pinned me to the bench and positioned himself between my legs, and my world was spinning as he pushed his way inside me and his lips met mine.

He was deep in the throes of fucking me within seconds. Hard slams as his flesh took mine. I gripped his ass and urged his thrusts, loving how deep he felt. I gasped with every slam, my pussy still struggling to take the size of him, and there was so much more to come. This was just the beginning.

His lips were like the whispers of the graveyard, so gentle as he brushed them down my neck. I held my breath as he kissed my throat, bracing myself.

Goodbye, life...

Bright sunshine warmed my face. Birds were singing. Children laughing.

With his cock buried deep, his fangs pricked my skin, and he bit down so hard that I cried out into sudden darkness, the pain splitting through my skull. He drank my blood with such ferocity that I gripped his shoulders in an attempt to stay steady, but it was futile. I wouldn't be able to stay steady for long.

Relax, Katherine, his thoughts said to mine. *Let your body die without a fight.*

I tried to focus on his thrusts in my pussy along with his teeth in my throat – a rhythm of life and death, both at once. His cock grew bigger with every drop of my blood he drank, until I was stretched to the limit, my pussy hurting in bliss, and then, in the pain, my pleasure rose. And rose. And rose. And fuck. *Fuck. FUCK. FUCKKK.* I came as he came.

He came in my pussy as he drank from my throat, giving and taking at the same time.

And then my body began to fade. I was dying.

Hans pulled his teeth out of my neck and blood dripped down his chin.

"Let it happen," he whispered. "You are at the point of death. Embrace it."

My ragged breaths turned into shallow wisps, my lungs trying their best to hang on to the air, but they failed. My love stroked my cheek as I struggled, and then he reached down to his jacket on the floor. He took out a long, sharp blade from the inside pocket.

I smiled inside, because yes, I was dying, but I was also ready to be saved.

I watched him slice his wrist with the knife, captivated as his vampire blood spilled free and fast down his arm.

My mouth was already open as he raised my head for me and pressed his wound to my lips.

"Drink," he said, and it came so naturally it was insane.

I sucked at his wrist and the taste of his blood was like heaven. Thick and metallic, a mixture of life and death. I swallowed it down and felt my senses returning, but they were different. Heightened in a new kind of way.

A magical way.

Magic.

I was feeling magic.

Hans' blood was like magic through my veins.

I could hear the whispers from the graves, and sense spirits all around me. Knowledge of lifetimes and ages gone by. I felt movement in the hedgerows and rumbles under the ground, as though I'd been reborn into a whole new world.

I guess I had.

But there was more. And more. And more.

I felt chants, and potions, and witchcraft. I understood the call of the seasons, and time, and the rhythm and sound in colour. I saw a whole chain of women before me with gifts beyond all reasoning, and I was amongst them. I was a woman who belonged in that chain.

I was a child of the light, and the oneness of all time. I was a part of everything, human, vampire, church, rock or plant. None of it mattered. There was only life.

Magic.

Love.

Joy.

Pain.

Everything blurred as one.

My flesh was screaming for human life as I drank the blood of an immortal, but I didn't hear the torment in it, just a symphony. There was only me. In life or death, as a human or a vampire, it didn't matter. I was still Katherine Blakely.

And so my body died, and my soul lived.

Hans pulled his wrist away from my mouth and I gasped as I stared at the world anew. This time it was me who gave Hans a blood-red kiss – red with his blood as well as mine. Perfection.

I was kissing him hard as a rumble sounded loudly underneath the bench. The walls shook on either side of us as something spluttered and gurgled, returning from the depths.

Yes, of course…

I felt the spray of fresh water.

It was flowing free.

Hans broke the kiss and turned me along with him to face the spring, and it was alive again. Like it should be. It was just another thing in the chain of things that were meant to be.

I recited the legend.

There will be nine witches from the bottom of Orcop to the end of Garway Hill as long as water flows.

I was one of the nine witches.

The water was flowing again.

My spirit was home.

Hans wrapped me in his arms, and I held him back, like I'd wanted to do as Mary. Her dreams were coming to life as mine.

"Happy Halloween," he said, and I laughed.

"The first of many more to come, I hope."

"Many, many more to come."

We watched the spring in silent harmony, loving our quiet embrace of our new life… until a voice sounded out like a screech in the dark.

"KATHERINE!"

I tensed in Hans' arms. What the–

"KATHERINE! GET HERE NOW OR I SWEAR TO GOD, GIRL, YOU'LL FUCKING REGRET IT!"

It was Grandma, and she sounded insane. Absolutely fucking insane.

34

*H*ans stood up from the bench and I felt the power in his stance as he prepared to face her for me, but I didn't want him to. I didn't *need* him to. I put a hand on his arm gently and shook my head as I rose to my feet myself.

"Let me," I said.

I pulled my dress back on as Grandma kept screeching from the other side of the grounds, but I wasn't frantic about it. I didn't rush to run to her, just walked slowly, enjoying the darkness of the night with my fresh new eyes.

"KATHERINE!" she screeched again, and then she started in shock as she saw me standing there.

"I'm here," I said, "and I won't be regretting anything. You'll never make me doubt myself again."

She was holding a crucifix and brandished it at me like I was going to curl up on the floor in agony, but it made me laugh.

"Oh, Grandma! God doesn't hate me. The higher power wants us to be true to ourselves, not living a lie for other people."

"THAT'S STUPID, GIRL!" she tried, but I shook my head.

"It's not going to work with me anymore. I'm not going to let you kick me with your criticism every time I want to be myself."

"Nor me," another voice sounded out, and wow, there was my mum, walking through the grounds towards us, wrapped up in her favourite thick green cardigan.

My heart soared.

Grandma looked between us like it was a conspiracy, but Mum was as calm as I was. She arrived at my side and took hold of my hand, and stared Grandma right in the eye.

"You either love us for us, or you don't love us at all. Your choice."

"DON'T BE–" Grandma began, but Mum shook her head.

"Which is it going to be? Do you love us or not?"

Grandma looked so hateful.

"And what are you going to do if I don't? Are you going to curse me and throw me to my death like you did your father?"

I clenched Mum's hand, but I didn't need to. She stood firm.

"Except I didn't kill my father, did I? It was your magic as well as mine that caused it. If I'm a murderer, then you are too."

Grandma flinched. Shocked. Because Mum was right. It wasn't just her roar of magic that had rocked the tower that night. Not at all.

"We're all witches," Mum told her. "Accept it, and you can accept the love between us all."

Hans approached from behind and stood beside us, all three of us looking at the woman battling her demons. We had none left of our own.

Grandma was still clutching at her crucifix as a car pulled up in the gateway. The glow of headlights blinded us all, and the figure walking towards us was nothing but a silhouette.

Wow. It was turning into quite a gathering. Who the hell was this now?

I heard one word. *Serena.* And my mum dropped my hand.

"Thomas?!" Her eyes strained to see him. "Thomas? Is that you?"

My God, I heard the love in her voice. The figure was walking towards us, but he didn't make it anywhere close. Mum went running to him in a full sprint and he was ready for her. He held her tight in his arms. I watched them open-mouthed.

"Time for you to meet your father," Hans whispered to me, and my undead heart pounded.

My father.

Grandma was mute as I took tiny steps towards the man I'd never had the chance to know.

"Katherine," he said and both he and Mum held out a hand to me.

Just crazy. Wow, it was just fucking crazy.

The tears streamed down my face as I joined my parents in their embrace. I let them hold me, the three of us together, and there were no words needed. The unspoken said it all, like it so often did these days.

"You're all sinners!" Grandma hissed, but I didn't care. None of us did.

My father broke the embrace and me and Mum stood by his side as he faced the old witch.

"All said and done, there's only one sinner here," he said.

Grandma held the crucifix to her heart, her lip twitching with disgust.

"Time for you to leave this time," my dad said.

Grandma hesitated, glancing from one to the other.

"Thomas is right," Mum said. "There's nothing for you here. Nothing but love."

Grandma recoiled at that and she spat. She actually spat on the ground in front of us.

"Sinners," she said, "this isn't the end of it!"

And with hatred burning in her eyes, she stormed away into the night, a fresh breeze washing over us as she left us behind.

"Goodbye and good riddance," Mum said.

Hans walked up and cleared his throat. My father stepped over and held out a hand.

"Good evening, Hans," he said. "Lovely to see you."

"And you, Thomas," he replied. "Sorry for the short notice."

They shook hands, and it was another round of crazy. These two men knew each other well.

My father pointed back to the car and the driver waiting there.

"Time to get back to the manor," he said with a smile. "Edwin has the merlot ready to flow, and well. We have a lot to catch up on."

He was holding my mum's hand tight as we walked the path, and I was right behind them, with Hans holding mine.

Yes, it was true. Finally.

My soul was home.

EPILOGUE

I checked out my fangs in Mum's bathroom mirror, beautiful pointed and white. They looked perfect. I was still getting used to the fact they were so much more pronounced now. I was grinning at myself. No doubt the novelty would last a long time to come. Quite possibly for ever.

"They do really suit you," Mum said.

"Thanks."

She wrapped an arm around my shoulders and landed a kiss on my cheek.

"Such a shame I can't make you any lovely jam sandwiches anymore."

As it turns out, I wouldn't want any jam sandwiches anymore. The very first moment I'd tasted blood, I was done for. The cravings were intense. Merlot had nothing on it, jam had nothing on it, and neither did rare steak; there wasn't anything that could compare to the insane taste of rich red life, fresh from the vein.

Hans had been keeping us close to the blood house. I'd been sucking at Sarah's neck so many times these past few weeks that I'd lost count. Hans and I had been having the time of our lives.

I wondered if he was taking a nip at Daniel while Edwin watched on, over at the manor, quenching his thirst a little as I embarked on my first ever Herefordshire coven adventure.

Maybe I'd take a nip of Daniel myself when I got back…

"It's definitely at the Garway community hall tonight?" Mum asked me, interrupting my thoughts.

"Yeah, it is."

"But you still don't know who is going to be there?"

"Nope. I have no idea. I can't wait for the surprises."

It had been almost a full month since the night in Garway church when I'd become an immortal, and the full moon was glowing bright outside. It was time for the witches to be meeting, and I – Katherine Blakely, of the long line of Orcop witches – was about to reveal myself as the ninth of them. The spring was in full flow and I was the latest in the family tree, about to take my place amongst the coven.

"Almost time," I said, and Mum took a breath.

"Are you ready for this?"

"As ready as I'll ever be."

I checked out my hair in the mirror, and smoothed down my dark green dress. I was paler now than ever as a vampire. My hair looked a lot, lot darker for it, and my eyes were hazel with a glow.

I was nervous as I walked down the stairs, the tension growing inside me as Mum got her car keys ready to drive me to Garway community hall. I felt like I was back to being a teenager driven around by a parental chauffeur, but it was nice these days. Our bond was growing stronger every day.

Just a shame Grandma didn't want to be a part of it. She'd disappeared off down south to some kind of holy refuge centre, no doubt preaching about us being sinners. Oh, the joy of a disjointed family.

On that note, I shot Mum a glance as I slipped into the passenger seat.

"Have you heard from him today?"

She blushed like she was even younger than I was. Her cheeks were bright pink, even in the dark. I could feel the heat from them. I could hear her heart thumping fast.

"Who?" she asked, but I laughed at her.

"You know who!"

She shrugged. "Yeah, a little. We've been messaging."

"A little? Right. Yeah, sure."

I knew she was underplaying it. Her grin made it obvious, not to mention I could feel the joy coming off her.

Who'd have ever thought that my dad would be dating my mum again after eighteen years apart? They could play it cool all they wanted, but it was a facade. Both of them wanted to end up together. Mum couldn't stop blushing as soon as Dad's name was mentioned, and Dad lit up like a beacon at the word *Serena* every time I'd seen him in London. They were as much fated mates as me and Hans were.

I could only imagine the weirdness of going out on double dates. Maybe one day…

"Are you still spending a lot of time with him?" Mum asked.

"Yeah. He's nice."

"You'd hope so. He's your father." She paused. "You look more like him now you have those fancy teeth, you know?"

I grinned to show them off. She was right. Everyone said it. I definitely looked like the daughter of the occult master of Britain, and I'd definitely inherited some traits from him. I was lucky to have been born of two bloodlines with such complementary talents.

Dad was quite a character, and I was still getting used to him. *Serious*, people called him, and they weren't lying. He was a very stern man on the outside, but I could see through that to his tender heart. Literally. I could see it beating when he was in the same room. It was a strong one. If I wasn't his daughter, I'd have probably wanted a shot of it.

Before I knew it, we were pulling into Garway community hall, the lights glowing out of the windows.

There were five other cars there…

Five. Hmm. Ok.

I took a breath, staring at the doorway. There were people already in there, I could feel them. But there were eight of them, not five.

I could hear all eight beating hearts.

"Wish me luck," I said to Mum, grabbing my bag from the back seat.

"You won't need luck," she said. "They'll be so pleased to meet you. But have some good luck, just in case."

"Thanks, Mum."

"Ping me a thought when you need a lift back."

I will, thanks, I thought as I walked away, knowing full well she could hear me. It was another great thing about being a witch with a witch for a mother. Mobile phones could get stuffed.

I arrived at the entrance to the hall and took another deep breath.

So, here goes nothing...

I pushed open the doors as Mum drove away, and my undead heart was pounding like crazy. I felt like I was stepping into some kind of trial – a newbie schoolgirl entering a schoolyard, with no idea who I'd meet. I was probably the most skittish vampire in the world right then.

I tried to be a psychic about the group and who was a part of it, but I had no chance. Even with my skills, the walls had been wrapped up tight with not an inkling in sight. I guessed these witches were good at it.

I didn't bother calling out a *hello* before I entered the main hall, somehow summoning up the courage to walk on in tall.

Sure enough, there were a circle of chairs laid out in the middle of the social room.

Nine seats in total, with one empty one right in front of me. The other eight were filled, and eight smiling faces looked right at me, without so much as a hint of shock.

They'd been expecting me.

I took my seat on the plastic chair like it was a crochet club meeting and cast my eyes around the group, trying to get a measure of them. And of course... I laughed out loud, honestly, because it was too obvious to be true.

My stupid guesses about local witches hadn't been stupid guesses at all.

There was Edna who walked her old Labrador every morning through Orcop village, and the goth girl who lived at the old pub in

Garway, with the faded sun tarot card as a tavern sign. And there too was Amy, who everyone knew as the *crystal healing lady.*

There was Jenny from the post office, and her cousin Jacqueline who lived with her at Hillside Farm, and the very elderly woman, Geraldine, from the apartment above the egg farm, who sometimes drove through the village in her electric wheelchair, even though she must have been going on 90.

And there were another two I couldn't place. They must have been sisters. Identical twins with long blonde hair down to their waists. New to the area, as far as I knew.

In the middle of the circle of chairs was an altar draped in a cloth of squares, and on the top stood a burning candle, a dagger, a wand and a pentagram. The beautiful smell of musk incense felt like a powerhouse.

"Hi," I said to them all, and they all grinned along with me. "How long have you known it was me? How long have you known I was the ninth witch?"

It was elderly Geraldine who answered me with a lovely deep shaky voice, her face lit up with wrinkles.

"Ooh, a long time now," she told me. "A lot longer than you have. So, how about we get started with the *pleased to meet yous?*"

I put my bag down on the floor, and began to make introductions. I learnt about Geraldine's first foray into witchcraft when she used to toss stones into Garway spring and make wishes, and I learnt about Amy's first experience with rose quartz where she felt the energy right through her toes, and I learnt about Edna's dog, Mollie, who was a spirit guide – and could talk to the other animals around her. Yep, my amazement went to a whole new level.

And then, once the initial introductions were done and we were well into the night, I took the hand of Jacqueline on my left, and Amy on my right, as we all locked hands for the ceremony.

I already knew the ritual in my vampire, psychic, witchy, ghost whispering soul.

I could picture my father casting pentagrams in the air and calling to the angels. I could feel the forces of the elements balancing all around him.

But then came more... ritual robes of white, and all-seeing eyes... and white roses... and... salt... I saw salt.

Edna grabbed my attention back by breaking up the hand holding and getting to her feet. She walked around us, speaking the holy names and drawing symbols in the air.

The room changed. The atmosphere shifted and we were in a space of pure magic, connected to the energies above. The rest of the world blurred and there was only us, the nine witches, at the boundaries of our own sphere. The centre of our combined energies and auras.

Edna sat back down when she'd finished casting, and she looked across at me with a smile.

"Here we are to welcome our ninth, Katherine Blakely, to our circle. Katherine, please take your place amongst us, and commit yourself to our coven."

It felt like an honour to stand in the centre by the altar.

Edna asked me the questions.

"Katherine, do you feel the connection to the spirits through us? Do you feel the force of the ritual within our group?"

I nodded emphatically with a smile on my face, because, yeah I felt it. I could feel it tingling through my vampire veins.

"Yes, I do."

"Katherine, do you vow to respect the privacy of the Garway lodge, and share no secrets with outsiders?"

"Yes, I do."

"And do you vow to explore the mysteries alongside us, bringing the forces of goodwill into the world around us?"

"Yes," I said. "I do."

"Do you truly want to walk the path of *know thyself* along with the rest of us? Do you vow to give your trust over to the higher powers to guide your way?"

"Yes, I do."

She took her hands in mine and gripped them tight.

"Then we welcome you to our circle, Katherine. You are now a member of the Garway coven."

The other witches clapped as I took my seat, and I was so happy to be amongst them that my soul soared sky high.

"Have you ever learnt the art of skyring?" Amy the crystal lady asked me.

"No," I said. "I haven't got a clue."

"How about we get started, then?" She handed me a clear quartz sphere.

Since I saw the patterns swirling inside it and scenes coming to life inside my mind the very moment it touched, I could somehow believe I'd be quite good at this witchy thing…

Having sex with a vampire literally is, out of this world. *Making love* with a vampire, even more so. But making love with a vampire when you're a vampire yourself is – mind-blowing? Sure. Seriously there aren't the words.

We were in the aftermath of our first session of the evening when Hans looked over at me with a smirk.

"So, how about you tell me again about the coven?"

I shook my head and poked my tongue out.

"Try to snare me into revealing secrets all you like, Hans, but it's not going to work. Not even in the afterglow."

He huffed. "Fine. I know, I know."

It was all in good humour. It made me laugh inside.

"Come," he said, "let me show you something really special."

"What the hell can be left to see?"

"Plenty," he replied, and lifted me from the sofa with a sparkle in his eyes.

This was my first night in his Edinburgh home. I loved the tartan fabrics he had everywhere, like he was living in a regal version of *Braveheart*.

"Holy fucking wow!" I said as Hans showed me into a room beyond his study for the first time.

It was quite a sight. A room full of taxidermy and artefacts from all over the world. So many animals, impalas, a tiger, a lion, a beautiful old zebra head up on the wall. So many birds of prey on plinths, all eyes on me. Some I didn't even recognise, like snapshots on the path of evolution.

He had stones, and fossils, and a sculpture of a winged bull on his dresser, and there were old tiles framed in gold up over the fireplace.

"Whoa," I said, doing a spin to take it all in.

"I like to preserve time," he told me. "Maybe one day this will be a museum of the true past. Quite a relic in the making."

"Sure looks like it."

"It's not just the spirits of humans who stay alive in the essence of the world," he said. "It's nature, too. Our world has so many kinds of life, none of them more valid than another."

I felt that. I felt it all through my new vampire senses.

It was like a whole new ritual when he laid me down in the centre of the room, spreadeagled. He teased me and licked me and gave me the dirty bite. Those souls of past times came back to life around me, so many hearts thumping, and it was bliss, only adding to my fascination with my vampire lover and all the time ahead.

I bit him right back, took his cock into my mouth and pierced it ever so gently with my fangs, sucking both his dick and his blood at the same time.

We were both a bloody mess when he fucked me after. A writhing tangle of limbs as the heat of the room pulsed along with us. And that's what it was, when two vampires made love – a pulse, as one, in perfect harmony, an orgasm of the *heart and soul*, go figure.

It was beautiful.

He was beautiful. My vampire lover.

"*We* are beautiful," Hans offered, his green eyes dancing with desire, my blood dripping from his chin.

He was right, of course.

He held me close, there on that rug, and our mouths met in a blood-red kiss.

Something I'd never, ever get tired of.

THE END.

ABOUT THE NOVEL

The myth *'there will be nine witches from the bottom of Orcop to the end of Garway Hill'* is a true one, and Garway church is surrounded by a great deal of speculation about its origins as a Knight's Templar church.

It's an amazing place to visit, and I've been there often. I'd thoroughly recommend it.

I live in Herefordshire myself, so it's been fantastic to be able to visit these spots as I write. I've loved every single second of it.

ACKNOWLEDGMENTS

Thank you to everyone who has helped me through this novel.

To my amazing editor, John Hudspith, who has been a constantly brilliant figure in my writing journey from the very start.

To Letitia Hasser for the fantastic covers – as always. You are a star.

Thank you to all my amazing readers, and everyone who has shouted loudly about getting absorbed in my novels. Every single one of you and your posts and reviews are hugely appreciated.

To my family and friends, who are always there for me, listening to hours and hours of book story talk on loop. You are brilliant. Couldn't do this without you!

ABOUT JADE WEST

Jade West is an erotic romance author, based in the English Herefordian countryside.

Best known for Sugar Daddies, Bait and Call Me Daddy, she began her career in 2015 with the launch of her debut novel, Dirty Bad Wrong - the first of the Dirty Bad series.

She is a dirty, obsessive fantasist, who couldn't hold back the words if she tried. Her incessant chatter on the topic of crushes and storylines can drive the people around her crazy, but they are plenty used to it by now. She's been doing it since she was tiny, but her fantasies have changed a little bit since then...

Outside of writing filthy romance novels, she likes sparkly things, black velvet and businessmen in suits. Late nights, and 90s game shows, and the dramatic lyrics of pop ballads.

Oh, and chocolate fudge cake. She likes that a lot, too.

Printed in Poland
by Amazon Fulfillment
Poland Sp. z o.o., Wrocław